Praise for Eliot Fintushel's

BREAKFAST WITH THE ONES YOU LOVE

"I ask you, gentle reader, who the hell could describe Eliot Fintushel's wild, wonderful, crazy (might I say madcap?), uncategorizable debut novel? Like Howard Waldrop, R. A. Lafferty, Avram Davidson, and T. C. Boyle, Fintushel is a one-off—and *Breakfast with the Ones You Love* reads like P. G. Wodehouse (on speed) collaborating with Isaac Bashevis Singer, Harlan Ellison, Woody Allen, and Barry N. Malzberg. What else can I tell you? Just go forth and read!"
—Jack Dann, author of *The Memory Cathedral* and *The Rebel: An Imagined Life of James Dean*

"*Breakfast with the Ones You Love* will enlarge your consciousness, tickle your soul, stop your heart, and make you laugh out loud. Although you board this interdimensional roller coaster of a book just around the block, before the ride is over you'll get a glimpse of the Promised Land—guaranteed! By conjuring up a gaggle of characters that give new meaning to the adjective 'quirky' and typing some of the most amazing sentences you'll ever read, Eliot Fintushel has established himself as the Master of High Strangeness."
—James Patrick Kelly, author of *Burn*

"Opening this book is like opening a box filled with wonders. Here are a talking cat, and old ladies who worship Satan, and a spaceship hidden in a deserted part of Sears and Roebuck—and Lea Tillim, a character with a real

voice, real sadness, so true you almost expect her to walk off the page. I could say the usual things—this book will make you laugh, it will make you cry—but, really, it might change your life."
—Lisa Goldstein, author of *The Alchemist's Door*

"If the world ended tomorrow and your soul was ready and your loins were sated, next you'd need a good yarn and a hard laugh. That's Eliot Fintushel's brilliant *Breakfast with the Ones You Love*. A deft, hilarious, and lovable apocalyptic tale that mashes the hard-boiled, the nightmarish, and the absurdly mundane like some new pharmaceutical with side effects that are equal parts joy, terror, and wisdom. Not a bad way to go."
—Patrick O'Leary, author of *The Impossible Bird*

"Eliot Fintushel masterfully weaves together the most unique and engaging collection of social outcasts, misfits, eccentrics, and God-fearing mobsters you'll ever meet—his characters are absolutely radiant, his prose flawless, and his story an unpredictable, enchanting journey. For those of you familiar with Eliot's stunning short fiction, you won't be disappointed. If you're not familiar with it, here's your chance to discover one of the few truly original voices writing in the genre today. This book is a pure delight."
—Nick DiChario, author of *A Small and Remarkable Life*

"This loopy, suspenseful, and profoundly funny book follows Lea Tillim as she tackles those three universals: how to love, how to control her powers of life and death, and how to accessorize. With his first novel, the ever-

awesome *Rebbe* Fintushel has returned from the unknown section of Sears and Roebuck's, bearing pancakes, wisdom, and extra syrup. What, we should be surprised by this?"
—Andy Duncan, author of *Beluthahatchie and Other Stories*

"A fantasy like no other. Certified *meshugge* Fintushel presents for our edification a Jewish comic knockabout metaphysical thriller, and gives to airy nothing a local habitation and a name. You should be so lucky as to own this book!"
—John Kessel, author of *Corrupting Dr. Nice*

Praise for Eliot Fintushel

"Eliot Fintushel and his nifty stories have been an ongoing joy for me for years."
—Harlan Ellison

"Eliot Fintushel is one of the most exciting, wildly inventive, and extravagantly pyrotechnic new writers to enter the field in many years. His work is madcap, bizarre, biting, brilliant, totally gonzo, and unlike anything else you've ever read. He is often very funny, and sometimes surprisingly profound. No one in the field, in fact, is producing work any more daring and totally original than Fintushel. His work goes beyond the cutting edge to what tomorrow's cutting edge may well turn out to be."
—Gardner Dozois, editor of *Asimov's* and *The Year's Best Science Fiction*

BREAKFAST WITH THE ONES YOU LOVE

Eliot Fintushel

BANTAM BOOKS

SPECTRR ™

BREAKFAST WITH THE ONES YOU LOVE
A Bantam Spectra Book / March 2007

Published by Bantam Dell
A Division of Random House, Inc.
New York, New York

This is a work of fiction. Names, characters, places, and incidents either are the
product of the author's imagination or are used fictitiously. Any resemblance to
actual persons, living or dead, events or locales is entirely coincidental.

Library of Congress Cataloging-in-Publication Data

Fintushel, Eliot.
Breakfast with the ones you love / Eliot Fintushel.
p. cm.
ISBN: 978-0-553-38405-5 (trade pbk.)
I. Title.

PS3606.I58B74 2007
813'.6—dc22

2006025660

Printed in the United States of America
Published simultaneously in Canada

www.bantamdell.com

BVG   10 9 8 7 6 5 4 3 2 1

For Ariel and Mollie and Noelle

CONTENTS

1. The Yid Paints the Ceiling of Our
   Spaceship Gold   1

2. I Become Reacquainted with a
   Couple of Muscles   19

3. Looks Could Kill   35

4. The Yid Measures My Talent   53

5. Indian Summer   74

6. Jack Kisses Me   88

7. Underground   111

8. We Make It to Bobson's   127

9. Mrs. Bobson's Hospitality   143

10. The Minyan Reconnoiters   158

11. Yakov the Bull Explains Me
    Everything   176

12. Rats   186

13. The Minyan Sings Ghi Diddy Di on
    Top of Mount Nebo   199

14.   Israel and Italy   214

15.   Mrs. Bobson's Marquetry Ladies   228

16.   We Establish <u>Vohu</u>   243

17.   The Coming of the <u>Meschiach</u>   257

BREAKFAST WITH THE ONES YOU LOVE

chapter one

The Yid Paints the Ceiling of Our Spaceship Gold

If you want to be safe, a person like myself, you have to kill your face. Otherwise people get their hooks in you, which, who needs it? I already killed my face by the age of twelve. Problem is, my tits invaded. I tried not eating, which I hear stops tits in their tracks, but I couldn't keep it up. In spite of everything, there is something in you that wants to keep you alive. It's like a disease that you just can't shake, no matter how hard you try. At least you can kill your face, see? Me, I can kill people, too. I can kill them whenever I want to.

My cat doesn't like me killing people. The ones I murdered, I figured, they're better off. Tule said no. I said, what, don't you like the blood, pussums, is that it? She said, no, even when there isn't any blood it's bad for you, it's just bad for you, honey baby, and I don't care about anybody else.

I'm no psycho. I know if somebody else had been there, all they would have seen was blinks and rubs, and all they would have heard was meow. It wouldn't have made them almost cry, like it did me. When you understand an individual, it makes you almost cry.

Like this one night that I was standing outside the kitchen door of this restaurant where I worked. Across the street some bag lady was slumped by a flophouse door—"By the Day and by the Week"—all bundled in rags and booze and snoring her death-rattle snore. My sleeves were rolled up; my arms were all wet and sudsy and steaming. The moon was steaming too, it looked like, playing peek-aboo through this moon steam; maybe it was the souls of my dead victims, if they had any.

I don't know what I was thinking about, but I was crying, and it was starting to sting my eyes, so I went back inside. Tule rode my shoulder. Sarge was in the kitchen, arms akimbo, nodding and tapping his foot and twisting that sausage puss of his and eyeballing Tule.

"Lea! Plates! Silverware!"

He *acted* like a sarge, so that's what they called him at the Wee Spot, but his name was really Serge. He was a Uky guy, big guy, the kind where you can't tell what's muscle and what's fat.

"You ever hear of health code?" he said.

"You ever hear of 'mind your own business'?" I said.

While he was chewing on that one, I pulled open the dish-washing machine—a cloud of steam rolled out and I piled a stack of plates onto a towel on my forearm faster than most people can deal cards. Tule jumped off my shoulder and disappeared under the butcher block. I grabbed the silverware tray and walked right past Mr. Openmouth to the waiters' station with the clean stuff.

I didn't kill him. I didn't maim him. I didn't knock him onto his knees or terrify him inside his own mind. I didn't do anything. I just put out the goddam dishes and silverware like he wanted. Like Tule told me to.

At 2:00 A.M. when all the tables and bus trays were wiped down and the floors were clean and steaming and the mop bucket was upside down in the sink, me and Tule slammed out the back door into the alley and hustled to the Sears and Roebuck, blowing white breath by moonlight. I mean, I was blowing the breath—Tule was inside my shirt and my leather jacket, where I held her curled up against my stomach, keeping the both of us warm. I climbed us up the fire escape onto the roof. I hated that dirty rust that made your hands red and gritty—it stung in the cold—but I was damned if I'd wipe them off on my leather.

Up top, my associate, the Yid, had stuff to wipe your hands on. He wasn't there yet, but I knew where his stash was. I wedged up the tar-papered plywood on top of the old elevator shaft and shimmied under. It was pitch-dark in there. The Yid always said, drop the feline down first, in case they ever move the elevator car—then you'll know not to jump and kill yourself.

I said, I'll drop *you* down first, Yid. I figured they would never move that old service elevator. It was probably rusted in place. The security dicks didn't even go over to that part of the building anymore. As far as me and the Yid could tell, it was walled off. Somebody had just drywalled off that whole section rather than deal with the shit and rot, probably before whoever sold it to Sears and Roebuck. That elevator wasn't going anywhere. I didn't even use a flashlight. I just jumped. My legs knew when to bend for the landing. The Yid always used a flashlight. He said, that's because of Auschwitz and Treblinka, where his folks had been, and he didn't trust anything anymore.

I said, I could take care of Auschwitz and Treblinka, no sweat, I could make those Nazis wish they had never been born if I half felt like it, and he said, I know, that's why I let you stick around, but I still gotta use the flashlight—for my nerves. I allowed him that.

I held Tule tight. "Don't claw me this time, pussums, okay?" I jumped. She clawed, like always, and I petted her special, like always. "Who loves you?" You have to reward people after they do bad; otherwise they just keep on doing bad; is the way I see it, because they stay unhappy. Cats too.

She relaxed. I felt around for the sliding plate on top of the elevator car. More rust and grit. I found the edge and pushed it aside. The scraping sound echoed in the elevator shaft. I still couldn't see anything but my own mind—red and blue points swimming around with that weird antiglow, as if there were another kind of light, the opposite of daylight, and the darker it gets, the brighter that gets.

Then I scooped Tule out from under my shirt and my jacket. "Hey! It's a girl!" I said, and I tickled her. The shaft said, *it's a girl, it's a girl, girl, girl.* Tule played at biting my fingers. I held her down the hole as far as I could without dirtying my jacket too much, and I dropped her into the elevator. She was okay with that routine. I heard her scratch around down there, smelling for mice. She'd find mice now and then. I don't mind mice. They keep the rats away. Then I lowered myself down a little and jumped the rest of the way.

It always gave me a kick to feel the car shake when I jumped in. Sometimes I'd imagine the cable breaking and the whole thing plummeting down to the bottom. Everything would get crushed, even if you jump and you're in the air—did you know that? The Yid explained that one to me; it's because your jump is falling too, like everything else. So you still wind up with your skull shooting down through your rib cage or whatever. Not Tule, though. I'd cushion Tule. I'd hug her, even if she scratched like hell. I'd be her shock absorber, see? She wouldn't starve, either. She could eat me till somebody shoveled her out. That would be okay by me. If the Yid was there, and she ate him too, and he didn't like it, well, that would be just too bad.

I went straight for the telephone box because the Yid always kept some wet-and-dry's in there with some rags that he called *schmattes*. I picked up the receiver and said, "I'm stuck between the seventh and eighth floor here. Can you send up a *schmatte*?" I grabbed a couple *schmattes*, said thank you, and hung up. I wiped off the grit—I wiped off the feel of the grit, is what I should say, because it was still pitch-dark, and I was doing everything by the feel of it, which is my normal mode anyway. Sight is an extremely overrated sense, in my book.

Tule was watching me. I felt her rub my calf. *That's right, wash up*, she said. *You gotta take care of yourself, keep yourself clean, keep yourself pretty. You know how to do it. When people see you, it will make them alive, instead of the other way.*

I said, "Aw, what do cats know, huh? 'I love you,' doesn't mean I gotta listen to your crap, Tule." But it got me thinking. I closed the phone box and wiped the metal casing with one of the Yid's *schmattes*. I knew what I was doing—no need to waste batteries yet. I polished it all up; I wanted it cleaner than what the Yid shaves by. Then I reached down to where I knew a flashlight was and I shined it up at my face to see if I was still pretty. You never know from one minute to the next. You think you do, but you don't. Especially if someone just died in front of you because you twitched a certain muscle inside, you want to check to see if you still look the same; sometimes you do and sometimes you don't. But now I was checking just for vanity or curiosity, like normal girls do who don't kill people. Tule meowed. Yes, that's the kind of thing she wanted me to do.

That's when I heard the board creak up top the shaft. I quick turned out the flashlight. I was damned if I'd let the Yid catch me doing a girl thing like that; I'd never hear the end of it. The Yid's light shone down through the hole in the top of the elevator car, and I saw my face on the phone box. My features wouldn't stay put, though—shadows danced across it like moon steam. And it was so dark, my face was nothing but shadows, so when the shadows changed, my face changed, as if some kid was trying to make a face in a ball of clay, and he didn't like it, so he kept smooshing it this way and that, and he still didn't like it.

That's when for the second time that dumb night, I started to get teary—so in spite of everything, I had to figure, I was still pretty. If you can feel a cat smile on your calf, Tule was smiling, the little bugger.

"Hey, *shiksie*, don't I get a hello today, hello today, today, day, day, day?" The Yid jumped down, and I felt the car shake, the way I like. I didn't say a word—that's how to spook him. It got very quiet. I could just see the Yid up there on top of the elevator, wondering what kind of shit he'd jumped into the middle of, if there was some Nazi bull waiting for him down below. I picked up Tule real quiet and held her close and shushed her in her furry cat's ear. The Yid's flashlight did a slow sweep of the places it could hit through the hatch. Real soft: "*Shiksie?*" I heard him sneak down onto his belly.

By now, with just that little bit of light spilling from the Yid's flashlight, I could see everything pretty well. I saw his curly head poke down through the hole like a rat's head out a hole in the mop board. His scarf hung down a little. His eyes were so big, they looked like skinned hard-boiled eggs. He was shitting bricks, believe you me.

So I said, quiet but with a lot of wind, "*Achtung!*"

I thought he was gonna blow out of that shaft as if it were a missile silo and he was an ICBM. The elevator shook like crazy. Tule yowled and jumped out of my arms. I'd never laughed so hard in my life. The Yid dropped his flashlight and scrambled back up the shaft. I heard the cover board creak open.

He must have heard me laughing then because the board crashed down again, and the Yid said, "Shit!" and the shaft said, "Shit, shit, shit, shit!"

The Yid was very reasonable, miraculously reasonable. It's all those rabbis in his genes, is what I'm thinking, figuring out if a chicken eats seed through another guy's fence, whose is the meat, or if a guy is born with two heads, which head he has to wear his yarmulke on—stuff like that. Anybody else would have gone ape, and I might have had to do something bad to him. But the Yid, he knew about my abilities, and he wasn't about to provoke me. He stayed reasonable, and he said, "Very good, *shiksie*—you know a German word. Now shine up a flashlight so I can climb down."

"No."

"*Shiksie*, be nice, *shiksie*. This is my spaceship I let you in on, isn't it? Shine."

"You know where the damn elevator is. Just jump, for crissakes."

"Shine. I'm asking you nice. Am I your friend or what?"

I just sat tight, enjoying my joke like a guy with money in his pocket. Then the Yid turned on the charm and said, "Who loves you, *shiksie*?"

It didn't have any effect on me. That stuff never touches me. I would have drawn it out some more, but Tule made me pick up the Yid's flashlight, which had dropped down through the hole, and shine it up the shaft.

"I thank you, *shiksie*." The Yid jumped down onto the elevator. He gave me a little size-her-up look through the hole, then shinnied down the rest of the way. He stood in front of me, and Tule stretched up against his leg. He picked her up, and she actually started purring, the traitor. He held out his hand, and I kind of found myself giving him his flashlight. "Thank you, *shiksie*. That was a pretty funny trick. You scared the shit out of me."

The Yid wasn't all that much older than I was. He was maybe nineteen years old. I was what—sixteen, I guess. He had curly red hair and hazel eyes and thick eyebrows that looked like they were stitched on, nice eyebrows, and a long face and a big nose like they have, and he was real tall, maybe a head taller than I was, so if I looked straight ahead, I'd be looking at his chest. He was pretty well built, I suppose. He wore granny glasses with stems the color of a root beer float. He wore combat boots and a trench coat except in the hottest months. He had a Guatemalan scarf that I darned for him once even though I can't sew worth spit. When he smiled he had big dimples and his lips curled down at the corners. I liked it all right when he smiled.

The Yid said, "You kill anybody lately, *shiksie*?" and I realized I'd been staring at him, and if my face hadn't been dead, I would have blushed then. I looked down, and he reached past me to the phone box for a *schmatte*.

"Tule says don't."

"Don't?" He wiped his fingers one at a time, the best way he could, without dropping Tule or the flashlight. Meticulous. Careful. That's how he gathered his power, is how I figured it, by taking time to do things, soaking up the extra seconds like a solar panel taking in sunlight. I tried it a couple times—never around him, mind you— and it works.

"Don't kill. Tule says don't kill anybody anymore."

"So you're understanding cat talk now, *shiksie*! Very good! German and Cat. You're becoming a linguist, a polyglot, a sophisticate. When the rest of my people come down here, you can interpret. You can explain to them what all the Earth guys are saying from all the different nations and peoples and tongues—and species."

I tried not to smile when he said that. I tried not to let it make me feel so good. I think I succeeded fairly well.

He handed me back the *schmatte* to put away with the dirty ones and said, "So, are you taking Tule's advice? 'Thou shalt not kill'?"

"I don't know yet."

"What else did she say?"

"Other stuff. None of your business, actually."

"Take the cat." He thrust Tule back at me, rammed her against my tits, felt like. I took her. "Let's go in, huh? Let's get out of the damn decompression chamber and get inside the ship. I'm tired to death of goddam Earthlings, aren't you?"

"Sometimes I want to just kill them all."

"But Tule says don't, huh?"

"Tule's not my boss."

"Anyway, it's too soon, *shiksie*. Don't kill them all yet."

"You're not my boss either." I let Tule jump down and prowl around and sniff things.

"You think I don't know this?" He pulled open the metal gate. He pulled open the big wooden doors with the steel braces and bolts the size of hot dogs. You had to be strong to do that, because of the rust, and nothing was on its right track anymore. Right away, I felt the warm air rush in from the unknown section of Sears and Roebuck.

The unknown section, our section, got heated up right along with the known section. We had running water in there too, and one outlet worked for a two-burner stove and a plug-in lightbulb. I wanted to get a gang plug for more appliances and stuff, but the Yid said no, if we ever blew a fuse, that would be the end of all our juice for good. We had a window too, the Yid and me, a little half-sizer that wasn't made to open. It was dirty as hell and had cobwebs clumped all over it, but you could see the moon in it tonight. The Yid wouldn't let me clean it, in case somebody outside should ever notice the difference.

Sometimes the Yid was *too* careful. But what the hell: It was his spaceship.

If you didn't know, if the Yid hadn't let you in on it, a person would probably never know that it was a spaceship. It just looked like a narrow, chopped-off piece of a warehouse, if you didn't know. Only thing was, it was extraordinarily clean in there—except for the window glass. It was hospital clean when the Yid first took me and Tule in, and since then, I'd scrubbed it down even better. We sanded the floor on our hands and knees. We Gymsealed it a little at a time so the stink wouldn't get too suspicious.

All that time on all fours, shoulder to shoulder, with *schmattes* and sponges, the Yid had never made a pass at me. He had never, what you call, taken advantage of me at all—lucky for him! Probably, he was scared to. Like I said, I knew I was pretty, in spite of the dead face and the crew cut and the scarecrow clothes, which I hear some guys actually find attractive.

The Yid had seen what I could do. He used to hang out at the Wee Spot before he entered the final phase of his mission, which required relative solitude. He used to talk about politics and religion and sell a little hashish. I kind of got to know him when I was bussing tables; I listened to him and his pals talk. Sometimes we shared a piece of cheesecake; I mean, because he wouldn't finish it, and I'd clear his plate, and then I'd eat the rest over by the sink, and he didn't know it. I can read a person's character from their table after they leave. I could tell he was from very far away. I didn't like him and I didn't not like him. I don't need anybody that much that I would like them or not like them.

Then one night when I'm dumping some garbage out back I see him with a couple guys in the alley. They look like college guys, football guys, frat guys—I mean, big. I don't know what I mean. They're half-drunk. They're hurting him. One's got a tire iron. He waves it and spits on it and laughs. They push the Yid against a brick wall. It's a hot night. Even the Yid is in shirtsleeves. They pull him up by the collar and slap him around. I hear him whining and sobbing after the excuses run out, and he can't pay them back their money, and he hasn't got any more stuff. One of the guys pushes him to his knees and lays back to kick him, when the guy gets a heart attack—if you catch my drift.

I shout at the other guy, "Lay off, asshole."

"Huh?"

The second guy looks at me and loses bowel control and starts throwing up. The Yid stands up. He's shaking. He wipes the back of his hand across his face and checks it for blood. There's only a little, on his mouth, but the next day he'll have a black eye. The guy with the heart attack is squirming on the pavement, hyperventilating.

Usually when someone sees you do stuff like heart attacks and seizures, if they aren't terrified out of their mind the way most people are, you have to kill them or ruin a part of their brains so they won't get you into trouble later. But I have this feeling that maybe the Yid is okay. I just stand there and watch him watching me. At first he looks completely blank, but pretty soon that smile of his sneaks out, like the moon from behind some steam, with the corners of his lips turned down—I can see how it might move some girls.

He threads past the two heavies. This Yid must have seen some wonders. Most people if they didn't just think the one guy tripped and hit his head and the other guy was sick drunk to begin with, they would be all gaga. Not the Yid, though; he's onto me. "You've got a talent, haven't you?"

"I don't know what you're talking about."

"Maybe we should call an ambulance."

"It wouldn't help."

He nods. He keeps looking at me. I don't blush. Then he says, "Take a walk with me. I'll show you some stuff."

I say, "Forget it. I got dishes here."

He just stands there smiling that way. I take off my apron and follow him down the alley, across the parking lot, up the fire escape, down the elevator shaft, to the spaceship. As far as Sarge is concerned, I had to knock off a little early.

I think the heart attack guy died. I never saw him around again. I don't know for sure; I don't follow these things up. Lots of people get hurt, lots of people die, you know what I mean? If Tule's not around to bug me, why should I care, is how I figured it, and I'd left her home that night.

I was worried that somebody had seen it happen, though. Stupid, huh? I mean, who would make the connection anyway between some drunk falling and dying and a dishwasher with a dead face standing fifty yards away? But I couldn't shake this feeling that somebody had been watching it all. I couldn't shake the feeling of these cold eyes on me. Sometimes they were cold and sometimes they were warm. I don't know what I mean. I couldn't shake it.

* * *

The Yid closed the elevator doors behind us. "What are you thinking about, *shiksie*? I smell wood burning."

"I'm thinking about the first time you ever took me up here, after you got beat up behind the Wee Spot."

"You make it sound like a date—*took me up here*."

"Just shut up."

He had reached our lightbulb. He screwed it in and suddenly everything was beautiful, more beautiful than ever. The Yid had painted the tin ceiling gold. It looked like a goddam chapel. I thought I was gonna cry again. I don't know what was wrong with me that night.

He said, "You like it?"

"It's okay."

I looked all around the spaceship. I looked at the east wall with all the black-and-white photograph posters of the Great Pyramid at El Gizah lined up like a sheet of postage stamps, every one the same and none of them peeling off or dirty or ripped. Those posters put the Yid back a bundle, and he even had to buy extras to make up for the ones that got ruined from dripped paste when he put them up. I had the ruined ones up in the room that I rented at the widow Mrs. Bobson's. They weren't that bad.

"My people built those," is what the Yid liked to say.

The southeast corner had the utility sink in it. I could see that it was flecked with gold paint and there were wet brushes and a roller in it. There were bundles of newspaper piled up under it that the Yid must have used for a drop cloth, because I didn't see a single speck on the floor. I could see my goddam face in that Gymsealed floor if the light was right.

I looked at the south wall: *Playboy* centerfolds. You couldn't make out individual girls too well because of the way the light reflected off the shiny paper; the lightbulb was plugged in underneath the Playmates on the south wall. The girls were trimmed around the dirty window. It was a mishmash of airbrushed body parts—lots of legs and tits with all different kinds of nipples and the hollows of shoulders and curvy flanks and eyes with long lashes and half-closed eyes, bedroom eyes, and lips, red lips, pouts and puckers and grins and little o's like blowing you a kiss, and tight little bits of clothing with pink skin around them or sepia skin around them, gauzy things with nipple dents, and every variety of hair on a person's head, but no pubic hair, because these were all from old, used *Playboys* that the Yid picked up second-hand. No armpit hair either. Lots of painted toenails and fingernails.

I shaved my armpits once. I didn't like it.

"That's my Fleshpot," is what the Yid liked to say about the south wall. "If you don't like it, don't look. It's not what you think. I'm not like Earth people. That stuff does not move me, *shiksie*. I simply study it in order to understand you *goyim*." *Goyim* is the word the Yid used for everyone living on Earth.

Once, I said, "I'm not a *goyim*."

And the Yid studied me, and he said, "Maybe! Maybe!"

I let the Yid watch me while I turned and looked at the west wall. The gold ceiling made everything look different, and I wanted to feel the room all over, to see how it had changed. I remember my high school got a new red curtain once, and when the principal walked out in front of it for the first time, her big head of white hair looked green. That's what I mean. The west wall was flat black,

black as a hole. The Yid kept extra paint in a can in the corner under the sink to touch it up whenever anything but black showed up on it. He wanted that wall to be invisible, like space with no stars in it. Only now it had a tiny bit of a shine to it, from the gold ceiling.

The Yid must have caught what I was looking at, because he said, "I'll fix that. I just have to think about it a little."

The west wall was Sears Roebuck's on the other side: *Catalog Orders* and *Returns and Repairs*. The west wall was the one that the Yid's people were going to come melting through when they linked up with his spaceship to take him away and debrief him and whoever he picked to show them—with me translating, if I felt like it. The Yid didn't know that *Achtung* was the only foreign word I knew, picked up from *Hogan's Heroes*, or that the only animal tongue I knew wasn't even Cat but just Tule, but I guessed I could take some Berlitzes if it came right down to it or just tell the Yid's people whatever the hell I wanted to—they wouldn't know the difference, because nobody can keep a poker face like the Fabulous Lea Tillim AKA Cadaver Dimples.

Point is, the west wall had to have zero albedo, no reflection, the opposite of the Gymsealed floor. Actually, that's how I wanted my face to be. The Yid called it a "Light Sponge" or an "antimirror." The *Meschiach*, the craft that was going to rendezvous with the Sears Roebuck once we got outside the Earth's atmosphere, couldn't join up with us if there was even a little reflection off that west wall.

Not that I ever believed any of that crap.

The north wall, which was opposite the Yid's Fleshpot

and between the pyramids and the Light Sponge, had two bookcases full of gitchy gewgaws and ratty, threadbare books in Yid language, one bookcase in each corner, and in between, which was most of that wall, there was the Holy of Holies, which I had no idea what it was because it was all covered with a purple velour curtain. The lumps behind that curtain could look like anything from an oversize treadle sewing machine to a bunch of football players rushing you to a giant bloody boar's head, depending on the light and on whether you'd had to kill anybody that day, which can leave a kind of sour taste in your mouth and make you imagine stuff.

The Yid knew what was back there, and Tule knew what was back there, because she burrowed underneath that curtain sometimes and sniffed around, which the Yid let her, for mousing. As for me, neither one of them would tell me anything about it, and it was taped down in a way that anybody would know if the curtain ever got lifted for somebody to go through. The Yid would "grind my *kishkes*," he said, if I ever peeked. I wasn't worried about that—I could kill him first, easy. Only, then he'd never let me up in the spaceship with him anymore.

Not that I'd really miss it.

I looked all around that spaceship, and I appreciated how the gold ceiling made everything look a jillion times better. It was like the Magic Fingers in your bed, when your father takes you away from your mother when you're a little girl because he says Mom's no good for you, how the Magic Fingers makes everything in that motel room, in all the motel rooms that the Magic Fingers is in the bed of, seem like a perfect fairy tale, and for just a quarter in the slot by the bedpost, so that, in spite of everything, his drinking and his sleazy girlfriends and his calling your mother a whore, it's almost okay.

All the time I was looking around, the Yid was looking at me. Who knows what the Yid ever had on his mind?

He said, "I've decided to tell you some more about my people. I think you might be able to help us, but it will be dangerous, and you'll have to use your talent. Would you be okay with that, *shiksie*?"

I said, "Tule isn't my boss. I'm okay with everything."

chapter two

I Become Reacquainted with a Couple of Muscles

I used to give myself a crew cut with a twenty-buck electric barber machine. When I was done, I would sit on the floor in the corner of the bathroom where the outlet was for the machine, and where I had wedged the second mirror. It's a double mirror job when you do yourself: one in front, one behind. I would sit there for a long time just holding the shaver against my head, under my ear, in the nape of my neck, on my forehead, all over, just closing my eyes and feeling it hum all through my head, till Tule got jealous and yowled at the bathroom door, and I had to let her in.

"Who loves you, Tule?"

I still looked kind of pretty. You know how you can tell? You kind of squint at yourself in the mirror. You try to see yourself the way a guy would see you. It's very tricky because every time you look—there you are looking, but what you want to see is how you look when your eyes are pointed somewhere else. It's like trying to tickle yourself. You can't. Nobody laughs when they try to tickle themselves.

I could tell I was still pretty because I felt sorry for the face I saw in the mirror. When there's feeling—that's how you know. Nobody cares about ugly people. I've got a nose out of Central Casting, small and slightly turned up at the end. My eyes are root beer brown, like my hair, when I have hair. My lips look like a Valentine's heart, but I would take care of them by pinching them together tight so guys like Sarge, my boss at the restaurant, wouldn't get the wrong idea and make me have to hurt them. I've got what they call bone structure, too; it means you can see my skull under my face.

I always had good color, extraordinary color, rosy red. It's a curse. Naturally, my skin would burn like hell whenever I tried to use any kind of makeup, so there was nothing I could do along those lines; so I just worked hard at deadening the facial muscles instead.

It's not so hard to kill your face that way. If you just throw all your attention, say, into the pit of your stomach and keep it there like a cold lead ball, not letting any feeling into your face no matter what happens, no matter how much your mother screams and your father slaps and the blood and steam spout, and people point at you and call you a freak, or throw stones or run away, well, you can pretty much get the moxie out of your face.

Maybe I'll make one of those workout videos in case there are people like me out there. The Fabulous Lea Tillim, Star of Morgues and Emergency Rooms, teaches

YOU how to make YOUR face look like a dead fish. We'll start with strengthening and centering exercises for the lower abdominal muscles. For the face, we'll do centrifugal shakes, to get it loose and flabby. Then there will be a series of graded mental exercises, clips of faces mostly: staring faces, starving babies, angry mothers, drooling Casanovas, mimsy poets, nurses, cops, all kinds of faces that want something from you. And you have to keep your face dead.

Along with my workout video there will be a free Lea Tillim Patented Twitchometer that you hook up to your puss with two alligator clips. When that baby cries or the cop barks, if you react—it zaps you. Just like real life. Any takers?

When your face is dead, people respect you. The tough cookies are easy—you're talking their language. The so-called nice people are more of a challenge. "Nice" people, if they don't get some reaction out of you, their natural response is to try harder, to really work those dimples and that glad hand. They try to crack you open as if you were a walnut and their greasy falsettos were nutcrackers. When they see that you are not softening, when they hear their dumb singsong bouncing back at them off your dead face—they get angry. I call that *respect*. I can work with that.

Mrs. Bobson was another story. Take that night up in the spaceship with the Yid when he was about to let me in on his whole mission. Nobody ever asked Mrs. Bobson to wait up for me. I never even told her my real last name, is how much I wanted out of that bag. It pissed me off that I ever even had to think about what she might be feeling about me, as if it was any of her business. I just wanted to sit and listen to the Yid, cozier than I ever was in my life, if you want to know the truth. But I could see Mrs. Bobson waking up at the hour of the wolf from one of her lonely old lady dreams and checking my room and seeing that I wasn't in there and worrying. I used to tape the bottom of the door sometimes the way I learned from seeing the Yid's curtain over the *Holy of Holies*, so I knew for certain that she opened my door when I wasn't there. I had to think about all that while I was sitting in front of the Yid.

The Yid was looking at me with those big, serious eyes, as if I were the only person in the whole universe. Halfway through, he even reached over and held my hand, and I didn't stop him, and I didn't cripple him or burn his brains out.

He's telling me probably the most important things in all of history—if you believe any of that crap—and I've got Mrs. Bobson's sorry-ass face in my mind, like I'm supposed to worry about her worrying about me. I was damned if I would.

Mrs. Bobson's one kid died in the Second World War, and her daughter died in a car accident, which had nothing to do with me. It happened before I was even born, and her husband died of lung cancer a couple years ago, and now she was all alone in her house that looked like a museum with lace and gauzy curtains and mahogany cabinets with glass doors and fancy cups and saucers inside them, so you could hardly take a step in there without being afraid of breaking something if you wanted to get up to your room at night. Plus I was sick and tired of her trying to hand me her daughter's old fancy dresses and frocks and ribbons and shoes and frilly underclothes, even if all those things were coming back in, like it said in

the *Vogues* she liked to leave all over the place. I mean—
look at me! I'd spent my whole goddam life not being the
type, but Mrs. Bobson only saw what she wanted to see.

Tule liked her, which was about the only point I had
against that feline.

That's the kind of slag I had to dump out of my mind
that night while the Yid explained his mission: "These are
the six keys to my power, *shiksie:* the Gold Sky, the Mirror
Below, the Pyramid Wall, the Fleshpot, the Light Sponge,
and the Holy of Holies. All this was here before Mr. Sears's
and Mr. Roebuck's ancestors were even down from the
trees. I just came along and made it visible.

"I am one of the Chosen of the Chosen of the Chosen.
Among all the peoples of the Earth, the Jews are the
Chosen. Among the Jews, the Kohanim and the Levites,
the ancient priestly classes, are the Chosen. Among the
Kohanim and the Levites, God Tetragrammaton, whom
the *goyim* call Jehovah, chose one family that all of cre-
ation was created to bring forth after generations and
generations of refinement and selection.

"That is *my* family, *shiksie, my* people."

I said, "You told me."

The Yid just went on: "There are now exactly sixteen
of us in the universe, two to the two to the two to the two:
thirteen on Earth as we know it, and three in the supernal
realms. The thirteen will gather here in my spaceship.
Then the three will come from the supernal realms in
their spaceship, the *Meschiach,* which will link up with us
just beyond the stratosphere, by means of the Light
Sponge. Our combined spaceships will take us away to the
Promised Land, to the true *Ish-ra-el,* which is above all
things and within all things, and of which everything on

Earth is a profane reflection, like the moon in muddy, broken water."

"What about *me*?"

"The *goyim* will stay below. You don't have to worry. For the *goyim*, everything will stay the same. You *have* your reward."

"I don't have any goddam reward, and 'the same' is a piece of shit, as far as I can see, and you said I could interpret."

"Maybe! Maybe! You have to have *k'vanna*!"

"*K'vanna*?"

"The six keys are all made of *k'vanna*. They *look* like walls, floor, ceiling, but they are really *k'vanna*. If you took away the *k'vanna*, they would all be empty of power."

"*K'vanna*?"

"Fervor, *shiksie*, the fervor of belief and devotion to God Tetragrammaton! And if I didn't think you were capable of *k'vanna*, I would never have risked the spaceship by letting you aboard."

"Do *goyim* get to go or not? You just said you wanted me to help you, and now you're leaving me down below with Mrs. Bobson and my stinking reward!"

"One or two *goyim* may get to come."

I shut up then. I didn't want to scotch my chances, I mean, in case he wasn't a complete fruitcake.

"If any of the thirteen ever come across one another, *shiksie*, you know how it's going to be?"

I shook my head, no. The Yid opened his hands wide on either side of him, palms facing, as if he were holding a medicine ball. He brought them together slowly until the fingers interlaced and the palms touched; it looked like praying.

"It's going to be like this. But everything has to be perfect in order to send out the signal to the other Chosen Ones of us thirteen, to meet up here. The floor is good. The Fleshpot is good. The Pyramid Wall is good. The Holy of Holies is perfect—someday maybe I'll let you see it, and it will change your life forever. There's a little problem with the Gold Sky and the Light Sponge, but I am confident I can fix it."

"Have you got anything to eat, Yid? My stomach's growling." When I say stuff like that, it's not because I'm stupid. Consider it a pressure valve. The Yid was getting hyper. He was practically starting to blaze, and I felt like I was turning to warm water and running down onto the Mirror Below or steaming up onto the Gold Sky, and I didn't want to. I wanted to stay right there with the Yid, so I slowed him down that way. I wasn't really hungry.

He reached into a pocket in his trench coat, pulled out half a bar of chocolate-covered halvah with the torn wrapper folded back over it, and slapped it into my palm. I saw him clench his teeth, but he didn't say anything angry. He just went on talking.

"*Shiksie*, the whole reason my people have been scattered, the thirteen of us on Earth and also the three supernal ones, this actual diaspora of which the Earthly diaspora of the Jews is a fractured, muted image, the cause of our being marooned like this among the *goyim* . . ." The Yid looked all around, then leaned closer and whispered as if he were afraid of someone spying on us. His shoulders were up to his ears. The little muscle under his left eye twitched. ". . . The cause is the Evil One."

He stared at me in a way that made me feel awful. I couldn't look away. I didn't want to look away. I liked it when the Yid locked eyes with me; I mean, it was interesting. But he was too hyper for me. I took a bite of the halvah.

"Do you understand what I'm telling you, *shiksie*?"

"Sure. You and your buddies are getting screwed by the Devil."

"That's right. By the Devil and by his agents, people you and I may see every day. I need you to take care of them for me, so that my people can come together again, and go back to the Garden of Eden."

"While I stay with Mrs. Bobson?"

"I'm telling you, I'll think about it! What more can I say? There are sixteen of us, and I am only one!"

"I want to go too."

The Yid stood up, pissed. He turned his back on me and flounced over to the Fleshpot. "I told you I have power of my own. I don't really need you, you know."

I said, "Fine." I had a picture in my mind of those college boys crowding the Yid and of him going down and down and down. I didn't remember that he used any power back then. I called Tule. She meowed and padded up to me from under the Holy of Holies. She sounded disappointed; I think she'd been casing a mouse. I could take the Yid or leave him, is how I saw it. I scooped Tule into my jacket.

Tule said, *Don't go.* I covered her under my shirt.

I went straight to the decompression chamber—no skin off my teeth—but when I pulled at that big wooden door, the damn thing wouldn't budge. I don't know why because I always could work it if I put all my strength into it. Of course, all my strength wasn't going into it. I don't know where all my strength was—stuck in my throat, felt like, or back there behind me with the Yid. And I just got mad at that big damn impossible door—if it was a person I would have steamed him—and I slammed into it with two fists, and it bruised my knuckles, and for the third time that ridiculous night, I cried, and Tule jumped out of my shirt and out of my jacket, and she scratched my stomach all bloody on the way, and I stuck my hand in there and I felt the sting, and I looked at it, just like the Yid had wiped his banged head and looked at his hand, and I saw the blood, and I said, "Damn you, you stupid feline!" and then I felt the Yid come up behind me.

He was reaching past me to the door. He was standing right up against my back so I could smell his halvah breath—sesame and honey—and feel his arm against my shoulder. He pulled open the decompression chamber door. Right through my back, I felt his muscles tighten and flex in his arm and even in his chest, his big, strong chest that he hid under that ugly, limp, ragged trench coat, and then the door was open, and he said, "Do you really want to go, *shiksie*?"

I was still trying to clean the catch out of my throat and get my breathing off the breakers. He put his hands on my shoulders and spun me around to face him, and I let him, but I wouldn't look at him. I looked at his stupid big feet in those combat boots. I saw a couple tears roll off me onto his shoes. I felt his hand on my head. He stroked my crew cut that Tule wanted me to grow like a regular girl's hair. I felt his hand slide back and forth over my head as soft as a mother powdering a new baby. I still didn't say anything. I could feel him listening to me not saying anything. I knew he was just looking at me, listening to me, thinking about me, and it was the most wonderful feeling in my whole life, and I wish I could have died right then and there and have the whole stupid thing over with. It felt good just to breathe, knowing that he was taking it in—my breath, my heartbeat.

He touched my chin. Ever so gently, he lifted my face with one finger, and I let him. I tried not to look up at first. My eyes were blurry with tears, but out of the corner of my eye, I saw Tule sneaking under the Holy of Holies again, and I looked up at the Yid, and I said, "Tell me your real name, Yid."

In his eyes, he looked like he was falling. Just for a second, he looked like he'd been climbing and he'd just lost his footing and he was startled and he wanted somebody to throw him a rope.

Don't look at me, Yid! You're my rope!

Then it passed, and I saw those dark brows wrinkle, then smooth out again, and there was a funny little light in his hazel eyes. I kind of let the weight of my head press down on his finger a little bit to wake him up from the thinking that he was doing. I don't think I ever talked to anybody that way before, not even to Tule—intimate. No words. It was like talking with your skin, by wrinkling or puckering—subtle, subtle—and if you just so much as narrowed your eyes a jillionth of an inch, that would be like thundering. I thought, *So this is sex!*

And he smiled this sad, shy, little smile, and he said, "Jack."

And I said, "Jack." If I could have smiled, I would have.

Then he took his finger away from my chin, and my chin fell a little, and that seemed to move him somehow, so that he had to quick touch my face again. He touched my cheek where there was a tear. And he stroked my cheek a little. He touched my face in different places. He said, "*Zygomaticus minor*, moderate crying and affliction; *levator labii superioris*, crying…" I felt his finger slide down past my lips, and I let them be a little heart and I didn't try to pinch them, and he said, "*Depressor anguli oris*, muscle of sadness and complementary muscle to aggressive feelings…" He touched my throat and whispered, "*Platysma*, fear, terror, anger…"

He shook his head like he couldn't stand being alive for another second. It could have been *me* shaking my head that way—I knew exactly what he meant. I must have shook my head that way twenty-three jillion times before I learned how to kill my face, because it's a stupid dead end to let yourself feel things. I was forgetting that for a minute, I guess.

Jack took a deep breath. He let it out fast, like someone about to jump off a diving board or a bridge. Then he touched me on another place on my cheek, then stroked my forehead just above my eyebrows. He looked at me so hard, straight in the eyes, that I could hardly see him. He said, "*Frontalis*, the muscle of attention; *zygomaticus major*, the muscle of joy."

I thought he was going to kiss me then. Instead, he said, "Are you going to help us?"

I said, "I don't care."

It was the best I could do.

The Yid told me to meet him at the Wee Spot early on Saturday night, which I had off from work, so that I would just be a regular customer and we would, like, eat something there, at a table and everything. We were going to sit in a window table and he was going to teach me about the Devil and show me a lot of the Devil's agents who would be walking right down Monroe Avenue. And he would fill me in some more on my assignment. We were going to meet more often from then on, and not just a few times a week like before. He was supposed to inventory my talent, using the scientific method, he said, like lining up bugs and stuff and experimenting how I could take them out or cripple them from how far away, how many, and so on, and then small animals, but not people yet, not *goyim*.

When I went home that night, by which I mean to Mrs. Bobson's place, my face was so out of control I was afraid for the first time since I was a little girl that I would get mugged, because I would look like such a *mark*, with so much of my insides showing for anybody to take advantage of. I ran down the streets, and when I got tired I walked fast. I slipped on ice a couple times, and Tule got very tense inside my jacket, but I made it okay, because I was happy.

I slowed down when I got to my block, because I wanted to hit the shadows in case one of Bobson's marquetry ladies was on the scene. It's unbe-goddam-lievable, but I would now and then run into one of them leaving Bobson's house after midnight, when I got home from the Spot. I mean: marquetry! —what is the appeal? Plus, if you ask me, with their human prune smiles and squeaks and nicey-nice, they showed an unnatural interest in yours truly, which I don't appreciate from the living dead.

When I finally got to Mrs. Bobson's front door and turned the key in the lock, I had to just stand there for a minute before I went in. My face felt so funny, I didn't know what to make of it. I combed through my memory to figure out if there was anything there that would give me a clue to what my face was doing. Then it struck me what was going on, and I had to laugh.

I was smiling.

It wasn't with my *depressor labii inferioris*, either, which is near the corner of my mouth, which the Yid showed me, which is for irony. I was smiling a smug, peaceful smile, a *buccinator* smile, like money in the bank, I don't know why. I must have been half-crazy that night.

I cut it out and went inside, into Mrs. Bobson's mausoleum of a living room, which she kept steaming hot, day and night, because she was always cold. In the room that I rented, I kept the windows wide open to make up for it, because the heat drove me crazy: What, was I still up my mother's hole or something? is how it made me feel. Plus everything smelled like rotten skin and Lysol.

I let Tule out. "It's a girl!" She padded off through the thick carpet, under the dining room table with the leaves and the felt pad and the fancy lace tablecloth that Mrs. Bobson had wasted her life making. She scooted past the armoire and the end table and past the glass-door scrollwork-leg mahogany cabinet with the good china and the family photos in velvet frames and the bowling trophies and war medals and the old box camera that nobody ever used anymore, into the kitchen for kibbles.

The light was on in there, which was a bad sign.

It was a bad sign because it meant that Mrs. Bobson had probably left a snack for me or done some other "nice"thing that I wished to God in heaven that she wouldn't. I had told her not to, maybe a jillion and a half times. Once she even tried to pump me about who my parents were, did I have any siblings, and other BS that was none of her nearsighted, hard-of-hearing business. The reason she took me in as a tenant was that her old lady neighbors told her it would be safer to live with someone. She was too fogged up to see what a bad bet I was from the looks of me. She should have left it at that—*quid pro quo*—but those old bags, their sentimentality always kicks in from all the disintegrating hormones or whatever. They have to make some kind of a thing out of it like you're supposed to be their little friend, which forget it!

So I went into the kitchen. Yes, she had an embroidery "God Bless Our Home" and a Jesus with his heart showing through his ribs and yellow wallpaper with spoons and eggbeaters on it. The light was left on to trap me into going in there, and there was a little kid's thermos on the table with Minnie Mouse on it. Next to that there was a plate of Mrs. Bobson's oatmeal cookies and an orange paper napkin folded into a triangle. There was also a note folded like a tent.

I didn't have the energy for it. I knew it would just get me angry. I opened the refrigerator, where I got to have half a shelf to myself as part of the deal, and I took out my apple. I took a bite of it, and I put it back. I stuck the rest of the Yid's wrapped-up halvah in there. I left everything else just the way it was, and I went upstairs without touching a single damn thing except the floor.

I didn't have to tiptoe past the old lady's room or not flush the toilet because she slept like the dead. Also, she snored louder than any noise I could ever make. I went into my room, and Tule flew in before me as soon as I opened the door.

I could tell that Bobson had been in there, because, besides the window being closed, which I was pretty sure I had left open, I heard a fly buzzing around. There had been a thaw the other day, the kind that wakes up some of the bugs at the wrong time, and I had seen these tired old farts of houseflies stumbling and buzzing in the upstairs sitting room. But I kept my room antiseptic, and when the window screen had ripped from Tule clawing at it, I sewed it with black button thread right away. In my room, nothing but nothing was alive except for me and Tule—and Mrs. Bobson, when she nosed in. So I knew this zombie insect must have come in with Mrs. Bobson.

I got so mad just thinking about it, my mind focused in on that fly before I could even stop myself, which I didn't care to anyway, and I felt a little snap inside me, like on your tongue when you spit, and the buzzing stopped.

Tule looked at me. Her eyes glowed, big and red in the dark. *Not good, Lea.*

I said, "Oh, shut up. You're probably gonna eat it now." She couldn't deny it.

Then she said, *Turn on the light and look at yourself in the window, honey baby. You're pretty.*

And I turned on the light, and the window turned into a mirror and I looked, and I was pretty. I decided right then to grow my hair long. I decided to wear some of the girl things that Mrs. Bobson had given me that I kept in some shopping bags in my closet. I decided to work on bringing back a couple of facial muscles, like maybe the ones for joy and attention, like the Yid—like *Jack*—had said. I took off all my clothes and I touched my shoulders and my back and my head and my face where the Yid had touched me. I touched a few parts of me where Jack *hadn't* touched me, too.

It's funny how your body has ideas in the skin, different ideas in different parts. If I put my palm on my belly, I feel like a baby; I remember somebody rubbing me there when I was a baby, is what I think, and it makes me feel drowsy and warm, which gets to be too much, and I have to stop. If I pet my tits, I get a kind of a melting feeling, and I feel like a heat wave coming off hot asphalt, the way the air ripples in the sun. If I touch my private parts I get fish memories, as if I used to be a fish, and I can remember squirming around in the deep sea, delicious and deathless and cool. It's all in the skin.

Then I had to go downstairs again to get that halvah that had been in the Yid's pocket out of the refrigerator, because I decided I wanted it with me in my room for some dumb reason. When I came back up, I opened my window before I got into bed. Even though it was pretty dark, I could make out the Great Pyramid of El Gizah on the dripped-on poster on my wall over Mrs. Bobson's tulip wallpaper, and I stared at it for a while, till I almost thought I was there on the desert watching the Yid's people build it. Then I snuggled under the cover with Tule, and I practiced locating and contracting my *frontalis* and my *zygomaticus major*, but it wasn't long before I dropped off and slept like the dead, just like Mrs. Bobson down the hall.

chapter three

Looks Could Kill

That Saturday night, the Yid got to the Wee Spot before me. When I came in off Monroe Avenue, Sarge was trying to throw him out, but the Yid was too smart for him. The place was packed and Sarge wouldn't come right out and shove him out the door, but he was trying to take the Yid up to that edge where the Yid would feel so red in the face, he'd throw *himself* out. I'd seen Sarge play that number lots of times, and it always worked. It worked because people have this pride that if you punch a hole in it and if they can't fight you outright—and nobody could fight Sarge on account of he's an ex–Russian Army boxing champion and even when he *likes* you, he looks like he wants to wring your neck—they have to find some little hole somewhere to lick their wounds and make themselves think they're hot shit again.

Sarge was not convinced that the Yid hadn't had anything to do with the dope smell in the john that cinched
his not getting a beer and wine license. Drug fiends and
dope pushers were not welcome at his establishment, he
said. He was not above an anti-Semitic remark or two, but
the Yid was fielding those okay. What Sarge hadn't figured
on was that when it came to head-to-heads, the Yid didn't
have any pride. You could say anything at all about him,
his mother, his people, or his God, and he'd just flash you
a shit-eating grin and agree; that's how little he gave a
damn about what any *goyim* could ever say. You had to
admire him for that.

I pushed in through the glass door and stood there
and watched for a long time before anybody even recognized me, because I looked totally one hundred percent
different from any way I'd ever looked before. I had a red
beret on, like from the cover of one of Mrs. Bobson's
Vogues, so you wouldn't even know I had a crew cut. I had
on a black turtleneck that showed the shape of my tits,
and I had a little red vest on over it and a short skirt that
was some color or other that Mrs. Bobson's daughter had
been into that wasn't red or black but it was the only thing
that was there in a short skirt. And I had on red panty
hose. Black patent leather pumps, too—it was all I could
do to balance on them.

I even wore some makeup, some nonallergenic
Revlon that would probably turn my puss into volcanoes
anyway, but not until tomorrow. My lips were blood red. I
had blush on my bone structure, on my cheeks and on my
forehead and on my chin. I felt like an asshole and I itched
everywhere.

Also, I hadn't been able to find a coat that would *go,* so I was freezing my buns off.

I'd thought once or twice of asking Mrs. Bobson to help me kind of design myself, but then I would probably have to find another place to live because she would take it as a big green light and glom onto me like athlete's foot or creeping crud. As it was, she kept trying to leave me notes all week, like I was getting a subpoena or something. I just stayed completely out of her way, so she never saw me, and I never touched any damn note. All of them could get rolled into stogies and burn, as far as I was concerned.

I just stood inside the doorway incognito. I was trying to keep my eyes open against the damn stinging eyeliner. The two waiters, Arthur and Sylvia, they didn't even know it was me, and Arthur said, "I'll seat you in a moment, Miss." Both of them were homosexual, but Sarge didn't know that about Sylvia. He was always coming on to her, and she put up with it for the job and because she liked the crowd. Sylvia always wanted to get me alone in the basement by the meat refrigerator, but I didn't give her the time of day. Right now she was looking at me funny, but she was too busy to add it all up, plus one of her girl-friends was eating tiramisu and wanted some more coffee to go with it.

Sarge was saying to the Yid, "You come in here, you talk to this guy and that guy, money is changing hands, maybe you're doing something you would rather do out-side my place, is what I'm saying to you. You know, you could go someplace *kosher*, where nobody has a foreskin and you won't feel too jealous, and you'll have a better chance with the ladies."

The Yid laughed politely, "You've got a point there, Sarge! You've got a real point there! But I like your place! I think you're doing a great job here…"

That's when the Yid saw me at the door. First he squinted, then he smiled. That smile of his wrecked me. It was as if all my makeup and fancy underwear and clothes dried up and got brittle and cracked off like a dead locust skin. I got all squirmy and like I was trying to see myself from outside—which you can't—because I was an ugly, dead-faced bitch made up like a two-bit *Rive-Gauche* whore.

Sarge saw the Yid smile, and he turned around to see what the Yid was smiling at, and he saw me at the door, and he put two and two together, and he said, "Lea Tillim, I'm gonna be a sonuvabitch, you turned into a *dish*!" Arthur heard and looked and dropped three dessert plates and a pot of coffee, and somebody shrieked.

Sylvia was a fox that night. She was dressed to make big tips. She had on her earrings that reached her biceps practically, that had moons and bows and arrows and other symbols of the Goddess, which she was into— which, get out of my face, is how much that stuff moves me. She was wearing low cut, and you can bet she had what to show above it.

Sylvia could definitely play it both ways when she felt like it. She had a deadly pretty face with eyebrows that slanted down toward the middle, like a hawk's wings when it's coasting and circling, and she had big, clear blue eyes and a little mouth. She always looked like she fit in her clothes too, and in her face, and she could make it do whatever she wanted. Me, I could only kill people or cripple them up. Her one funny thing was her complexion,

though, which was pale as a slice of frozen cucumber under all that makeup that she was an absolute expert at. I
caught her touching up one time after she was crying for
some goddam reason, so I know.

Sylvia everythingokayed her tables and she said something in French to one and Italian to another, like she
does, and she came right up to me at the doorway, where
my skin was practically steaming from the cold, and she
put her hand on my elbow and she said in her Mae West
voice, "Honey, what *happened* to *you*?" She looked down
at my pumps. She looked up at my beret. She looked at
everything in between, and she raised her eyebrows, and
she nodded.

I'd been doing some practicing in Mrs. Bobson's bathroom mirror, but right now I just couldn't find my joy
and attention muscles. Sylvia had a sudden case of the
runs. Her face went slack, then she was quick threading her way through the tables to the ladies' room in the
basement. Arthur picked up his shards and mopped up
his spill. He kept his eyes glued to me the whole time, trying to riddle me out, while the guy with the coffee in his
lap sang about how he wasn't mad and everything
was okay.

I just walked over to the Yid's table by the window on
my damn heels, like a circus act. All around me I could
feel people losing their appetites, the bastards, if you
know what I mean, but I thought about Tule and I didn't
pull anything heavy. Sarge stood there collecting flies
while the Yid got up and pulled out a chair for me. At first
I didn't know what he was doing with it, but I got the idea
in a minute; I mean, I worked in a restaurant—I'd seen
people do that, for crissakes. So I sat down. I checked out

who was looking at me. Outside the Yid and Sarge, nobody was looking at me. They were all thinking about their own problems now. They weren't well.

I said, "Thanks, Jack."

The Yid smiled, and I looked at my place setting. The silverware had water stains on it.

Sarge looked at the Yid. I let him alone; the three of us were all too close together somehow. Sarge kept twisting that sausage-muscled face of his. He looked at the Yid. "She your date?"

The Yid shrugged. Sarge smiled. It was like the sun came out. I hardly recognized the guy. He laughed, but it wasn't a mean laugh. He laid his two beefy paws on the table, and he leaned in toward us and he said, "You're on *me*, on the house! We got praline pie, you'll think you died and gone to goddam heaven!" He gave me a wink, and I just sat there and let him while I tried to find my *buccinator*. He shook his head. "Holy cow! For you, Tillim girl, we give the Heeb the benefit, huh?"

He stood up and barked Arthur over to take our order.

People were getting up and leaving. I wonder why. There were plenty of shades of green in those kissers. Arthur wasn't feeling so good himself. Arthur just managed to stay vertical while he said, "May I take your order?" just like someone at a fancy place like a Denny's or a Howard Johnson's.

I said, "Oh shut up!"

The Yid ordered us the pie and some cappuccinos. He ordered it for himself and he ordered it for me. He ordered it for me too, is what I'm saying. He gave Arthur *my* order for me. He told him what to bring me. And Arthur nodded and went away. The Yid was ordering what I wanted for me, and Arthur never blinked an eyelash, and it all seemed so completely natural that I almost believed it myself, as if I were a *girl*. Something happened to places on my skin that made me forget where I was for a minute.

The Yid said, "You're so pretty, *shiksie*!" He really meant it. It came out like a cough or a hiccup that you don't want to, but it just comes out. Nobody can lie that well. "That's twice you've saved me, once from your dark power and once from your light power."

"You mean once from being a black magic bitch and once from having tits and eyeliner." I couldn't stop it from coming out that way. I'm what they call *honest*. "Don't get too happy. Sarge still hates your Yid guts. He's just down-shifted to show me some class so he can hit on me later. It could have just as easy gone the other way."

"I know." He kept those hazel eyes on me a second too long, and my ice was starting to melt and drip, but then he whipped his head around to look out the window, like he was already there but he'd had to go back and fetch his eyes, which had gotten stuck on something. On *me*, in fact. So he was looking out the window at people walking by on Monroe Avenue when he said, "I can't let myself get distracted. This is not just about you and me. We came here so I could show you the agents of the Evil One, some of whom I am asking you to take care of, either by the light or by the dark."

"By the dark. By the dark. Only the dark, Jack." *The light is just for you*, is what I heard in my head, and it startled me so bad, I actually shook my head like trying to get burnt crumbs out of a toaster. It was like a soap opera had snuck in there when I was asleep or something. I hated myself for even thinking that. I started to feel sick, and that scared me, because I realized *that I had done it to myself* just like I'd done it to those boobs that had been giving me the fish eye. I'd gotten so messed up in my mind by having a stupid soap opera thought echoing around in it, and it made me hate my mind so much that I'd twitched a muscle that the Yid didn't know the name of, and now it made my stomach feel like an ingot.

When I looked up again—I hadn't known I'd been looking down—the praline pie and cappuccino were set in front of me on the red-and-white-checkered tablecloth, but I tried not to look at them because it made me feel dizzy. I was holding my stomach inside me like a mug of beer that could foam over if you're not careful. Tule's cat voice was echoing in my head, saying, *You could make people live instead of die—ever think of that?*

The Yid was sipping his cappuccino and staring out the window and talking. It was like listening to the radio from another room, where you can hear the tunes and get the feeling, but the words—they could be practically French. The Yid was pointing across the street to the barbershop where a card game was going on. Then he was nodding in the direction of an old couple walking by, probably from a concert. The old fart was wearing a tuxedo, and the bag had on a black fur coat with frills sticking out under it that looked like the bottom of a fancy lamp shade or the border of a wedding cake. She looked like one of Bobson's marquetry geeks, but I could be wrong.

Then the Yid pointed at a cat that was sitting on the hood of a parked car. Then he wanted me to look at a station wagon that was stopped at a signal light, at the lady who was driving it. You could hardly see her, but you could see the little red fire and the smoke of her cigarette for a second when she puffed.

I would look at the Yid, then I would look at where the Yid was looking. The Yid had slipped off that trench coat of his and draped it over the back of his chair behind him. He was wearing a white shirt with no buttons and no collar, but it had embroidery around the neck and the cuffs, and the sleeves were a little puffy, like guys on the cover of a Harlequin Romance that have their lips in some broad's cleavage on top of a castle.

His hair looked nice. I could smell cologne. His face was as smooth as a baby's tummy, except around his jaws, where there was the tiniest bit of stubble. Even movie stars have that. You can fall into those little spots on their faces and it makes you feel like someone is polishing under your belly with a chamois, I mean, with that masculine skin that you're looking at, if you are the type.

I looked at the Yid, then I looked where he was looking. Little by little, the Yid's French turned into English and the foam settled, and he was saying: "Don't focus on the individuals, *shiksie*. The individuals don't matter—how tall, how old, how fat or skinny, what species even, or male or female—all this could change in a second, in less than a second. Focus on what *is* this that's tall or fat or a dog or whatever. If it is of the Evil One, and you are watching the body but missing the evil spirit, then the spirit can move on and catch you unawares: you have been looking at the wrong thing. But if you are watching the evil spirit, then you can defend yourself. It won't evade you.

"You've got a talent. You can see what I'm talking

about. If you couldn't see it, you couldn't do what you do. You could never find what to do it to. Ordinary people see old folks or a cat or a woman in a car at a stoplight, but we know better."

I looked away then. His cologne and the warmth of his face were making me drip and puddle inside, and I just wanted to get a grip. But Jack thought I was checking to see who was watching us. He said, "Don't be afraid. We can say whatever we like. Ordinary people think we are talking philosophy or religion—something unreal. We are invisible to them, and we don't even have to try. Do you understand what I'm saying?"

"I understand everything plus."

He sighed then. It took me by surprise. He looked straight at me. I had to quick harden up my eyes. He looked sad. He shook his head the tiniest little bit. "Why do you always have to talk tough?"

I didn't have anything to say to that. What was I supposed to say? I felt like a sap. I don't know why I didn't make him turn inside out. I would have once.

"I'm going to take you through this step by step by step, okay, *shiksie*?"

I kind of had some trouble with my face, but I nodded. I think I rubbed my nose a little. I didn't cry. For some dumb reason I wanted to do whatever he said.

"Tell me, *shiksie*, when you hurt somebody, what do you hurt?"

In spite of how he said we were invisible, I had to practically whisper. I felt like I was making one of the Yid's drug deals, like everybody was looking at us, and we would be busted any minute. I said, "It's like a worm. It's like maggots in garbage sometimes, and sometimes it's like new puppies wiggling and sucking their mommy's tits. It's like what you see when you look at the sky and there are little squiggly things swimming around on your eye that if you try to make them stand still, you can't.

"*I* can make them stand still, though. It took me a long time to figure out. It's like finding the muscle to wiggle your ears. You have to kind of sneak around inside your mind until you find it. You have to want to a lot. You have to want to more than you're scared of dying, because to be able to do it, you have to jump off a cliff practically."

"Tell me what kind of a cliff."

I didn't see anything but Jack's hazel eyes. It was kind of wonderful. It was like watching a movie in a dark theater all by yourself, the whole place to yourself when you go some afternoon because you're working the night shift at the Wee Spot, or like watching the sky when you're coming out of a tunnel in a roller coaster.

"There's this cliff that's at the edge of everything that everybody thinks is true and good. As long as you stay back from the edge, it's kind of okay. Only, once in a while something happens to a person that they're *not* okay. They jump. Most of the jumpers die or go crazy, is what I think."

"And the rest?"

"*You* know."

"Say it."

"They get what you call a talent."

"I saw what you did to everybody in the restaurant." His voice was like a heat vent that you sit on in a cold house to warm yourself up. His knee touched my knee under the table for a second, but then he shifted it away. I didn't move mine.

"I did it to myself too. I slipped!"

"I saw that. How could that be? It seems to me that a person couldn't do it to herself. Are you sure it was you that time?"

"Am I sure? Who the hell else would it be? Tule?"

"Okay! Okay! I don't know everything! That's the point, isn't it? But I jumped off some cliffs too, *shiksie*, more cliffs than you did, in fact, but different cliffs, different talents. I can't do what you do, but I can see what you do."

"I did it to myself, Jack. I'm scared."

"Don't be. We're going to take care of all that. We're going to map your talent, *shiksie*, like it was the Antarctic and we were Admiral Byrd. You'll never get lost again, see? And I'm going to learn to do it myself: not just to see it, to do it. We'll be company for each other, *shiksie*. You'll help me?"

I nodded, *yes*. Inside me a voice was screaming so loud I was surprised everybody didn't hear it and turn around to look. *You sap, you don't know this guy! You're climbing back up that cliff you jumped off to become Cadaver Dimples, the Star of Morgues and Emergency Rooms, don't you know it? Right back to all the assholes who slapped the Valentine's heart off your mouth in the first place, while you stood there, little sucker, with your eyes closed and your lips puckered. You're going to lose everything you jumped for!* But I nodded, *yes*.

The Yid finished his cappuccino. It made me look at mine, which I hadn't touched, and I finally drank some. It was the best thing I ever drank in my life. I tasted every bubble. I tasted the bitter and the sweet of it all over my tongue, and it was still warm, too, sliding down my throat.

It made me want to eat some pie, and I ate some, and it was good too. Everything was sweet. Some of it crunched, and some of it melted and stuck, and it was like a whole life story there in my mouth. The only other time I'd ever had praline pie was in the kitchen, leftovers, and you can't taste it when you're between bus trays.

The Yid said, "Those squiggly things that you can make stand still, *shiksie*, you kill one—and a person dies, whoever it's in when you kill it. But the thing is not the person."

"I'm not a brain like you. You're giving me a headache."

"Later we'll go to the spaceship, and we'll talk. I have something to do there anyway, and you can help me." He reached down into his trench coat pocket and pulled out a little pamphlet, it looked like. He took my hand, which I liked. I liked it a lot and I didn't care who knew it, goddammit to hell, and he put this thin little pamphlet in it.

Only it wasn't a pamphlet. I turned back the cover and the first page was all shiny gold, and all the pages were shiny gold, thin as a cobweb. If you just held your finger near it, the corner of the page would curl up to touch you. It made me smile like a baby. "I know what this is for."

"It's gold leaf, German, the best kind. Very expensive. I acquired some quantity of this from an associate of mine."

"This is for the Gold Sky, isn't it?"

"Yes. You can help me put it up. The paint I used isn't good enough. It isn't working like it should. My people aren't getting my transmissions."

"The thirteen."

"Yes. The thirteen and the three."

"I love it. It fills your eye up, Jack. Thank you." I found

my *buccinator* a little, and I think I might have smiled and showed a little joy.

"*Shiksie*..." His eye twitched, like when he had talked about the Evil One. His voice was like the wind. He looked like the wind. His face was like the place the wind comes from.

"What?"

"Nothing." He stopped, the way a gust stops after it blows around the dead leaves. You know it's going to pick up again. It's going to gust and gust until it gets its way and it's winter and everything is scattered and dead, and there's snow.

"What?"

"Kill for me. Kill for me now."

I looked out the window. I felt the Yid watching me real close. The cat was still on that parked car, across the street in front of the liquor store. I zeroed in on it. I could see every hair. I could see every flea. I could see the cells in its blood and the nerves in its brain. I could see more and more of it, until I couldn't see it at all, like when you look at the print in a book under a magnifying glass, and it isn't letters anymore, but just black blotches on a field of bumpy snow.

Then I saw the thing that made the cat live. For the tiniest second, it saw me seeing it there, and it was terrified. If that thing had had a mouth and eyes, you would say, the mouth and eyes opened so wide that they popped like soap bubbles that you blow too hard. It tried to get away, which they never can, and then it was gone, and that cat just fell flat. Later on the guy whose car it was came out and pushed it off his hood with the sleeve of his coat.

It fell into the gutter, where the garbage trucks would get it sooner or later.

The Yid said, "Good."

Can you believe that Sarge sang us a song? I can't. He stood there by our table, in front of the three or four tables that filled up again after all the customers had left sick. He stood there in his cowboy shirt with his stomach that you could see his belly button in like it was clay and somebody had made a dent there with his thumb, and he did it:

"You are my spring.
Your family gives me goats and chickens,
So many that the czar will be jealous,
But I don't care about them.
At the well, all the women want to kill you
Because you are too beautiful.
Even the moon wants your looks, dear.
Everything inside me is blooming
For the love of you.
All the men wonder at how strong I am.
It's because of you.
It's really great."

I must be hallucinating the whole thing, is what I was thinking. If I would have believed it, I would have made him stop. He sang in fits and sputters, because he was translating in his mind from Ukrainian as he went along, and sometimes he would stop and say some Uky word over and over until he thought of an English word that would translate it. In the whole song there weren't two notes that went together in the same key, and Sarge had a voice like a rolling fart. A couple of people applauded out of sheer embarrassment, and Sarge turned around and flashed them his gap-toothed grin. Then he pressed a little envelope into the Yid's hand.

"You like the fights? Hell, everybody gotta like the fights! This is two tickets for Wednesday night, two weeks, Denny Love gonna knock the shit out of some nancy-boy from Detroit name of Ruiz. I own a piece of Denny Love. You go, you take Lea, you have a good damn time."

I said, "I gotta work Wednesday, Sarge."

Sarge wagged a finger at me. "You switch with Sylvia. You got the night off." Then he turned to the Yid, like it was the men deciding what was going to happen with the women, I mean, with *me*. "You gonna insult me, turn down my present?"

The Yid folded the tickets into his pocket. "No, no! Thank you, Sarge. I love the sport of boxing. We're definitely going to go, that is, if Lea wants to."

"Sure she wants to! What, are you crazy? You like the pie?"

"Fabulous."

"You better believe it!"

Sarge beamed at me. It was pretty disgusting. For a minute I thought he was going to pinch my cheek. I felt like the whole world was going crazy. I didn't dare move my face. "You're a dish," he said. Then he barked at Sylvia and Arthur to go do coffees. He left the Wee Spot then, probably to get drunk somewhere.

Sylvia dipped by and said seven words, though she

didn't have to take the trouble, as far as I was concerned. Out of some goddam sense of civic duty, seemed like, she said, "He left a teenage daughter in Russia." She filled the Yid's water, and she gave me an extremely strange look, which was a good thing, because it was more respectful than the fox eyes she used to sizzle into me. Arthur grabbed her elbow to take her to the waiters' station to gossip, but I didn't give a frog's puke what they talked about.

I looked at the Yid. It was like I was starting to get used to the water. It still made me melt, but I was getting used to melting. What's wrong with melting? Ice melts and it's still ice; it's just liquid ice. I mean, really.

I said, "The fights?"

The Yid shrugged. "Let's go." He left a dollar and a half for Sylvia. I wasn't supposed to have anything to do with the money part of anything. I was the girl. He put on his coat, and we went out onto Monroe Avenue. I still had the book of German gold leaf in my hand because I didn't have any accessories. I crunched it up in my hand before I knew what I was doing, it was so cold, and my hand just did that. I was freezing cold, that I hadn't been able to find a coat that would go, and I tried to hide it, but Jack saw how cold I was, probably because my shoulders went up to my temples and I was shivering, and he did the most extraordinary thing that anybody ever did to me and lived. He took off his trench coat and he kind of hung it over my shoulders and wrapped me in it, and I felt warm. It was warm from his being in it, and he put it on me, and I couldn't believe it.

We went to the spaceship like that. We passed the dead cat. I mean, I noticed it, but so what? What can you say about it? It was still dead. The point is, I was in the Yid's coat.

We passed some agents of the Evil One. They looked like ordinary people. You couldn't tell, but the Yid would just nudge me or give me a look. One was even a cop; the Yid shivered and looked down. After we passed the cop, he said, "We already got one of them. It was in the cat. They're sniffing around. They know something is up, but they don't know it's us. They never heard of the Chosens doing something like this. You've got a very special talent, *shiksie*."

I said, "I love your coat."

When we got to the fire escape at Sears, he stopped and he put both his hands on both my shoulders and he looked me in the eyes and I could have died and he said, "Now there's no going back. The Lord God Tetragrammaton is a priceless friend to the friends of the Chosens, but he is a jealous God as well. Do you understand what I'm saying?"

"No. I don't understand anything, Jack."

"You've got to stick with me. That's what I'm saying. It's begun now. You can't change your mind."

"I don't want to change my mind."

He didn't kiss me. He turned around and walked up the fire escape, and I walked up the fire escape after him. We ducked into the top of the shaft, and he reached into the pocket of the trench coat that I was still wearing, and he got out his flashlight, and he saw that the elevator car hadn't gone anywhere.

And we jumped.

chapter four

The Yid Measures
My Talent

I love gold leaf. It's so thin you can't pick it up between your fingers or it all bunches up. You pick it up with a brush by means of static electricity, like how a balloon sticks to a wall if you rub it against your head. First you paint on some stuff called "sizing." Then you hold the gold leaf near what you have sized, and it sort of shrink-wraps whatever it is. It's beautiful. I love it.

I was laying gold on gold for the spaceship. The gold that the Yid had painted wasn't gold enough. He had boxes and boxes of books of gold leaf from Germany and buckets and buckets of sizing in cans and lots of brushes, big ones for the sizing and little ones to pick up the gold leaf, which I love. He had two ladders, and I don't know how he got them in there, but they were brand-new and they still had Sears and Roebuck tags. He set them up with a board across the top so you could size and gold leaf on your back, like Leonardo da Vinci, the Yid said, and your neck didn't get stiff till after a couple nights of it. And he had a big Sears and Roebuck electric fan blowing the fumes of the sizing out the elevator shaft, where he left the door open and the top of the elevator car open and the cover of the shaft up on the roof halfway open too. Those fumes were not meant for the store dicks at Sears and Roebuck, is what we're talking about here.

Sometimes, while I worked on the Gold Sky, the Yid worked on the Light Sponge. He tried a different kind of black paint. He tried tar paper. He tried roughing it up with emery cloth. We had to get that albedo down to zero for when the *Meschiach* came for us, even though the ceiling was getting shinier and the floor was already shiny as could be from maybe three layers of Gymseal. It was a big problem for the Yid, the "Albedo Dilemma,"—he lost plenty of sleep over it.

Other times, he lay up on top of the ladders next to me, sizing and gold leafing. The old tin ceiling had shapes stamped into it of stars and circles. Once you sized them, those stars and circles sucked up that gold leaf like a wet T-shirt on some bosomy broad. And he was right next to me doing it. And every night I wore something different from Mrs. Bobson's dead daughter, who was petite.

I didn't care if I got sizing on them. There were bags and bags of them.

He saw me wearing those clothes, brother. He didn't have to say anything for me to know that they were doing something to him. He would see me and he would start to move differently, like imagine a fish swimming from fresh water into, maybe, tangerine Jell-O, how it would whip its tail in slow motion and nose around with a different wiggle, and its eyes would act like a whole other animal living in its head. That's the Yid when he got an eyeful of those clothes of Mrs. Bobson's petite daughter. They showed everything that I've got, everything I never wanted to even *have* before this. And my hair was growing the whole time. And he would lie right next to me on top of the two ladders, and we would size and we would gold leaf.

Which is how I came to understand the Yid's integrity, because he didn't make any moves. His people were the main thing on the Yid's mind, the Chosen of the Chosen of the Chosen, who were marooned by the Evil One, and who I could help with my talent and who I could maybe go with to the Garden of Eden and translate the *goyim* for.

I could see how he was holding himself back from having that much to do with me on a personal, physical level, even though, probably, if it was just us, I don't know, he might get fresh, and I might have to decide whether or not I had to do something to him; I don't think that was what was stopping him, because he probably thought that I wouldn't—and I think he was right. But my clothes were definitely crippling him, and my body inside my clothes was crippling him, in the way that *normal* girls cripple guys, and I didn't want it to stop. But you had to respect him and admire him and want to help him, and I did.

During the daytime, I went to the library and listened to language tapes on earphones in all different languages, and sometimes I fell asleep, but I kept it up. I was supposed to be the goddam interpreter on the spaceship. The Yid thought I was a linguist, a polyglot, and a sophisticate, all of which I looked up, and pretty soon I was *going* to be those things, because if he was going to the Promised

Land, so was I. Over there, he could probably relax and concentrate on me. *L'amour est triste, n'est-ce pas? Ich bin ein Berliner. Mira! La dolce vita!*

I hardly was at Mrs. Bobson's at all those days except if she was asleep and snoring—*habe sueño*. I just took all those notes she left me on fancier and fancier stationery, with my name written bigger and bigger each time, and I threw them away.

Late at night, I learned other stuff—from the Yid, in our spaceship. He tested me and he taught me. Most of it, I could have cared less—he talked to me like a baby—but the point is, we were getting in a lot of proximity, me and Jack, late at night, alone.

Once he made three clay dolls, Skinny, Fatty, and Lumpy, each one of them the size of a birthday cake cowboy. Skinny was the pretty one. The Yid stood them up in a row on the floor on their little clay feet, and he laid down a kitchen match next to them. Each of them had half of a gelatin capsule for a head—I guess the Yid used them for his drug hustling, to fill with uppers or downers, though I never asked him about it. He showed me a brown bottle of rubbing alcohol from under our sink, and he poured some into a shot glass, which I bet he used to measure marijuana, one shot to a nickel bag. Then he stabbed his thumb with a pin.

"What are you, crazy?"

"Shh!"

I watched a little drop of blood form at the fat part of his thumb. He let the blood fall into the shot glass and it spread through the alcohol and turned everything pink. He was like a magician; he would look at me, and he would look at his stuff, and he would do something. Then he would look at me again to see what I thought of it, and I would locate my *buccinator* and give him some encouragement so he would do the next thing.

The Yid eyedroppered the pink stuff out of the shot glass and squeezed it out into Fatty's head. Then he picked her up and poured out her head into Skinny's head. He poured it into Lumpy's head next, then the Yid just poured it around from head to head for a while. "This liquid is an agent of the Evil One. He's in this person, he's in that person."

Now the pink stuff was in Lumpy's head. The Yid said, "Suppose I see that this person, Miss Lumpy, is furthering the designs of the Evil One against the Chosen. I decide to take care of her. But meanwhile, the evil spirit moves on to another." He poured the pink stuff out of Lumpy's head into Fatty. Then, quick enough to make me flinch, he laid down Lumpy and smashed her with his fist. He looked at me. I smiled. He peeled her off the edge of his hand. "Wrong one! You see?" Then he smashed Fatty. The pink stuff was beaded up on the Gymseal next to her squashed body.

"No good either. It still lives." The Yid eyedroppered up the colored alcohol and he filled Skinny's head with it.

"*This* is what you have to do." The Yid picked up the kitchen match. He opened his mouth and he lit it on his tooth and he looked at me and I nodded. Then he touched the corner of it to the top of Skinny's head, and the inside of her head burst into flame. It sizzled and it burned, and the gelatin started to melt and burn. Skinny's head dripped down over her shoulders. Bits of her head oozed and burned. The tops of her little shoulders charred and crumbled.

I said, "If they had stronger heads, you could kill the evil thing, and it wouldn't kill them."

He said, "They don't have stronger heads."

I said, "Yeah, I guess I knew that."

It was quiet for a minute. We were right next to each other. I didn't know what to do. He didn't know what to do. I wanted him to do it though. But he didn't. He scraped up the clay and put everything away under the sink.

Then he said, "Don't be squeamish."

I said, "I'm not squeamish." Then I said, "Are you squeamish?"

He said, "No, I'm not squeamish."

We were talking about different things.

Here is how the Yid gave me his talent test. It was Monday night, and the gold leaf looked like a million bucks where it was up already in our spaceship in the unknown part of Sears and Roebuck. The Yid had told me to be sure to leave Tule at home. *No problemo.* Between you and me, Tule was getting to be a pain. It had started Sunday morning when I got home in my *Rive-Gauche*-whore costume that had crippled everyone at the Wee Spot.

All I could figure was, it's the weather. There was this warm spell, Indian Summer, fattening us up for the kill. I mean, who did it think it was fooling? The days were *still* getting shorter and shorter. I always think, they're not going to get longer again this time.

But a south wind blew in this warm couple days from down where they don't know about real winter. Real winter pummels you and kills you and makes you say uncle and then still never lets up till you forget what the sun is. Then one day you feel this funny tingle and you think it's a headache and why won't it let you alone and you reach for an aspirin. But then you realize you're warm again, and it's not a headache—it's the sun.

The ice was melting and the dog shit was starting to stink—I bet that's what did it to Tule. She really knew who loved her, only the smell of dog shit turned her against me. Like every spring, when she acts crazy for a week or so, just when I'm reaching for that aspirin, that's what it is, if you ask me—the stench of spring.

Anyway, Tule wasn't talking to me, and she was showing me her asshole every chance she got. I would say, "Who loves you, pussums?" and she would stalk off to Mrs. Bobson's Lysol-and-dead-skin bedroom, flicking her tail at me like I was some kind of criminal. Who needs that from their cat, you know what I mean?

The first part of the talent test was the interview part. "This is for my people," is what the Yid said. "I have no personal interest in you or in your past." I knew he meant the opposite of everything he said, and I was wearing a yellow vinyl jacket and I had an accessory of a black purse with long fringe on the bottom that makes men think unconsciously about what it would feel like to get tickled by something, is my take on it. The Yid pretended not to look at it. "How did you first come to be aware that you have a special talent?"

"How did *you*?"

That stopped him. But then he thought for a minute, and he said, "Sure, okay, I'll tell you about myself, *shiksie*. I'll tell you so you'll trust me and you won't hold anything back, because my people need you to cooperate fully," and it was like Mrs. Bobson drinking *Diet* Cokes with her pounds and pounds of sourballs and marzipan. That excuse was the Yid's Diet Coke, is how I saw it; and *I* was the sourballs and marzipan, sitting there looking at him from inside my killer clothes. People do what they want to do, is one thing I figured out a long time ago, then they think up reasons for it. It's okay by me. I don't care what a person's motivation is as long as he does nice things for me, and the Yid was looking at me and talking to me and I was the happiest I ever was in my life.

He said, "I was brought up an orthodox Jew. Both of my folks came from Poland when they were kids. They were kids in the concentration camps in Poland. They went first to England, then to Canada, then the States. They didn't know each other until they arrived in Toronto, in their twenties. They got married up there, and they moved to New York, then here. I've lived my whole life in this city, according to the ordinary understanding. According to the supernal understanding, of course, I have been all over the universe, looking for the thirteen and for the three, trying to find the way back to *Ish-ra-el.*

"My family, way back, on my mother's side were Cabalists. One of them, Sabbatai Levi Hagodol, was a friend of the great Abulafia and wrote a book called *Zohar Hagoyim*, which means *Brilliance of the Nations. Zohar Hagoyim* was an explication of the secret spiritual relation between the Chosen People and the other peoples of the world. No copy exists today—they were all destroyed by the Evil One in fires and floods—but I have read it many times in my dreams, and I have also discussed it deeply with Reb Sabbatai. I have studied *Zohar Hagoyim*, and I have carried the work forward.

"My father was a Kohayn, Nathan Konar, from the ancient priestly tribe, but for him it was purely ceremonial. Although he had no understanding of the meaning of any of it—no *k'vanna*—he did all the things a Kohayn is supposed to do in the Jewish religion. For example, he never stepped foot in a graveyard, because it's forbidden if you are a Kohayn. Of course, my father's father was also a Kohayn, and even in the war, in the camps, my father told me, when they had to handle corpses, some of the other prisoners, the observant ones, would do my grandfather's work for him, because the priestly class is not to be soiled with death.

"On holidays, the Levites, who today may be Levis or Levins or Levinsons, would help my father and the other Kohanim take off their shoes. The Levites would wash the Kohanim's hands for them, too, with water from silver goblets. Then my father would mount the altar among the Kohanim, and they would sing:

"Ghi di di di! Ghi di di diddy di di!"

"When I was a little boy, and I heard that sound, *shiksie*, my hair stood on end, and my whole body shook like a ribbon whipping in the wind. Nobody was supposed to look at the Kohanim when they did that, when they blessed us all, singing and stretching out their arms. You would go blind from the holiness.

"With their fingers the Kohanim made the sacred sign, holding the ring finger and the pinky together, away from the other fingers, making a sort of v-shape like *this*, as the Song of Songs says: 'My beloved is like a young deer or like a gazelle who peers in through the latticework.'"

The Yid stretched out his arms and made that sign and looked at me through his fingers and he was a young deer or a gazelle and he was my beloved. Then he blushed. He folded his hands in front of his belly. His fingers were interlaced like how it would be when he came together with one of the thirteen, which I never forgot.

He said, "My father showed me how to do that. In the synagogue, I never looked, and since I never had a bar mitzvah, I was never allowed to do it myself with the Kohanim up there. Something happened to me first. I saw the truth, then everything was impossible. I found out about my true family, the Chosen of the Chosen of the Chosen.

"We are like dwarfs, *shiksie*. Dwarfs are not born of dwarfs, but they are born of ordinary people. We Thrice Chosen are born some to Kohayn families and some to others, even to *goyim*. This was revealed to me, as it is revealed to all the Thrice Chosen, precisely at puberty." He kind of mumbled the word "puberty." If he hadn't, I might have had to leave then, because it would have given me the creeps that he would say that, but since he mumbled it, it meant that it gave him some creeps too and he wasn't a pervert, and it was still okay between us, between Jack and me, between us two together, me and him, the couple of us. I liked the sound of that when I said it to myself in my mind.

Puberty. Let's not talk about it.

"I was twelve and a half, *shiksie*, and suddenly I didn't have a father or a mother, and my sister was a stranger, and everyone in this world was a different kind of creature from me."

"Except for the thirteen."

"The thirteen and the three, fifteen besides myself—my true family. I was in eighth grade then. Can you imagine, *shiksie*, trying to go to school and talk about civics and algebra and predicate adjectives, or songs or sports or girlfriends, all that, when your mind and heart and soul are afire with another reality, a reality so vast that if any of your teachers or classmates glimpsed it, they would go mad or try to kill you just to close it off?" The Yid was knotting up in his stomach and his chest and his arms. His whole body curled in like wood shavings when they dry up and burn. His face got ugly the way people's faces get if they have to shout at somebody while they're crying.

I said, "Can I imagine? Can I imagine? It's the story of my goddam life!"

He eased up and looked at me for a minute without talking. His face was dried out, all the feeling drained out of it, like after crying (but he never cried that night). Then he said, "It's not the same."

We just breathed for a minute. Up on the roof, ice was melting and dripping down the elevator shaft—*plip, plip, plip*.

The Yid said, "Reb Sabbatai talked to me through many mouths. He told me what to eat and what to drink..."

"And what to smoke?"

"Are you making fun of me?"

"Did he tell you to do dope, is all I'm asking you, Jack. I'm not trying to be funny here."

"Yes. He told me to use marijuana and hashish to open the doors of my senses to perceive the supernal realm, but not to use any other substances and not to eat meat any longer, only fruit and vegetables and dairy."

"Are eggs okay?"

"Eggs are okay. This was for me, *shiksie*, not for the *goyim*."

"Do you still think I'm a *goyim*?"

"Maybe. Maybe. So try this diet if you want to. I won't stop you. It wouldn't hurt you."

"I'm going to. But not the dope; I don't like it."

"Okay. I'm telling you how Reb Sabbatai was riding on my shoulder day and night during the time when I was becoming a man. This is the critical time for each of the thirteen—either we come into our own at that time, or else we die: the light goes out in us. We walk and we talk and we have jobs and families, but inside us, there is nothing."

"Can one of the thirteen be a girl?"

"Yes. Some are women." He must have caught the way I was biting my lip. Sometimes you chew your lip when you are chewing on a thought, is what I notice. He said, "Not you. You're not one."

I was angry for a second, then I let it go. After all, was it up to him?

"Reb Sabbatai shepherded me through. My father became to me a screaming, crazy monster. I wouldn't do what he said anymore. I wouldn't eat the same food as the family. I failed everything in high school. My sister tormented me, why don't you have a girlfriend, why are you alone all the time, why can't you this, why can't you that, the same as my mother, as if I didn't have Sabbatai Levi Hagodol sitting on my shoulder showing me the way to *Ish-ra-el*, as if I were not one of the Thrice Chosen.

"Uncle Sabbatai opened up in me the power to see the supernal realm, which is why I am aware of how you use your talent, maybe more aware of it than you are. I don't yet know how you do it, though, *shiksie*."

"Where are your folks, Jack?"

"Dead."

"Dead? Both?"

"Both."

"Car crash?"

"Dead *to me*."

That shut me up for a minute. "What about your sister?"

"Gone, married, far away."

"I'm sorry."

"Don't be sorry. I told you it's not my real family. My real family is going to be right here as soon as I get the spaceship right, the geometries on four levels, physical, emotional, intellectual, and spiritual. It must be done through the six keys, the Gold Sky, the Mirror Below, the Pyramid Wall, the Fleshpot, the Light Sponge, and the Holy of Holies. Reb Sabbatai instructed me in all this at the time when I might have died if I had given way to my gross appetites and worldly inclinations.

"Now that you're here to stop the Evil One, to knock out his agents, everything will be easier, do you see? And I want to learn from you everything I can."

"From me, Jack?"

"Yes. From you."

"I want to learn from you too, then."

"Okay."

It was like a wedding ceremony.

* * *

This is what I figured: When the Yid had told his story, which even if it was total BS, like, compared to obituaries or the high temperature for the day, or what's the capital of Idaho, it had to be true in his heart, and in my heart, because of how it melted him to say it, and because of how it melted me to hear it, which who cares about the exact words. It's like when a wino gives you some line about bus fare to Poughkeepsie, and you know he's lying through his ratty teeth, but it's true in his heart because he really does want to go home to whatever his Poughkeepsie is, only he'll never make it past the liquor store to the bus station. You give him the money anyway, unless you're me, which, when it came to bums, like almost everything, I had a heart of black stone.

When he was all done telling his story, the Yid said, "Now you."

And I said, "I don't have a story."

There was a noise in the elevator shaft, and the Yid said, "Shh!"

Plip...plip...plip...!

Then there was a scraping and scrambling noise—a mouse? Maybe some twigs from the rooftop loosened by melting ice, falling down, blowing around? We quiet-as-could-be sneaked over to the decompression chamber and looked around inside and looked up through the hole in the top and nobody was there. But the Yid climbed up while I shined the flashlight for him. He pulled the cover board shut, and we didn't do any more sizing that night. While the Yid was monkeying around up there, I found a piece of something on the floor of the decompression chamber that made me feel sick.

"Hey, keep shining that flashlight up here, *shiksie!*"

"Sure! Sorry!"

It was a piece of tin or aluminum the size of a half-dollar, but it was stamped and cut in the shape of a quiver with arrows in it, and it had a little hole in the top with a broken piece of wire through it. I stuffed it into my inside vest pocket, like a gun into a holster.

I didn't want to show it to the Yid. I didn't want to talk about it. I felt too angry and scared and mixed up. When the Yid lowered himself down to the roof of the elevator car and made it shake the way I like that makes you think the cable is going to break and that you're about to fall and get smooshed and die, I couldn't even enjoy it.

The Yid shinnied down into the decompression chamber. "Nothing. Nobody. A mouse."

As soon as we were back inside, the Yid smiled that smile where his lips turned down at the edges instead of up, and he said, "Now you have to tell me how you found out about your special talent. Come on, *shiksie*. Give."

I gave. First I reached my hand inside my vest the way I'd seen some guys do that makes you think they have a gun, but I was feeling in my pocket for that quiver-and-arrows thing. It was in there along with a ticket stub from a show Mrs. Bobson's daughter went to, and it couldn't have been with a guy or she wouldn't have had the stub, is how I figured it. I just kept fingering that thing, thinking about it with my fingers like it was Captain Hook's teardrop that wanted to poison my Yid.

It was from Sylvia's earring. Sylvia had been spying on us. If I had seen her, I would have killed her right then. Period. What the hell did she want from us? I couldn't really think straight for all the red I was seeing.

I gave. It was almost like somebody else talking. I was

feeling too much, and it flipped a breaker or something. I heard myself say: "It was Sunday morning. We were all of us having breakfast together. I was eleven. Julian was only eight. James was fourteen. Daddy was making pancakes. He had on a red-and-white-checkered apron. He had on a white chef's hat for a joke. Mom was humming 'Sunny Side of the Street' and pouring milk in our glasses, and coffee in hers and Daddy's, and James had half coffee with half milk. We were all laughing.

"The sun was so bright, it was like melted butter pouring in through the kitchen window. We all ate a lot of pancakes, but Daddy ate the most. We had practically lakes of maple syrup on our plates. Later on, Julian swung, and James and I took turns pushing him."

Plip...plip...plip...!

The Yid said, "And...?"

My breaker flipped back on. I said, "And nothing. That's all I can handle right now, Jack. Okay?"

He nodded. "Okay." He looked so sad. For a minute, he could feel things in my heart as if it were his—that's what I thought.

I took my hand out of my holster and I touched the Yid's chin, I don't know why. He turned his head away. He said, don't, and I decided to forget all about it and to forget all about the bitch's quiver until later when my head was clear.

I could do that.

We sized and we gold leafed and we roughed up the Light Sponge. Being as we'd had a thaw, we didn't freeze our buns off from the draft that we had to keep that shaft open for the fumes. Sometimes I got dizzy. My ears rang. The tips of my fingers tingled. It was okay though. The Gold Sky was getting more and more beautiful, and the Yid found a nongloss finish to try on the Light Sponge.

I killed stuff for the Yid. He was measuring my talent. I killed cockroaches. I killed mice. He watched me do it. I liked it that he watched me.

I bought a full-length mirror for twelve bucks and change, in the known section of Sears and Roebuck, and I put it in my room and I used it to look at clothes to see what would go. Tule was giving me the cold shoulder, but she would watch me, which why not, since she was the one who said I should wear pretty clothes in the first place and go out with guys? Some of those clothes were killer clothes, that I knew would have their effect.

And all the time, my hair was growing.

I figured out my own color chart, and blues look like shit on me. I have a spring palette actually, and pinks and reds and peaches love me to death, and I found the bag with all the accessories in it, and I accessorized. There were belts and bags and change purses with chains and straps and beads and fringe and every sort of you can't imagine the kind of dough Mrs. Bobson's daughter must have blown on all this stuff just to get hit by a car and killed when she was still an old maid.

The Yid brought in a microscope one day, extremely fancy, with matte steel turrets and hinges and dials that his gold leaf friend got for him. It was beginning to look to me like the Yid was fronting money for a little thieving operation, but who cares how people make their living if they're nice to you?

He showed me a drop of water on a piece of glass in

the microscope. I saw amoebas in there, and some of them were splitting in two and they looked like a rubber peanut, and vorticellas, which looked like a jellyfish on the end of a string, and other tiny animals.

And he said, "Make the amoebas sick," and I made them sick.

And he said, "Kill them," and I killed them—but the vorticellas died too.

And the Yid said, "*Shiksie*, I bet you could cure cancer."

"That's what Tule says." I looked in the microscope again at all the dead stuff floating around. "But the vorticellas died too. It's like the gelatin burning with the alcohol: the cancer would be dead, and the person would be dead. Big deal."

The water was drying up from the heat of the lightbulb underneath. It was a microbe graveyard. All these dried-up microbe skeletons stuck to the glass in a scummy splotch.

"Do you ever get sick, *shiksie*?"

"Yeah. All the time. I never get well, either."

"I don't get what you mean."

"Let's gold leaf."

The Yid made notes on me and charts and graphs and kept asking me questions, how did I feel when I did this, what was I thinking about when I did that, and I loved all of it. It was like having breakfast with somebody you love, even though he wasn't ready to let himself know it, but I did. He did a lot of stuff with numbers. He said, "*Shiksie*, thousands and thousands of years ago, out on the desert, someone pounded a rock with a stick, and ten people listened. Nine of them said, 'One! One! One! One!' but one of them said, 'One! Two! Three...!' That made the whole difference in the human race forever. There are the nine, and there is the one.

"I'm going to understand what you do. I may be learning now. I think I may be getting it a little."

"Show me, Jack." *Jack, show me. Jack, Jack. Jack show Jack. Jack me. Jack, Jack, Jack, Jack ...*

He narrowed his eyes. We had a mouse in a jar that we trapped in a thing that just catches them inside it but it doesn't hurt them. The Yid's eyes closed. I got to look at him then. He had smooth skin. The hair on those rust-colored sideburns of his was starting to get long and curl. I counted his freckles that he had between his nose and his eyebrows: fourteen. His lips tightened, then relaxed. He looked like a baby asleep and dreaming baby dreams. Nothing happened to the mouse.

He opened his eyes. "It's with your stomach more, isn't it, and a little, say, angrier?"

"I don't know."

"I'll get it."

"What for? I can do it for us."

"I'll get it."

He made me hold tin cans that he had wired to something that looked like a barometer with a rotating drum and pens that made lines on a piece of graph paper. "Skin conductivity," is what he called it. He said it was a crude measure but that his contacts were not able to get him an electroencephalograph machine, and he couldn't get a magnetic resonance imager in through our decompression chamber. Anyway, the magnetic field of an MRI would make all the cash registers and metal stuff in Sears Roebuck fly off their housings and hit the hull of our spaceship, which could screw up the albedo.

But the tin can data would be useful when we got to the biofeedback rig that the Yid had in mind. A person could shoot for the same patterns I got on my rotating drum, even if they didn't know which of my nerves was making my skin conduct. Like you can draw a picture somebody else draws without knowing how they move which fingers, but if you draw it to look just the same, probably, you used the same fingers the same way.

When I did that thing inside me that made creatures squirm or sicken and die, I got peaks on my rotating drum. The Yid adjusted the scale so my line wouldn't go off the edge. He kept my charts in a binder in one of the bookcases next to the Holy of Holies. He did my temperature. He did my pulse and blood pressure. He put them in different colors on one chart. He stared at it.

He said, "I'll get it."

I didn't think so. I kept killing stuff and he kept watching and measuring and writing things down. We worked on the spaceship too. The Gold Sky got brighter and brighter. The Light Sponge got darker and darker. The place filled up with moon steam of dead creatures.

Sometimes I would come in there and the Yid would be wired up to the gizmo, trying to concentrate and make patterns like my patterns on the drum. And he would say, I think I understand this, or, I think I understand that, or, I think I'm getting it.

He wasn't.

Like I said, Mrs. Bobson's daughter's clothes were doing their work. I was starting to appreciate how you can do some real damage, so to speak, the normal way, with your looks, but the Yid, he was interested first of all in my talent. Looks were a lubricant, let's say. So I was glad he couldn't do my talent, because if he could, even though I had bone structure and tits, he would drop me.

Love is *one* thing.

chapter five

Indian Summer

Tule knew right off that something was wrong. She said, *Somebody's hunting you.*

I said, "Get off my back. Nobody's hunting me. It's just dog shit smell getting to you."

I was just about ready to bury myself between the sheets and sleep the sleep of the dead, when I heard Mrs. Bobson's voice from downstairs: "Is that you, dear? I've been leaving notes for you, Lea dear. Someone's been trying to get ahold of you..."

I hadn't known Bobson was awake. It was maybe three in the damn morning. Must have been she was in the downstairs bathroom taking an old lady crap when I came in. Bad dream? Insomnia?

Sometimes she said things in her sleep, but who could make out what, with all her gurgling and lip flapping and wheezing? She would go downstairs for a glass of water or the cream sherry she pretended was for cooking, but every week there was a whole other empty bottle of it in the garbage, four or five bottles a month and fifty-two bottles a year.

She would hang out in her little glassed-in room, filled with mementos of her dead family like an evidence room at a cop station or like a morgue; like I said, her whole house was practically a mausoleum anyway. She had her framed marquetry up on the wall in there, which she made from tracings with her human prune marquetry circle, and her favorite one of them was a Bing Crosby doing the soft shoe with the cane and the straw hat in *White Christmas*. She would rock and rock and stare and stare at Bing's soft shoe dance made of slivers of glued wood, all different colors and grains. Old ladies being what they are, she would end up in the downstairs bathroom reading *Modern Maturity* and waiting for her bowels to move.

I am never going to be old, is what I decided. Period.

I didn't say a word. Sometimes Mrs. Bobson would hear me and call to me, but then if I was real quiet, she would just think her old lady ears were out of whack, which they were anyway, and she would leave me the hell alone.

I was sitting on the edge of my bed. My silk pants had sticky spots of sizing on them. I was tired from sizing and sanding and doing my talent all night. Tule jumped into my lap, the inky, warm fur ball. She stretched her front legs up my chest and spread her paws the one toe from the other. Cute. She kneaded me under my collarbone where the softness of my glands starts, where any kind of pressure—this is what I figure—makes me feel maternal, the little sneak.

Who loves you, Lea?

"You do, Tule. You and Jack."

Somebody's hunting you. I smell it. You're anxious. What's in your pocket?

"Somebody's earring, is all, dammit. Bug off. I hear Bobson coming upstairs."

You're looking pretty, Lea. I'm happy how you're getting to look. Your heart is getting warmer too, honey baby. I feel it through your skin. I told you, though, you gotta stop killing. It's bad for you. (Kneading, kneading...)

"It's just bugs and mice."

Are you telling me you didn't do a cat?

"It had an agent of the Evil One in it for crissakes. I did it for Jack. It's all for Jack. I'm not mad at anybody. I don't want to kill anything. It's just a test, for crissakes. Trust me on this one, will you?"

Who do you trust, Lea?

"Jack. I trust Jack. He's gonna marry me."

The door was half open, but Bobson knocked on it anyway with her bony fist. She had on a nightgown and, over it, a pink terry-cloth bathrobe with the collar turned up. She had on pink old lady slippers that must have been a jillion years old, but I gotta say, they went. "Are you up, dear?"

"I'm just going to bed, Mrs. Bobson. I'm real, real tired."

"Oh dear, of course you are! It's an ungodly hour for a human being to be awake, isn't it?"

Tule jumped down from my lap and padded over to Mrs. Bobson. She rubbed up against her varicose legs that were like piano legs in pink coasters. Tule was a sucker for that old dame's bubbly falsetto. Bobson giggled and cooed and ratcheted herself down to pet Tule.

I yawned loud.

Bobson said, "Your cat is such a comfort to me sometimes. Do you know, she cuddles up to me in my bed sometimes. Why, I even found her sitting on my head one morning when I woke up."

"I'm sorry about that, Mrs. Bobson..."

"No, no! Land sakes, I like it!" She inched the door open a little more and shuffled in on her stiff legs almost as if they were stilts. "I know how tired you are, dear, but can I come in for just a minute and talk to you?"

"I'm real tired, Mrs. Bobson. I don't know if I could stay awake."

"Dear, there's no place to sit down. Can I sit down beside you on the bed for just a minute? Would you like me to give you one of my nice bentwood chairs for in here?"

And before I could say no to one thing or yes to the other, her skinny butt had landed beside me on the mattress, and I was smelling her permanent, which I didn't want to. She had one of those smiles ironed onto her face that let her do whatever the hell she wanted to do without noticing what anybody else in the world wanted. She looked me up and down while she pretended to catch her breath from lowering her skinny butt down onto the bed.

She said, "I'm so glad you've started to wear Lillian's clothes. You look just wonderful in them, Lea dear."

I couldn't help it, I knew it could get us into a conversation, and I didn't want to, I just wanted her off my bed and out of my room, but I had to say, "Do I? Do you really think so?"

And she said, "Yes, indeed! You seem to have put together such a nice outfit, too! Such a nice ensemble!"

"That means 'together' in French."

"Does it? Well, that makes sense."

"I put together what goes, didn't I?"

"Yes, you certainly did. You have a fine sense of color."

"I do, don't I?"

"Yes, you do. Oh"—leaning closer, looking sad— "you've got a little stain on those pants. Would you like me to get it out for you, dear?"

"No, I'll do it, Mrs. Bobson." No, I wouldn't. I was going to trash them. There were plenty more.

"You're so pretty. You have a cute figure." She laughed a hiccuppy laugh. "You have a pretty face, too. Can you smile for me? I just want to see what you look like when you smile—you know, just one girl to another."

I didn't throw up at the thought, which I should have. It was like Tule kneading my tits, I guess. I think maybe the break in the weather was turning me into a sap. Maybe that's where that word comes from, like how sap rises in the spring, and you tap a maple tree, and it just pours on out. I just poured on out. I found my *buccinator*, and I gave her my best one.

She looked at me hard, and she smiled. It wasn't like the constipated smile she hobbled in with. She smiled hard and her eyes kind of twinkled and she nodded and she said, "Lovely! Lovely!" and I have to say it made me kind of happy, and then I wasn't in such a hurry to kick her out.

Which was maybe how she was playing it. There was a little voice in my head, and it said, *Sap*, but I didn't listen. She was stroking my things.

Mrs. Bobson touched my chin with her arthritic, knobby finger and she turned my head this way and that way. She said, "Bone structure."

I said, "I know it."

Tule jumped between us, her little black butt up against Mrs. Bobson's thigh and her little chin on mine, and she purred and she purred. And Mrs. Bobson said, "Will you let your hair grow?"

I said, "Mm-hmm. I'm gonna."

She said, "It's better than killing, isn't it?"

I said, "Huh?"

And she said, "When it grows in you must let me help you do something with it."

"What did you say about killing?"

"I beg your pardon, dear?"

"Nothing. Never mind. I'm real tired, Mrs. Bobson. Did you want to talk to me about something?"

"Oh, land sakes, yes! Did you talk to that man?"

"What man?"

"Why, the one who left you all the messages!"

I'd thrown out all those messages. I'd never looked at a one of them. I didn't know they were from somebody. Who did I know who would leave me messages? I figured they were crap from Bobson about leaving the window open.

"I didn't get a chance to look at them. What was his name? What did he look like?"

"He had a ring through his nose, but he seemed very nice."

"What did he say his name was, Mrs. Bobson?"

"I'm not sure I remember his name. He only said it once, and it was windy. He never came in the house, you know. He always talked to me through the front doorway. I don't let young men into the house unless I know them. He kept coming back, though. I thought that was sort of charming, only the window was a bit much."

"The window?"

"I saw him staring in at the window once or twice, but when I checked, why, he'd be gone, like a little rabbit. He did it once when my marquetry circle was here, and one of the ladies saw him. She wasn't scared, though. Nothing scares my marquetry circle ladies. They are a lot like you, dear. You should come sometime."

"I don't think so, Mrs. Bobson."

"Is that young man your beau, Lea?"

"He's not my beau, Mrs. Bobson. What did his name sound like? What did he want?" My heart was starting to pound. My throat got tight as a reed. Times like that you wish you still had a big brother to protect you—even if, when it comes right down to it, they can't.

"Land sakes, I don't know! Do you know a Shane or a Shamus? Maybe it was Chad. He must have signed his name to the notes. I wrote your name on the outside, but he wrote his messages himself on paper I gave him out the door. Didn't you read them?"

"I said I didn't. How old was he?" It could be the college guy from the alley, the live one, I was thinking, the buddy of the one that had a heart attack.

"Oh, a little older than you are, dear. Are you in some kind of trouble...?"

"No."

"Because if you are, well, you may think I'm just a weak old fossil, but I can be very helpful sometimes." She was stroking Tule from her ears down to the tip of her tail, and Tule was Jell-Oing up to slide under her hand and purring and purring.

"I'm not in any trouble."

"I have ways of doing things to people, dear. I have ways of protecting myself and of protecting people who are my friends."

"You keep a gun?"

"Land sakes, no! But trust me, dear, I have ways. No one ever hurt me, dear, and no one takes advantage of me, even if I am older than dirt." She sidled up to me on the bed. Her thigh touched mine. I didn't mind. "Tell me what's wrong, honey."

"Nothing's wrong." I was that close to opening up to her. What a season, that Indian Summer! Something in the air makes a person crazy inside!

She said, "We're not so different, you know, except for me being so old. That's why I let you into my house. Lots of people wanted to rent my room, but I rented it to you, because I could feel something the same in you and me. I felt it right off, first thing, and I never cared if a word you said was true or false, because I recognized you, dear. You're like me. Let me help you, Lea dear."

"Please let me go to sleep now, Mrs. Bobson. I'm tired."

"Why aren't you living at home with your mother and father, a young girl like you? They aren't really both dead, are they? You're not really from far away either, are you? I think you're from this very town."

"Everything I told you is true, Mrs. Bobson. I gotta go to sleep, honest. I'm dead tired. If that guy comes around again, get his name for me and ask where I can get ahold of him, okay?"

"Of course, dear." She got up. You could see how hard it was for her even to get up off the bed, her with her "ways" that she had, and Tule poured off of her like black-strap molasses, and she had to lean on the wall for a second to catch up to the pain in her joints. "You look lovelier and lovelier, dear. Lovelier than Lillian, I think, and Lillian was a beauty! Come to me when you need me, even if I'm with my things."

"Your things?"

"Mr. Bobson ... Lillian ... Harold ... all my pictures, my keepsakes, my memories, in my room behind the glass door. Don't you have any keepsakes, dear?"

"No. I don't like them."

"Oh." She stood there for a second, wrinkling her saggy forehead like she found something in her mouth that she didn't remember putting there—a prune pit or a piece of candy wrapper—and she had to swallow carefully. Then she did that magic tweak that old ladies can do with their withered brains, and she forgot the whole thing, everything that rubbed, right on the spot, like amnesia. She brightened up. "Well, remember that I'm there for you, dear."

"Sure, Mrs. Bobson. Thanks, Mrs. Bobson."

She left and I tried to sleep. Tule stayed with me a while, and then she got tired of my tossing and went in with Bobson.

I dreamed about James. I dreamed that he was a bob-cat. He followed me around like Mary's lamb. He hid in the bushes and when somebody gave me a hard time, he'd jump out and eat their throat.

My brother used to do that for me, actually. He was like Superman. He'd come out of nowhere—"It's a bird!

It's a plane! It's Superman!"—and some bully would get a mouthful of knuckles. That was James. He was my protector. He kept an eye on me. I was just a kid then.

Now I have Tule.

I went to the Wee Spot by myself. Tule didn't want to come. Tule wanted to stay home with the old bag. I showed up during the afternoon setup, when Sylvia was taking the chairs down from the tables, which I am never around for. She was having a little trouble because she was dressed for making tips, not for setup. She had on her usual ten pounds of makeup and a wraparound skirt and heels, with this purple top with a bertha collar, like a choirboy, and she was holding things away from herself to not get dirty.

Sylvia said, "Hi, honey." She acted normal.

I said, "Don't give me that, Sylvia. Why were you spying on me?"

"I don't know what you're talking about." She was so cool. She asked me to hand her a clean ashtray from the waiters' station, honey. I handed her the quiver and arrows instead, and she shut up. I could see the wheels spinning in her head. She was figuring out that there was no point trying to BS me.

She said, "You're not going to hurt me, are you?"

I said, "Now *I* don't know what *you're* talking about."

She looked me right in the eye, but I could see she was really scared of me. I kind of liked that.

"Look," she said, "I'm not some gangbanger chick like you. I'm not tough, and I'm not after anything. I was curious, okay? I saw you in the parking lot, and I was curious to know what anybody could be doing in the back of Sears and Roebuck at night. I wasn't the only one."

"Huh?"

"I wasn't the only one. Somebody else has been spying on you. I heard him a couple of times through the elevator shaft, rustling around on the floor just below."

"Mice."

"I don't think so."

Definitely mice.

"Well, what did you find out about us, Sylvia?"

"I saw you with Jack, that's all. You were painting or something. What is it, a clubhouse?"

It threw me that she knew his real name. I know it's stupid, but I guess I'd felt like I was the only one who could call him that. "How do you know the Yid?"

"What do you mean? He comes in here, doesn't he? Jack's a dopehead. He sells. Everybody around here knows him. Look, I'm sorry, okay?" She tried to put herself together with a deep breath. "You know, I guess I'm a little attracted to you..." She put her hand on my shoulder. I just had to turn my head and look at it and she took it off quick. "I'm sorry. Okay?"

"What did you mean, not to hurt you? You think I could hurt you, Sylvia?"

"No." That made her nervous, I could see. Her eyebrows shot up to her little bangs, and her voice got higher. "I mean, the way you dress, or the way you used to dress, the way you move, I thought maybe you had gang friends, Lea, you know? I mean—how those guys in the alley got hurt! I don't mean you did it. I mean, you look like maybe you're friends with some people who could do things like that. I mean, you look really beautiful. I like the way you look..." She was like somebody who finds herself up on some high pole and she doesn't know how she got there or how the hell she's going to get down. I loved that.

Then she surprised me. She said, "Stay away from him, Lea."

"What?"

"Why do you hang out with Jack? He's a dope-head. He's not going anywhere, and if you hang out with him, you'll just get messed up. Jack doesn't care about anybody."

I stared at her. I couldn't understand what I was feeling. Nobody ever got inside me to the place where she was getting to. I could hardly recognize my own guts if she was there inside them that way, talking about things that actually made a difference. Only Tule could do that. This was bad. This was real bad. It was like, this is what can happen to you if you flunk out of Lea Tillim's Dead Face Course and let assholes under your sheet, into your Holy of Holies, mousing.

All my circuits were blowing. I said, "He's gonna take me with him in his spaceship."

Sylvia laughed, and then I was the one up a pole.

"Jesus, listen to you, Lea! You're just a kid, aren't you? You don't know anything! You don't know that guy from Adam. Let me tell you about Jack Konar..."

"You just hate guys. You got nothing to tell me."

"Honey, I've got so much to tell you, I think you should move in with me just so I'll have the time!"

I was out of control. I'm never out of control. I don't let that happen. I don't let people past my face. I don't let people mouse inside me.

Suddenly, the bitch didn't look so well. She grabbed

one of the upside-down chairs, but it slid off the table and she fell on top of it. She got right up, but the chair legs had poked her chest and her groin, like a knight falling on his sword in the movies, and she was rattled and she was shaking and she didn't laugh anymore.

She said, "Jesus, Sarge was right!"

I said, "Sarge was right about what?"

And she said, "I'm so clumsy! It must be my period." There was a little catch in her throat, like a sob, which I didn't really understand it. "You do what you want to with Jack. It's none of my business."

"Sarge was right about what?"

Then I heard Sarge's voice behind me. I hadn't known he was even in the place. He was coming up from the cellar with a crate of Pepsi-Colas from the big refrigerator, and he said, "I told her, sonuvabitch, you're on the rag, stay home, Sylvia. Arthur can open. Look at this pain and suffering, huh?"

Which struck me funny, now that my brains were working again, because I thought Sylvia was just now noticing that maybe it was her period, but Sarge made it sound like they'd talked about her period before. It didn't add up.

Sarge said, "Hey, it's the dish! It's Lea, the looker! Jack gonna take you to the fights Wednesday, right?"

That blew me over the edge again. "Goddammit! How come all of a sudden everybody and his goddam brother is calling the Yid 'Jack'?"

It got real quiet. Sylvia stared at me from one side, and Sarge stared at me from the other. Or were they looking at each other? Sarge was tight in the face, angry. Who at? At Sylvia? What for? When I looked at Sylvia, she looked away. When I looked at Sarge, he smiled. Phony smile. Wrong muscle there. Muscle of irony and insincerity. I know all about it.

I took a couple oaths and then I left. I took one in French. I took one in Spanish also. I was slamming the door when I heard Sarge say, "You're a dish, Lea, a genuine dish!"

Goddam Indian Summer!

chapter six

Jack Kisses Me

The Yid took me to the fights. It was cold as hell that night. The nose ring guy hadn't come by again; it had been a few days, and I was starting to figure that maybe he was nobody. Maybe he'd gotten my name off a bathroom wall that one of my enemies had put there. Nothing to worry about. That's how your human mind works: Everything fuzzes over. Your dome gets gold leafed. You can only take so much aggravation and all the bad thoughts get gilded. Same thing with Sylvia and Sarge. My motto was, I can kill them whenever I feel like it. All I was thinking about was the Yid and the fights and what I could wear that went.

I told the Yid about Sylvia. I didn't say what she'd said about him, which I took for lesbo BS, I didn't mention her other guy who was spying on us, which was definitely mice, and I didn't say I'd mentioned the spaceship. I felt kind of bad that I'd said it, but she couldn't do a damn thing to stop the Chosens. She thought it was a joke anyway.

The Yid got a little nervous about Sylvia spying on us, but I told him about my show of force, let's say, and he was satisfied she wouldn't come nosing around anymore. The Yid was very curious about Sarge, though. He was very curious about Sarge and Sylvia. I told him it was all about Sarge wanting to get in Sylvia's pants. I could see he wasn't satisfied about that. He was like the way you say, "Mm-hmm!" to somebody stupid, instead of, "Shut up, that's dumb," and then you just clam up and think about it yourself.

The point is, he took me to the fights. The point is, he showed up at Mrs. Bobson's door, and Mrs. Bobson answered it, and she called up to me, and I was getting Lillian's thigh-high stockings on and I was checking out this red cloche in my mirror, which looked a little like those half of a gelatin capsule heads the Yid set on fire, only upside down and with a cute brim. I looked pretty great, I have to say. I called down, "Just a minute!" and I felt like I was a normal person, I couldn't believe it. I felt like the Brady Bunch. I felt like Miss America, only with a crew cut under her cloche. And I was smart about the whole thing, that if we sat up close and the boxers splashed blood on me, it wouldn't show because I was in mostly red, which is on my chart anyway.

And I used some nonallergenic blush and some lipstick, and probably tonight the Yid would have to kiss me, and I decided to let him.

I put Tule in her wicker basket—the only place she

was going to be was in there or under my coat the whole time—and I put some towels in there to keep her warm. The whole thing didn't really go, as an accessory, and Tule was pissed that I was even taking her, as a kitty cat, but I had to have her with me for crissakes: I was having a date. Life was not going to be the same, and I wanted her to be in on it.

Mrs. Bobson intercepted me at the bottom of the stairs, near her room with the glass door. The glass door was open, and her prehistoric record player was playing a scratchy old seventy-eight. I recognized the voice of Bing Crosby, Bobson's favorite.

"My heart is in your hands, dear.
I hope you'll treat it well.
I don't know where I'd land, dear,
If it ever fell.

"The notes I used to write you,
The ones you never read,
The ones you wrapped your fish in—
You'll never know they said,

"My heart is in your hands, dear.
My heart belongs to you."

Something like that. Bobson stuck her old lady body in my way like a goddam halfback, which is what they do, and all the time they get so much percentage out of looking frail like they do, and she clucked her tongue and she whispered, "I don't know, dear."

I said, "He's my friend, Mrs. Bobson." I walked right

past her to the door. I almost wanted to introduce them. I don't know. I guess it would have made it so nice! It would have been like, I don't know, like breakfast with the ones you love. Normal. I wished Lillian could have been there to see it. I felt so good!

The Yid was standing just inside the door in his trench coat, which had been dry-cleaned and looked positively chrome stiff, the way a new furnace looks, and he had his navy blue sock cap bunched up in his hands in front of his crotch, like a soldier or a priest. I figured, someday I'm gonna teach him his chart and what goes.

I said, "Hi, Jack," and I felt so gorgeous I could bust. I'd kept my coat open till then so he could see my ensemble before I buttoned up and it would stagger him and make his knees wobbly, but the Yid was all business. He didn't look up, hardly: A girl has the advantage. Looks could kill.

He was already cowed. He was going to kiss me for sure, whenever I wanted. I could maybe hold him up through six heats and finish him in the seventh, is how they would say it at the fights.

Mrs. Bobson was right behind me. She wanted to check him out some more. She mentioned all kinds of varieties of herbal teas she had in the kitchen, but the Yid had all his no-thank-you's lined up and we got out of there quick, out into the eye-clinching, shoulder-hiking, vicious cold. And guess what? There was a goddam taxi out front waiting for us.

The taxi driver opened the door for us before we even hit the sidewalk. We didn't have to close it either: he did it. The Yid had already told him where we were headed and everything, so nobody had to say a word. It was really warm back there bundled next to the Yid, feeling the car purr through that cushy seat.

The Yid mumbled, "Sarge paid for this." Which struck me funny, but I gilded it.

I sat next to the Yid, waiting for something to happen. Nothing happened. Then Tule got restless and the basket started to squirm next to me like a Mexican jumping bean, and the Yid said, "You brought the cat?"

I said, "Yeah. She'll be okay."

He said, "Dammit! Dammit!" He looked like he was going apoplectic on me. He got red in the face, and he practically foamed at the mouth. " 'Okay?' How could she be 'okay?' They'll never let her into the arena. You can't bring a cat to a boxing match, dammit!"

"Nobody's going to know. She'll be in the basket or she'll be in my coat. I got it worked out. We do stuff like this all the time."

"This isn't all the time! This is tonight!" He leaned forward to read the time off the clock by the speedometer. "We can't go back and drop her off; it's too late. We'll have to leave her somewhere."

"No! Relax, for crissakes! Tule'll be okay. She's always okay."

"She's gonna blow everything." He was looking every which way, whipping his head around, looking out all the windows, left, right, behind. He even looked up at the roof and down at the floor, but he wasn't finding what he was looking for. What he was looking for, I figured, was me. But for some reason he couldn't let himself in on that. Guys.

"You're just nervous. Look, you can kiss me right now if you want to. That's it, isn't it? Well, you can kiss me.

Then you can relax. It's okay, really! Here..." I turned in the seat so my knee was practically on his thigh and my tits touched his shoulder and my face was in his face and I closed my eyes and I waited.

I could hear the slush flying under our wheels. Cars honked. Frozen mud spattered the windows. The windshield wiper went on, and then it went off.

I opened my eyes.

The Yid said, "You would do anything for me, wouldn't you?" He looked completely surprised.

"Yes, Jack."

Then he kissed me. Nothing touched except our lips, lightly, like how you might touch a wound that was still tender, nursing it, worrying it, loving it, to make it heal. Outside, it wasn't Indian Summer anymore, but inside, everything was melting. I tilted my head this way and that, and Jack did the same thing, as if we were trying to get each other into focus. As if we had to milk every little drop from whatever the hell was rushing between us in the backseat of the cab on Plymouth Avenue South headed toward the Memorial Arena at West Main, a ride of maybe fifteen minutes, and five of them were already wasted.

I was melting and burning, like if you set fire to a plastic bag, how it drips flames. My arms and legs wanted to clamp around Jack like a crab at the end of a poking stick. They wanted to gobble him up and burn him up, and the more I kept them back, the hotter and hungrier they got. He sobbed. I could hear it and I could feel it through his lips. He was burning too, and he was tight holding himself back from burning me and eating me up. But just our lips touched, and lightly.

Tears pumped out. I was back there, in the yard, after breakfast, with James and Julian. I still had the taste of maple syrup on my tongue. I was pushing Julian. James was rolling on his back on the soft earth, like a flipped-over turtle rocking and rocking and laughing. James used to say, "Who loves you, Lea? I'll always be with you. I'll always take care of you." I was singing "Sunny Side of the Street," just like Mom. I saw Daddy through the kitchen window. He was washing dishes. He still had on that white chef's hat, but Mom snuck up behind him and she pulled it off and he laughed. I saw through the window. And they kissed. It was my turn to push Julian, and when his swing came back toward me, my voice vibrated in the taut chain and echoed back at me, which I liked, and I liked Julian swinging and James laughing and all those pancakes in my stomach, up in the air so blue.

Then I was back in the cab. It had stopped, but the meter hadn't stopped. Jack had told the cabbie to stop, and Jack was saying, "Listen, *shiksie*, I mean Lea, listen, Lea, you know that everything I do, I do for my people, for the Chosen of the Chosen of the Chosen. You understand that, don't you?"

"Sure, Jack. The thirteen and the three. You have to. I understand that. Why wouldn't I understand that?"

"Sylvia was spying on us…"

"She's got the hots for me, is all. You know about that girl!"

"No, that wasn't it. Sarge put her up to it."

"Sarge? What for?"

He leaned very close and talked very low and every now and then his eyes darted in the direction of the cabbie to see if he was listening, and of course the cabbie could have cared less—he was looking at a magazine like they do and smoking a cigarette. He was making good money off us.

Jack said, "He saw you and me together at the Wee Spot. It was stupid to meet you there. I made a mistake. God! I made an awful mistake!"

"What are you saying? Are you saying you didn't want to kiss me?" I was walking on the edge of a fence, teetering this way, teetering that way. I wanted to kiss him and I wanted to kill him and I wanted him to do stuff to me. The cabbie's blue smoke was curling back between us. The smell of it made me feel cheap.

"No! Listen! Sarge saw you and me at the Wee Spot, and then he put two and two together. He knew that dead guy in the alley had something to do with me, and he knew there was something funny about you."

"Yeah, you're right. I think he knows I can do stuff to people. He doesn't know much, he hasn't really seen anything, but he's, you know, kind of respectful of me, and, believe you me, Sarge is not that kind of a guy that he's respectful of you if you don't have a lot of dough or a gun."

"The day after he gave us that little serenade, Lea, Sarge collared me on Monroe Avenue, and he talked to me—'man to man,' is the way he put it." Jack looked down at his feet. I could see his face working, that pretty face of his, like something was killing him inside and he just couldn't stand it. "He wanted me to do something for him. He wanted to use me to get to you, to get you to do something that would help him out."

"What are you talking about?"

"The fights. He wants Denny Love to beat the Ruiz guy. He wants it real bad, like tens of thousands of dollars' worth of real bad. Sarge is a betting man, and the odds are very, very long. Denny Love is washed up. Nobody expects him to win. He thought you could swing it."

"So you told him no, right? What, did you smack him or something?"

"How the hell could I smack him? The guy is a monster. He was the boxing champion of the Russian Army, Lea! He could beat me to a pulp. He could get me in a lot of trouble, too, if he felt like it. He knows about my little hashish trade. What the hell does he care if it's all to finance the coming of the *Meschiach*?"

"You want me to do something to Sarge?"

Tule was scrambling inside the basket. I saw her little nose peek through the crack under the toggles, then her paw, and she meowed. I don't know what she was saying, though. I had things on my mind.

Jack said, "No! For God's sake, Lea, no! You don't know what you're dealing with there. You think Sarge runs the Wee Spot with his own money? Sarge works for somebody else. He's got all kinds of connections. He does things for them, and they do things for him. They make all this money doing something else, and they have to, you know, do something with it. The Wee Spot is just one of their little investments.

"Believe me, every time I move a quantity of hashish around, there are people I have to check with, and they're all friends of Sarge. Lea, if you mess with Sarge, you better be ready to mess with a whole army. And for what? Sarge isn't the Evil One. Sarge is nothing. None of this stuff means anything. It's a diversion, see? It's just something that's slowing us down . . . Shit!" Jack saw Tule's head poke out, and he reached past me to push the top of the basket down and it squooshed her back inside and taught her a lesson, I guess. I didn't really feel that good about it, but he'd kissed me.

"So what do you want me to do, Jack?"

"Look, Sarge is a jerk. He has no idea what you are. You are going to be one of the Righteous Ones who help the Thrice Chosen herald in the *Meschiach*. Through your talent, Lea, you're going to preserve the people of God Tetragrammaton, our Father and our King. All Sarge wants to do is tap you to make a few bucks, then he's quits."

"So what do you want me to do, Jack?"

He looked out his window for a second. He looked at the cabbie's clock again and at the dollars turning over on his meter. "That's up to you."

"Did you kiss me because Sarge told you to?"

"Is that what you think?"

"No."

I took out my little compact that I kept in my black bag with the fringe that was over my elbow, and I opened it, and I looked at my mouth. I have this really pretty mouth. Anybody would say so. You can't fool a person about a thing like that. Lips like mine, the power they cast over guys when I take care of myself and wear what goes and so on, it's undeniable.

Guys are imperfect. They're weak and they do stupid things, but they love you. You have to help them out sometimes. I said, "Let's go to the fights."

"What about your cat?"

"She's coming with us, but she'll stay in the basket, don't worry. I'll keep her out of sight."

He said something to the driver. The guy butted his

cigarette and headed out. Actually, some kid in a rusty black Chevy Impala sideswiped us when we were pulling away from the curb. The cabbie rolled down the window and swore at him and gave him the hi-sign, but the kid was already gone. The cabbie just rolled up the window again and shrugged. He said, "It happens all the time."

Did I mention that Jack kissed me? That's the main thing.

When we got to the arena, Jack told the cabbie to go around back to Valhalla Street for a minute, and we drove into this alley by the loading docks of the arena, right over the river. Jack said park, and he parked, and Jack took out a long-stemmed pipe with a little brass bowl, and he said, "Do you want some smoke?"

And the cabbie said, "Sure," and he turned off the meter.

I said, "Jack, I want to do whatever *you're* doing."

He looked at me. He knew I never did anything. His brow kind of wrinkled a little. That thing happened to his hazel eyes where they looked like two little planes that the engine suddenly shut off and they dived, as if the world was all shot to hell and nothing was worth a damn. But then they looped up again—desperado, is what I'm thinking, where you know the world stinks but you have to take your stand somewhere, what the hell—and he looked at me and the wrinkle was gone and he nodded. It all happened in maybe a couple seconds.

Jack put a tiny black chip in the bowl of his pipe and he lit it and we passed the pipe all around. We smoked, the three of us, in that frozen, windy alley, where there wasn't a soul in sight to begin with, and the more we smoked, the fewer and fewer people there were. I had never done a drug before. There were a couple of things inside me that I didn't feel like lubricating. I figured, if people think you're a narc because you don't do their shit with them, that's their problem. But with Jack, everything seemed okay.

It didn't feel half bad. After the first hot, rough drags, it went down like maple syrup, and the whole world that was a stinking muddle of stuff that doesn't fit together and hasn't got any time for you, it all fell into four-four time. Everything that happened, breathing, heartbeat, ice spray, cans clacking against the curb, voices drifting in from the crowd around the corner, every plink and bang and sizzle—fell on the beat, exactly on the beat: four-four.

I was right about Tule getting in past the ticket takers, especially because we had the most expensive seats you could get. They were right down in front where you can smell the fighters and you can hear the grunt they make every time they throw a punch and you can see the sweat spraying off of guys' faces when the glove hits. You can see them crumble and break down inside, two or three rounds before anybody in the cheap seats knows it's already over. That was the kind of seats we had, and the guys who tore our tickets could never afford them. They were so misted by the price of those tickets, I could have had a cow in a basket at the end of a tow rope, and they would have waved us on through.

Jack put his arm around me and took me right to our seats like he went there every day and it was nothing to him, which I knew it really wasn't; he was nervous. When a guy has his arm around you, which Jack had his arm around me, which was so warm and comfy that I wished I could have moved in there and just lived there in the crook of Jack's arm and forgotten everything else, when a guy does that to you, you feel what's going on in his head. You feel it right through the inside of his arm and through his hand on your shoulder—which I love—and he was nervous.

The place was like a crater lined all around with bleachers in two or three balcony sections. You came in on the first balcony level and walked through a train station, is what it felt like. Guys were selling hot dogs and sodas and beers and program books and T-shirts and jackets, with even the french fries two or three bucks. It echoed like you were inside a big drain pipe; I'd slept in a couple once upon a time right after I ran away and decided to become my own guardian.

Then you went through a hole into the bleachers. You could be crawling in through the pore of a rotting orange. There were plenty of little kids up there. It was a family entertainment, like. Everybody was eating something and talking about their favorite fighter, and who could beat who with his gloves laced to his shoes, and everything was still four-four.

There was already one fight going on when we came in, Jack and me, him with his arm around me, Jack's arm around my body, and you could see them way down in the ring, these tiny little guys beating the crap out of each other, and the ref dancing around in his bow tie and rolled-up sleeves, like a fruit fly over a banana peel. Somebody was making a movie, because all around the ring were these gorgeous silver umbrellas and huge, hot lights on account of which the management opened up a lot of windows because of the heat of those spotlights, but then the freezing cold wind came in, and customers in the cheap seats were freezing their buns off.

While Jack and I were threading through the balcony to the stairs down, one of the fighters landed a big one to the other guy's skull, and all around us you could hear them gasp and grunt and everybody stood up and some lady was shouting, "Finish him off! Hit him hard!" It was like twisting down through a wormhole, going down those stairs, smelling everybody's smell, and smoke and spilled beer and burnt wieners and tiny kids chasing between your feet. Who knows what they were doing there. Their mothers and fathers were probably scarfing burgers and screaming their throats out and couldn't care less.

By the time we got to our row, that fight was over, but down where we were, one of the high rollers in the folding chairs was saying the whole thing was a "barnie" and that Kid Mansfield was so stupid about it, he even hit the canvas when Charlie Furman landed one on the referee. Our seats were behind this guy. He had on a black-and-red bowling jacket. He had a neck like an ox's, and he was wearing a thick black toupee, and he said, "Everybody knew it, too. A couple hours before the fight the odds in the West Side poolrooms went from five to four for the Kid to two to one on Furman."

Then the guy he was talking to got really pissed and jostled the toupee guy and started swearing at him, why didn't he tell him before he threw away a hundred bucks on the Kid. And the toupee guy said in a real low voice, well, don't go ape-shit because you're going to make it all back on Denny Love—which he'd told him already, hadn't he?—"because that's a hot one, and a lot of the so-called mavens don't even know it."

We said excuse me and settled in, because there was hardly knee space. The toupee guy and his string-bean partner turned around and looked kind of alarmed, because they hadn't noticed us back there, but you could see them loosen up and smile when they saw we were not the type to pack heat or to use what you say against you in a court of law.

Down in the basket, Tule was tight as Bobson's bowels. She felt like a bowling ball, all scrunched into one corner, and she didn't move. I leaned my head close to the wicker basket, which was in my lap, and I whispered, "Who loves you, Tule?" She hissed.

Jack was not relaxed either. He took his arm back as soon as we sat down. The toupee person was saying, "Remember Johnny Tendler, the one that come up from the clubs? He flattened everything in sight, and when it come time to cash in, he told all the big boys, 'Nothing doing.'"

The string bean said, "Sure. That fellow was a bruiser, Jew boy from Joseph Avenue, am I right? Very scientific fighter, fast on his feet, left hand like a goddam torpedo. I saw him deck Fazio in three in this ring right here, what, two years ago last July. Hey, Benito, whatever happened to Tendler?"

"Somebody doped his tea."

"See? That's what happens when you put your own private interest ahead of the interest of the sport as a whole."

"That's exactly what I told the guy's widow."

We had great seats, all right. There were only maybe five rows in front of us, and then there were three card tables right next to the ring, where there was a guy with a clock and a judge taking down notes and a doctor who I wouldn't want to patch my pretty face, he looked so drunk and shriveled. The families of the boxers were in our section, too. None of them seemed too broke up over their situation. Their husbands or fathers or sons could have been, like, getting a haircut, and these folks were just waiting for them to be done so they could go home. I guess you get used to everything.

Tule picked that moment to agitate herself. She was scratching inside the basket and clawing at the wicker and trying to push her head out under the toggles, right when a guy in a tux was announcing Denny Love and Orlando Ruiz the Detroit Pile Driver. I didn't even get to see them climb into the ring because everybody stood up and applauded then and I had to stay down cooing to Tule. My beat which I got from Jack's pipe was starting to syncopate by that time, and everything was a little mixed up, so I had some trouble cooing, because I would start to giggle, and then Tule would get restless again.

I saw Ruiz's wife through a forest of bodies. She was a pretty black woman in a green bolero jacket, if you can believe it, and a tight sheath skirt. She stood up when they announced Orlando Ruiz, and she laughed and shouted. She got so excited she had to bite her lip. She made a fist and raised it and she blew him a kiss. Then she sat down and the woman next to her handed her over this little two-year-old kid to sit on her lap.

Ruiz was undefeated in eighteen pro fights, is what the announcer said, or else it was eighty or else he was talking about something else entirely, because my concentration was syncopating a little bit. The guy with the toupee and the ox neck stood up and applauded with everybody else. He said, "Orlando Ruiz is beyond reproach."

The string bean, who was standing beside him now, said, "We got no lack of bona fides here, Benito."

Then Benito said, "I hear he drinks tea, though," and they both laughed, and somebody else laughed, and I turned around, and it was Sarge.

Sarge said, "Don't say hello. I'm not here. You just enjoy the fights, nice couple like you. Beautiful couple! Sonuvabitch! You just have fun." Jack turned me around and sat me down. He didn't say a word to Sarge. His arm was around me again. Benito looked past us at Sarge and winked at him and gave him a thumbs-up.

Jack said, "Don't be afraid."

I wasn't afraid, and I said so. Why should I be afraid? I was the dope in Orlando Ruiz's goddam tea. I was about to win my first professional heavyweight bout. No skin off *my* teeth. I wished I'd put some of my own dough on Denny Love, was all.

The applause Denny Love got was what you call polite. When the announcer counted off Denny Love's big accomplishments, like winning a decision two years ago over a guy who used to be a contender at one time, somebody called out, "Mr. Ring Rust!" I was still hugging Tule's basket. I would have liked to see the look on Denny Love's face then, not out of meanness, but I was just curious to see if those big bozos were moved by that kind of guff.

Well, it started off slow, and I could hardly tell the one from the other. I couldn't see Mrs. Ruiz, to see which one she was rooting for, and I didn't remember which color

trunks was supposed to be whose. I was pretty well opi-
ated. Plus, they were clinching and trading little powder
puff jabs, and half the time the one's biceps were tucked in
the other's armpits. It was pretty exciting anyway. Jack's
hashish put me right in the ring with them. They were
just measuring each other, see? They were looking for an
advantage. All this time, Jack was sitting as still as a
corpse. His face was the color of the ash at the end of a
cigarette, and his arm that was still around me was as stiff
and dead as a crash dummy's.

Just before the end of round one, after they hit the
plank for the ten-second warning, the one of them con-
nected with a short, left-handed sock, and the other guy
floundered around while the first guy smashed him in the
breadbasket till the timer hit the bell and his trainer ran
into the ring to escort the guy to his corner. He crumpled
in a heap, and everybody loved it.

Tule was giving me grief so I could hardly concentrate
but I had to make sure she didn't yowl and bolt. I figured,
Prince Valiant, the guy with the hard left, has got to be the
Detroit guy Ruiz that I'm supposed to take care of. Sarge
leaned forward and whispered something to Jack and Jack
whispered to me, "He goes down in five."

Round two started, and Jack began talking to me in a
low voice that nobody but me would pick out in all the
ruckus that the fans were making, now that one of the
boxers looked to be on the run. "Do you feel it, Lea?
The evil spirits in this place? This is why Tetragrammaton
destroyed Sodom and Gomorrah. Don't do anything,
though. Save it for Ruiz."

He kept talking but I kind of drifted off. It was round
two and it was round three and somebody was getting

belted all over the ring and they both of them got dropped at one time or another. I kept my hand on the basket and I said, "Who loves you, Tule?" over and over like a lullaby, but she wasn't buying it.

Right in the middle of everything, this guy in a thick, black overcoat and a wide-brimmed black hat came into the ring from out of the movie lights. He just kind of twinkled in like dew when it steams up and then chills and streams down again. He had side curls and a beard down to the middle of his buttoned-up chest, which that beard branched off into two parts like a river at a delta. He had a thick black book under his one arm. There were bookmarks hanging out of it, ribbons of all different colors and pieces of notepaper that I could see the writing on them even though I was pretty far away, and it looked like snakes.

He cleared everybody out of the ring just by the way he breathed, and the whole Memorial Arena shut up like a bunch of monks. I could hear the wind blowing in through the open windows up by the cheap seats. I could hear the metal casings of the spotlights tinkle from the hot and the cold. I could hear the guy's beard whisk his collar when he turned his head to look around.

He held up the book to read to us from it, and I saw the rib, and it wasn't English what it said, but I understood it anyway:

"ZOHAR HAGOYIM"

And then I knew that this guy was Sabbatai Levi Hagodol and my hair stood on end and the whole arena turned the color of blood and my heart pounded like a jungle drum and I didn't know if maybe I was going to die and did anybody realize what was going on? I couldn't find my head to turn it to ask Jack what I was supposed to do.

Sabbatai Levi Hagodol read:

"God Tetragrammaton looked at the Earth and the Earth was corrupt before God Tetragrammaton. The Earth was filled with violence. And the sixteen saviors, the Chosen of the Chosen of the Chosen, were dispersed, thirteen on earth and three in the supernal realm, and they did not know one the other.

"And God Tetragrammaton said: 'Build a space-ship in the hidden section of the Sears and Roebuck Building on Monroe Avenue. Cover the ceiling with gold leaf and the floor with Gymseal. The south wall, let it be covered with all manner of female images, air-brushed on glossy paper and pleasing to the eye, but without beaver and with shaven armpits. On the north wall, place you my Holy of Holies hidden from profane eyes by a purple cope. On the east let there be many images of the pyramids which my children built in the Land of Egypt, the House of Bondage. And on the west let there be a hole, a vacuity, an opening— vohu—through which the Meschiach *will come, the vessel which God Tetragrammaton has enjoined the Thrice Chosen of the supernal realm to form, in preparation for that day.*

" 'And when the spaceship which God Tetragrammaton has commanded you to build is perfected in all its aspects, then will congregate the thirteen in that spaceship which God Tetragrammaton has

commanded you to build. And the congregation of the thirteen will call up the congregation of the three. And the congregation of the thirteen and of the three will fly above the firmament and below the firmament to all parts of the Earth and of the heavens to inquire of all the creatures there and to judge them whether they are worthy and what part of them may enter the Promised Land Ish-ra-el, which I have promised unto my Thrice Chosen ones.

"*'And there will be a* shiksie *to translate and to interpret all the tongues of all the peoples and the tribes of the* goyim *for my Thrice Chosen. Unto her therefore will be given the final understanding of the brilliance which God Tetragrammaton has hidden in the peoples of the Earth,* zohar hagoyim, *which is the sanctification and glorification of that which is violent and corrupt.'*"

Then the timer climbed up onto his card table at ringside, and he had a ram's horn, and he blew it and blew it about a hundred times, and I knew it was to fool the Evil One into thinking that the *Meschiach* had already arrived so he might as well pack up and leave us all alone because his game was up. And Reb Sabbatai went on:

"*'The* shiksie *is not really a* goy,*' saith God Tetragrammaton, 'for she will decimate the minions of the Evil One to speed the way for the coming of the* Meschiach, *and she will sit at My right hand, along with Jack Konar, on the Day Of Judgment, for it's the fifth round. I said, it's the fifth round—anytime now. Lea, are you listening to me? What's wrong? Do you need anything? Can I get you anything? You've got to do it now. Lea! Lea!'"*

"Huh?" I looked at Jack. He was squeezing my arm. People were yelling and screaming all around me.

Benito and the string bean were laughing and shaking their heads. "Who'd have thought the guy still had that much?" is what Benito said.

And the other guy said, "Is this a slugfest, or what?"

I heard the leather walloping flesh and the hiss of the fighters' breath and the grunt at the other end of each punch. Somebody was getting knocked silly, spinning across the ring, then curling up with his back to the turn-buckle and his knees wobbling like plates on a stick. The Ruiz dame was on her feet with that toddler in her arms.

I blinked myself awake. Tule was half out of the basket, yowling and scratching. I concentrated as hard as I could. Like through a zoom lens, I could see the red gloves pounding into the guy past his own gloves, which his arms felt so weak he could hardly keep them up, and I could feel the attacker like a machine gun, full of sparks and gunpowder. Then it was like it switched to an even higher-power lens and there was nothing but squiggles and urges, but I knew the guy on the ropes had one good punch left in him—desperado—so I waited for it, and when he threw it, I did what I had to do, and Ruiz went down.

Jack shot to his feet. "Jesus, God, what have you done?" He looked like he was scared shitless. People started shoving and stampeding down toward the ring. Folding chairs were collapsing and getting kicked around. Some fights broke out in the expensive section.

"I knocked out Ruiz just like you said."

"No, you didn't. The guy you knocked out was Denny Love."

"No, Denny Love was the weak guy, the guy on the ropes, the guy that was losing. Otherwise, why did you want me to hurry and do it?"

"Because it was the fifth, dammit. It had to be in the fifth. The round was almost over."

Sarge was still sitting down. I've never seen a darker face. He was fuming so heavy, you could practically see smoke coming out of his nose and ears. Any minute he was going to blow. And the two guys in front—which now I figured they were seated there especially for us, to surround us there so we got the message of how everything definitely had to go—they were standing up, staring at us, and they were not happy either.

And Jack said, "Run!"

chapter seven

Underground

Tule sprang out of that basket like she was on fire. She jumped and she scrambled from head to lap, through legs and past tumbling metal folding chairs. People shouted and shoved and massed toward the ring. The ref had got hold of the microphone, and the feedback was enough to bust a dead person's eardrums that was already rigor mortised and six feet under:

"All bets are off!"

I could still smell Sabbatai Levi Hagodol's black cloth coat, a musty, mildewy smell, with a trace of something sweet—wisteria? —and something strong and burning—ether? I had this crazy idea that Tule might be heading for Reb Sabbatai and Reb Sabbatai would take care of her, or else I wouldn't have let so many seconds pass before I ran after her.

"Not that way!" Jack hooked my arm and yanked me toward the stairs.

I yanked back. "Tule—I gotta catch her."

On Jack's one side Sarge was standing with his fists on his hips. He was working those sausages in his face. On Jack's other side Benito, the ox neck guy, was practically levitating his toupee with the steam coming out of his head. Jack gave up yanking, and he dived into the crowd with me. Those two bruisers tried to run after us, but everywhere we snaked, the crowd closed up behind us. Namely, we were young, and Sarge and his buddy were decrepit farts—as long as their knuckles weren't up your nose.

Then it seemed like there were other hoods after us, all guys with shoulders made of beefsteak and foreheads made of shoe leather, grabbing for us and tumbling in after us, swiping customers out of their way. Everybody was falling over somebody. Things were too crazy to think about using your talent—your mind's got to be in one place for that.

I saw Tule then. A little boy had clawed her up off the floor, and he was shaking her and laughing. I squeezed through to him with Jack close behind me, and I slapped the smile off his stupid face—"Mommy! Mommy!"—and Tule squirted out of his hands.

I crawled under somebody and grabbed her tail, which I don't like to do, it being disrespectful to a cat to grab its tail, but I got her and I reeled her in and I clutched her tight. Jack yelled, "Straight ahead!" and I looked, and I saw the archway where the boxers came in. We beat it to the archway, which the security guards at that point didn't know what was going on better than anybody else, and we got through into this sweaty hallway. We found a staircase, we avalanched down it, and then we were underground.

Nobody but us was down there. You could hear all the feet stampeding overhead and the shouting and the grabbing for the microphone and chairs scraping. Nobody knew who was supposed to have what seats anymore, cheap or pricey. But Jack and me and Tule, we were in a different world. Down where we were, you could hear water dripping from the pipes louder than that whole riot.

I held Tule tight. It was like holding a handful of greasy springs that wanted to explode in every direction. Tule said:

Death! Death! Death! Death!

Everything down there was made of dust. The light was made of dust. The dust walls were no-color, like black-and-white movie walls, and where light came in the air shined, because the air was dust.

Jack jerked his head around like a chased bird, and where he saw the air shine, he said, "This way!" We came to a stairway with glass double doors at the top that led out to a terrace over the river, must be on Valhalla Street. We ran up the stairs and pushed through the first set of doors. There was a little space in between, then another set of glass double doors that opened out onto the terrace. We were in the middle, on a big black rubber mat that looked like a kajillion hinges spattered with muddy water and broken skins of ice. We pushed against the bar to open the outer doors, and they rattled but wouldn't go. We looked down: They were chained shut with a padlock the size of Tule.

Jack said, "Shit! Can you do something?"

I said, "You know I can't do a thing. I can only do it to a person."

We turned to go back into the hallway—and the inner doors wouldn't open. They only opened from the other side. We were stuck in the vestibule between the doors. I thought, it's like the dinosaurs in the La Brea Tar Pits. All they would find would be our bones, little cat bones, big boy bones, and girl bones with nice bone structure in her skull.

For the second time, Jack said, "Don't be afraid." I leaned all against him, and my head was on Jack's shoulder and my side was on his side and I could feel the fuzz of his coat on the fuzz of my coat.

It was cold in there. The wind blew in off the river through the outside doors. The doors chattered in the casement. "God won't let us die here, Lea—but if we do, it's not your fault. Everything's gonna be okay."

I felt so drowsy, I could have fallen asleep standing up, leaning against Jack, in spite of how it was cold and a lot of guys in that place wanted to fricassee us. Thing is, they could get in at us but we couldn't get out unless somebody let us. It was like goddam Death Row. And I felt so drowsy that if one of Sarge's buddies came by, I didn't know if I could find my talent to do him, even if Jack let me.

I said, "I don't want to smoke that stuff anymore, Jack."

Then we heard someone whistling in the hallway. A guy came around the corner. At first I thought it was

Sabbatai Levi Hagodol, and before Jack could stop me I started banging on the inside doors. The guy came out of the shadows. It wasn't Reb Sabbatai. It was some old guy in a baggy gray-striped jumpsuit pushing a pail on casters at the end of a mop. He didn't seem to hear me banging, but he saw me, and he stopped in front of the stairs leading up to our glass coffin. And he horse laughed.

He let go the mop and he climbed up the stairs and opened the doors. He was a bald guy with salt-and-pepper whiskers like bread mold all over his face. "What are you kids doing in there, making out?"

Jack said, "Could you open the lock for us? We just want to get out."

And the old guy said, "What?"

And Jack said, "Could you open the lock for us? We just want to get out."

"This ain't a public exit, y'know."

Jack, he practically shouted, "Please open it for us. You'll have a portion in the Promised Land." The guy practically fell over laughing.

The old guy said, "Hey, what in hell is going on upstairs, huh? Did somebody get murdered or something?"

Jack and me looked at each other. I don't think it had crossed our minds, either of us, that maybe Denny Love was dead, but now it did. I wasn't too sure one way or the other. I had been under the influence.

Then the old guy said, "Aw, you kids don't care nothin' about the fights. What, did you think this was supposed to be a rock concert?" He fished out a key and he reached past us to the outer doors and he started to unlock the padlock and pull the chain out from behind one of the push bars, one goddam link at a time. He saw Tule then, which he had been laughing too hard before, which Tule was still tight as Bobson's sphincters, saying, *death, death, death, death*, and the guy said, "Is that your cat or was he down here?"

I said, "It's my cat Tule."

He said, "What?"

Then I said what I'd said again, only louder, and he said, "Well, it puts me in mind of Sam Patch, who, y'know, he jumped off a cliff into the river not fifty yards from where we stand, but it was a hundred years ago, and he had a trained bear with him."

Down behind the old man there was a ruckus because some big fellows were hauling their fat asses through that hallway, and one of them landed a foot in the old man's bucket. It gave him a little ride till he slipped and fell on his butt, but it wasn't loud enough for the old man to hear it through the closed doors behind him.

A broad-shouldered guy in a boxing club jacket, guy with a chin like a milk carton stuck to the bottom of his face, he tripped over the guy in the bucket. Then he got up, and he got the other guy up, and the ones who had run ahead, they all ran back to where those two were. One of them saw us up in the vestibule and he pointed and they all looked.

Jack yanked the rest of the chain out of the push bars. He shouldered out through the doors, and he pulled me and Tule out with him.

And the old guy said, "Don't you forget my portion of the Promised Land, now!" just before the wind slammed those doors shut on his laughing ass. The five thugs rammed up into the vestibule, their pants full of soap suds, and the old guy went down, and the big fellows bulled, yelling and screaming, out onto Valhalla Street, and Jack and me and Tule to my bosom were heading like a sonuvabitch down toward the frozen river.

Jack pulled me along by my hand. When he tugged I could feel it all the way down my arm and through the tendons in my armpit right to my heart underneath my tit and then the rest of me to my legs. I was feeling a little dreamy and groggy, but I ran like hell. The point is, he was holding my hand. And I think I said, "Aren't you going to kiss me again?"

He kept running. If I had let up on Tule for a second she would have crawled up my face and jumped off my head into the goddam river. Jack shinnied under a dumb, wooden fence with rotting, broken planks and a NO TRES-PASSING sign, and I shimmied after him. It was cold rock underneath it, and it stung where it touched my skin where my coat got pulled open and my thigh socks got scraped down, but I made it. Then there was a stone staircase down into the dark.

We were clambering down into the dark, and he said, "You didn't kill him, did you?"

"I don't think so."

We were running hard, and I heard Jack sobbing while he pulled me after him down the stairs and along the rocky edge of the river. Way up overhead there were streetlights and cars rumbling on a steel bridge, and I heard some guys shouting, but we were young and they were fat. There was an old aqueduct, and a train was going through it, or else I was getting a killer of a headache. All at once we were jumping across icy water from one plank to another, then we were underneath some building with old, pissed-on brick walls and bum trash underfoot and the ashes of old campfires, and we stopped.

Jack rested his hands on his knees. He hunched over like that and breathed slower, slower, slower, until he could talk again. He said, "It's not your fault. I should have learned to do it already. I can see it, but I can't do it. With the biofeedback and with the watching you, I'm sure I can get it, but it's taking me time, and the first thing has always got to be the spaceship. My people are waiting for me, Lea."

"For us."

He looked up at me then. "Come again?"

"For us, Jack. They're waiting for us. Jack, Jack, I saw your Uncle Sabbatai! He appeared to me at the fights. He read to me from the *Zohar Hagoyim*. There were ram's horns and heavenly lights. He said I'm not really a *goyim* because of how I will help the Chosens and polish off the Evil One and I'm going to sit right next to you on the Day Of Judgment, the both of us, you and me, at the right hand of God Tetragrammaton. That's what Reb Sabbatai said, right in front of everybody, near the end of the fifth round."

"You saw him?"

"That's not all. What's *vohu*?"

"Wait a minute. Let's go someplace warm." He stood up in front of me, and I was smiling now because I remembered I had some great news for him. He held my arms in his hands and he looked at me hard and he cocked his head. Then he led me along a brick wall to a huge pipe, as big around as a couple of cows, and with a pipe joint, which there was steam hissing out of it. It was warm there. "Now, what are you asking me, 'What's *vohu*?' How do you know *vohu*?"

"You tell me what it is."

"If you mean the word I think you mean, it's a Hebrew word, a Biblical word. In Genesis, it's what the world was before God made day and night: *vohu*, dull, black, and static. That's what the Light Sponge is—zero albedo."

"I know it, Jack, but that's not what Reb Sabbatai said about *vohu*. Reb Sabbatai said *vohu* was supposed to be *a hole, a vacuity, an opening*."

Jack's eyes went as wide, practically, as that steam pipe. He hit his forehead with the heel of his hand. "*Vohu!*" The corners of his lips curled down, then his cheeks hiked up, and he smiled. "*Vohu! Vohu!*" He took my hand and he did a little dance and I did a little dance with him.

He said, "We have to bust through the west wall!" and for the second time in one night—he kissed me. He held my cheek in his palm while we kissed. Then he slid his hand up to my beret and pushed it back off my head. He stroked my crew cut, which was already longer. He stroked me and stroked me and we kissed and kissed. My back was against a part of a wall near that warm pipe, and I felt like cheese melting between two slices of bread in a sandwich grill. I sneaked my hands inside Jack's coat and held him around his waist. I could feel the shape of his back and his spine, the small of his back down to the swell of his little buttocks and then up, like the backs of two smooth shiny swordfish curving out of the sea to his shoulders, or like wings beating and beating while he stroked me and he stroked me and we kissed and we kissed.

We stopped to catch our breath and I said, "It's like being on a swing. I can't stand it—I love you! It's like pushing somebody on a swing, up and up, and singing, and there's love in the kitchen window, and there's laughing on the ground, and everything is perfect, and then..."

"Shut up, I want to kiss you!"

"This is important..." But then we were kissing again. My little fringe bag that I had on a strap over my shoulder through thick and thin the whole night, the strap must have broken because I heard it slip down and hit the mud. I didn't know where my beret had gotten to. My makeup, it was probably smeared all over my puss, but we kissed and kissed. My fingers tickled up his back and even came up through his collar. I felt the nape of his neck and the round tops of his shoulders. His hands were doing similar to me in back and in front, and I said "Mmmmmmm!"

And Jack said the exact same thing.

Then his fingers pushed down under the elastic of Mrs. Bobson's daughter's panties, and I said, "Tule!"

Because she was gone.

Our eyes got used to the dark. There was some light down there reflected off the river. It shone down from floodlights off the backs of buildings through rotted, broken boards overhead. Sometimes you were in a crawl space, feeling your way along the steam pipe in the nearly pitch-dark, and you would look down and you could see the river through the boards between your feet. Other times you were out in the open on a steel beam ledge that jutted out of the embankment under an old factory.

I kept shouting *Tule, Tule, Tule,* and why she didn't

come to me I don't know, because I saw her four or five times scooting around a corner into a shadow or out of a shadow. Jack saw her once or twice, too. Now and then I heard her—*death, death*—and I told Jack, "This way!"

We also saw a lot of bums down there, but they didn't bother us. They were like dead people. They stared at you from a perch along the wall, looking halfway dangerous and halfway pitiful. They'd got their piece of steam pipe staked, and you could pass but you couldn't tarry. They had droopy, shadowy ghost clothes and Halloween globes for eyes.

One said, "Who's Tule?" but we didn't answer.

Another one said, "What's this 'death, death' stuff?"

So we were underground, I was wild afraid for Tule, I was pulling Jack along by his hand while he warned me from behind, go this way, don't go that way, because he knew all these passages from when he was a kid and Sabbatai Levi Hagodol led him through all these places and taught him about the Devil and the Land of the Dead.

We were climbing down some rickety steps to a huge, echoey dark chamber where the dripping water sounded like thunderclaps, and he asked me, "Lea, how many people have you killed?"

I whispered, "She's down here." We stood real still. The black turned to gray and I could see broken concrete pillars, practically a Parthenon of them, but worn down to the steel rods inside them and with chunks cracked away and sitting underneath in pools of water. A couple times I said, "Who loves you, Tule?"

Then I said, "I only killed one this year. That was the guy who wanted to bust you up. Last year, nobody. It would have been nobody this year too because I can control it better. Now I don't have to kill them—I could just cripple them or give them indigestion. Before, I could only kill. I was in a kind of a panic, though, when that kid was all over you. I got clumsy."

"You saved my life, Lea." He gave my hand a squeeze. He never let go.

I wasn't looking at Jack, though. All the time I was talking, I was looking around the dark chamber, pillar to pillar and along the concrete walls and back and forth to the rusty heaps of, must have been, furnaces and pipes, for Tule. "The year before last, a guy got fresh with me when I was hitchhiking, guy in a suit—you wouldn't expect it, you know? He took me to the park by the lake and he parked and he held my arm and lay down on top of me but I hardly had time to get scared and he had a stroke or something. It was a long walk home."

"My God! I read about it!"

"Everybody read about it. What was he, the mayor?"

"A councilman, I think."

"Figures."

"You can be so tough! Why are you so tough?"

"Then, the year before that, there were two, maybe three—I'm not sure." I stopped talking because I thought I spotted Tule, but it wasn't Tule. It might have been some more stuff crumbling and splashing. I could see better and better every minute I was there, and I saw more outlines of things, then I could see inside the outlines. There was no way Tule was going to get out of that chamber without me seeing her.

I said, "It was on this street I lived on for a little while. I was scared. There was a lot going on. There were guys with guns running around, and you didn't know which ones were cops. Somebody was screaming. This girl was already lying in the gutter with blood gushing out of her, but I didn't do it to her.

"I had to get home, two blocks ahead, filled with crazy people. There was nothing behind me but screaming and shouting, Jack. Then some people fell down dead in front of me, the way they do. I didn't even know if they were cops or bystanders, but my way was clear to run home.

"Anybody would have done the same thing if they had a talent—I couldn't help it. I'm more accurate now. I'm a better weapon. I'm cooler."

"You had to take care of yourself, Lea. It's a law of nature."

"That's not what Tule says."

"What does Tule say?"

"Don't kill."

"You were only thirteen, right?"

"I guess. The year before that, when I was twelve, hell, a lot of people died. Adults do not respect children, Jack. They don't. They hate children. They take advantage of them. I didn't have any home. I didn't have any mommy or daddy. I didn't have anything. And every place I went, every place they put me or that I ran to, people just wanted to push me around and use me up like a foil packet of ketchup that you squeeze onto your hamburger and then you crush it and you throw it away and a dog licks it and then he spits it out and then a car runs over it. That's how they treat you. CPS is the same..."

"CPS?"

"Child Protective Service. They're the same. One of them died trying to get me into the goddam car. I didn't want to go in that car, I wanted my goddam mommy.

Only my mom was the same—squeeze you and crush you and throw you away. She's alive somewhere, but I don't want to know about it, because maybe, in spite of I'm so goddam accurate nowadays, she wouldn't last so long once I caught sight of her.

"And Daddy was the same, wasn't he? I know I'm the one that started everything, but he didn't have to hit a person and drink till he practically fell on you when you came home from school. He didn't have to break a chair over your mommy's head one time, then take you for a ride where you end up in cheap motels for days and days, until he died too."

I kept looking and looking—no Tule. Partly, I kept looking so hard to bleed off some juice from what I was thinking about. I wanted to finish telling Jack what I was telling him—and what I was telling me. I knew that if I looked straight at it, it had snakes for hair, and I would turn to stone.

"That was my fault, anyway, because he wasn't like that before James and Julian and I went in the backyard swinging. I saw him in the kitchen window. He was wearing the white chef's hat. Mom sneaked up behind him and swiped it off and he kissed her—that's how happy we were! And James was rolling on the ground laughing and laughing. He always said, 'Who loves you, Lea?' and 'I'll always be there! I'll always protect you!' And I was singing and pushing Julian—this was the first time I did my talent. I never knew anything before that. And I was pushing Julian, and do you know what kind of a breakfast we used to have? We used to have pancakes piled so high, it was up to your nose practically and you used up half a bottle of

Vermont Maid just on your own plate to get them all wet with it, which is the only way pancakes are any good, which everybody knows. And Mom was singing 'Sunny Side of the Street,' and I was pushing Julian, and he kicked back one leg a certain way that he had which I must have told him a hundred times not to do that because it caught me in the chest, and James stopped laughing, and I got so mad at Julian, because his foot hurt my chest, and I wanted to scream, but I didn't scream. Instead of screaming, it was like the whole red-hot volcano lava river of screaming at Julian got shunted someplace else inside me that I never even heard of, and he fell out of the swing, and he was dead."

Jack was still holding my hand. Our arms were like the lifeline that deep-sea divers have. He reeled me in, like, and when I was in, I was in his arms, and he looked at me so soulful and kind. He hugged me tight. He said, "Shhh! Shhh!" I cried so hard I couldn't stand up by myself anymore, but Jack held me up.

I said, "Where was James? 'Who loves you, Lea? Who loves you?' How come James didn't stop me?"

Then I said, "I gotta keep looking out. I can't lose Tule."

Jack said, "I'll look out for you," and I closed my eyes and I wished I was a baby in Jack's arms. That's all I ever wanted.

I heard Jack's heartbeat, soft and deep, and somewhere far away a dog barked and Jack said, "Shhh! Shhh!" He rocked me in his arms, and I was happy.

Water dripped like kettledrum beats, the dog barked, Jack's heart thumped, my breath whispered in and out like a spring wind through clean white laundry swelling and beating on a clothesline in the sun, and somebody said, "Yakov, is it you?"

I heard Jack's voice through his chest, like he would hear his own voice, from inside, and he said, "Abie! Are you still alive?"

And Abie said, "No! I'm long gone," and he laughed.

chapter eight

We Make It to Bobson's

Abie was a small guy, almost a midget. He walked downstairs into our chamber and sloshed nearer, puddle to puddle. When he walked, one hip wheeled to pick up his leg and plant it down again like it was a wooden leg. When he got close he fished a flashlight out of his pocket. He held it at his arm's length and he pointed it at himself and he turned it on. "This is me." It was like he wanted to put me at my ease.

He had the ugliest face I ever saw, which I warmed to right off, as it had the best developed *buccinator* and it had twinkle marks at the corners of his eyes so deep you would think a backhoe had dug them there. He had a face like a bunched-up rag and there was a different feeling in every fold, like this guy had been around the block a kajillion times, and he was still going around the block, and he liked it.

Who knows how old Abie was? Old. He had on white painter's pants —you could still see the white here and there if you looked hard maybe. He had sneakers on with galoshes over them. He had a worn-out brown aviator's jacket over his shoulders which the sleeves dangled down and he had a lot of shirts on, one over the other, and the top one was a flannel pajama top which was embroidered, "Sleepytime," under the collar, and he had on a sock hat with a pompon, and, believe me, nothing went.

Jack said, "You come by the river now, the ten men?"

"Yeah, by the river. We feel like the time is getting closer. Is it getting closer?"

Jack nodded.

"We felt it. So we come by the river, like you and me from before. Under the city, Yakov. Under." He kept shining that flashlight on himself, at his arm's length, from above. It was like watching a circus guy in a spotlight. "Yakov, it's a long time you haven't come to see us."

"It's worried you?"

"We know you have your reasons, but we worry. Are you in trouble, Yakov?"

"Always, but God Tetragrammaton will preserve me."

"Amen!"

"Have you found a replacement for poor Menachem?"

"A young fellow! A miracle! He wasn't even a Jew, and he came to us, and he believed, and he had signs: three rats died at his feet. They were the Devil's. Rabbi Metzger gave him to have a *mikvah*, a bath of purification in a grotto between the columns under the Court Street Bridge, and we asked him questions and he answered well. They call him the Bull . . . Don't you want me to tell you about your father, Yakov?"

"Is he alive?"

"Yes, he's alive."

"When he's dead you'll tell me."

"Whatever you say, Yakov."

Abie turned the flashlight on us for just a second—it made me squint—and then he turned it off. He said, "Girlfriend?"

Jack said, "Yeah."

He said, "She's not Jewish."

And Jack said, "No."

After the flashlight, my eyes had to get used to the dark all over again. I couldn't see anything, but I heard Abie go, "Tsk, tsk, tsk!"

I said, "Jack's Uncle Sabbatai Levi Hagodol said I could go."

Jack said, "I didn't tell her that. He told her. He came to her and spoke with her and read to her from the *Zohar Hagoyim*."

Abie snorted. "*Bubbe meisehs!*"

"No. Not old wives' tales! Afterward, she knew things. *Vohu!*"

"What, *vohu*? The west wall, you're talking about? The Light Sponge? It's finished finally? It's dull? What do you mean, *vohu*?"

"We mistranslated it. It's not supposed to be just dull. It's supposed to be void. That's been the whole problem, Abie. That's why the other twelve have not been called and the *Meschiach*, with the three, is delayed. Reb Sabbatai told her."

"When?"

"Just now. At the fights."

From behind a pillar somebody shouted, "The whole thing, it was a fix-up job! I heard it on my Panasonic. Denny Love took a dive, *und fartik*!"

Then somebody else said from another part of the chamber, "It wasn't a dive. Denny Love couldn't beat my cousin Esther."

Somebody else said, "Leave Esther out of this."

And another person said, "Shut up, all of you! They're talking about the spaceship! About the spaceship they're talking!" Then everybody was quiet for a few seconds and the same guy said, "Mavens!"

"*You're* the maven!"

"Shut up!"

"He thinks he knows it all!"

"Don't start!"

After a few more cracks, with more and more of a pause between them, like a faucet squeezing shut, they all shut up.

Abie laughed. "The *minyan* is here."

Jack told me, "They come here at night. They pray for the coming of the *Meschiach*. They pray for the sixteen. Ten men make up the *minyan*. These men are the thrusters for my spaceship. Their prayers are the fuel. They know why God Tetragrammaton made human beings. They know what they live for, and they do it, God bless them."

"We know what Abie tells us," one of them shouted. "If it's true, God only knows!"

Another said, "Probably it's all *bubbe meisehs* and every one of us is a lunatic!"

Another said, "Shut up and let the boy get a word in edgewise!"

Abie laughed.

Jack went on, "Abie here, I know him from way back. I met him when I was twelve. I used to come down here to be alone. Everybody had me thinking I was going crazy, with the dreams and the visions and the raptures, but Abie listened. Abie believed. I wrote down for him the parts of the *Zohar Hagoyim* that I remembered from my studies with Uncle Sabbatai."

"That was the proof," is what Abie said to me, "just like your proof was the word *vohu*. A word like this, no *shiksie* could ever know from it."

The voices were coming nearer, but I still didn't see anybody down there:

"She's a *shiksie* what the Thrice Chosen brought into our *shul*?"

"If even a *Kohayn* can't be with even a convert for a girlfriend, can a Thrice Chosen take up with a *shiksie*? Shame on him!"

"Shame! Shame!"

"Look at her, she's got a bone structure like the Bull! Such a face!"

"Take her away from us, the *shiksie*!"

"Let him get a word in, I'm telling you!"

"A *shiksie*! A *shiksie*!"

I shouted, "*Vohu!*" as loud as I could, and it completely shut them up.

Abie laughed. My eyes got used to the dark again, and I saw the *minyan* poke their heads out of the shadows like so many dogs that had pissed in the wrong place, and now the master is home. They weren't used to a person shouting at them, I guess.

They had yarmulkes on and silky shawls, blue and white, with fringe at the ends, hanging down around their necks all the way to their knees. I counted eight *minyan* guys, which made nine with Abie, which they said the Bull had gone off somewhere, so it was ten altogether, just like Jack said.

Some were old, like Abie, and one was even older with maybe three teeth in his mouth and maybe four, but a few *minyan* guys were in their maybe twenties or thirties and could have looked pretty sharp in the right clothes and all. One of them I even recognized from the Wee Spot, which he'd been there with his wife one night for flan and café au lait, and Arthur had made a big tip off him, which he bragged about, and so I'd found out that he owned a chain of dry goods stores name of Noah's Ark, and this guy's name was actually Noah Solomon, if it was the same guy.

Jack kissed me on top of my head. "Are you okay, Lea?"

I said, "I feel like shit. I don't know anything. I told you something about Julian that I never told anybody, not even any cops or social workers or even me, actually, maybe. But listen..." I cuddled against him. I buried my face in his chest, and who gives a good goddam what the *minyan* makes of it, is what I was thinking. "I've never been happier anytime in my life, and I don't want you to do anything different from whatever you want to do, Jack."

And he kissed me some more.

He said, "*Liebe brider*, my beloved brothers, listen to me. The law for the Chosen of the Chosen of the Chosen is not the same as the law for the Children of Israel or the same as even the law for their priests. Sabbatai Levi Hagodol, the righteous one, precious in the eyes of God Tetragrammaton, appeared to this girl and gave her a message for us. Because of this message, the day of our salvation has been speeded along. We have to knock through the west wall of the spaceship, right through into Sears Roebuck, even into Catalog Orders and Returns and Repairs, in the known section of Sears Roebuck. I never understood this before. Then the sixteen will gather, and the Garden Of Eden will open up to us, as God wills."

Abie said, "This is why we live."

And the other nine, all of them together, said, "This is why we live."

I said, "But, Jack, do they get to go?"

And Jack said, "No."

I looked at Abie, and Abie nodded. They all of them nodded. I never saw so many people nod together, like cows that face you when you walk to their gate and they chew and they nod. And the *minyan* looked sad, but their eyes were bright and their shawls were beautiful. Whatever light there was, their eyes caught it and the prayer shawls caught it and they looked sad and they nodded. I looked at them. You had to. They were the thrusters.

One of them said, a younger guy who was probably, from his haircut and his diction, an insurance salesman or an abstract-and-title person or a loan officer at some bank, he said, "The *minyan* will come. The *minyan* will axe and shovel and claw or do whatever you want, Yakov.

If you need dynamite or drills or whatever, you know who to ask." They nodded and nodded.

Suddenly I heard that dog again, I heard it growl and bark and make a noise like it was shaking something in its teeth, and I realized that I'd forgotten all about Tule, and Jack was supposed to be watching for her, but he wasn't watching. He was thinking about the thirteen and the three and the ten and I don't know what all, because when I said, "Tule!" he said,

"Shit!"

Jack said to the *minyan*, "Have you seen a cat?"

They said to one another:

"Who's seen a cat?"

"Someone's seen a cat?"

"A what?"

"A cat!"

"So now we're looking for cats? I haven't got enough on my mind that I should be looking in the freezing cold for a cat by the river?"

"So do you want the *Meschiach* or not?"

"I suppose it depends on a cat?"

"He's talking cats! The Thrice Chosen One would maybe like to get a word in edgewise! Did you ever think of that, maven?"

"Who's a maven?"

"A cat...?"

Abie said to Jack, "Go where you're going. Down here, in the dark, you'll never find a cat. We'll be here awhile longer; if we see it, we'll keep it safe for you, this cat. If not, believe me, you wouldn't find it either." He was going to say some more, but he stopped in the middle of a breath. He came close, he looked me up and down, then he held my arm.

Abie said, "She's got a talent!"

And Jack said, "Yes."

And Abie said, "*Baruch habaa!* Blessed is the coming! She will keep the Evil One at bay up until the time."

And Jack said, "Or teach me how! This is our hope." And he turned to me, and he said, "Lea, let's go. He's right. If they can't find Tule, we won't."

I felt a hot iron ball in the back of my throat, and I couldn't get one thought to follow another one, but they all came crowding in like cattle through a gate and I said, "But nobody can understand her. I'm the only one. A dog'll eat her. She'll freeze to death. That's what she was talking about—*death, death, death.* You wanted me to drop her down the elevator shaft! She's my cat, Jack. If I let her die, what the hell good am I, will you tell me that?"

Abie said, "The *minyan* will find your cat, honey, if your cat can be found. Any friend of Reb Sabbatai's is a friend of ours. Go."

Jack said, "Come on, Lea," and I didn't want to, but I was so mixed up, I went. He took me back upstairs the way we'd come down, and he called back to Abie, he said, "I'll be in touch. It's coming soon. Don't plant any trees."

Down below, I heard one of them say, "Now he's talking about trees," and we were out on the embankment again, a stone lip above the river. There was a rapids below and it was white in the security lights and even though it was night and it was winter, pigeons were circling through the light over the water, and it was so beautiful it made you want to jump.

We saw agents of the Evil One all along the river. They scurried through the dust and stink on four legs under greasy backs with tails like ugly pointy fingers. Their red eyes were everywhere, under heaps of rusting machinery and junked car upholstery and looking up from holes underfoot in packs of twenty or thirty. Some of them had two legs and a face like yours and mine, only if you looked at them too long, they would fold you away inside them and you would feel lost for a long time till they let your soul out again.

Those you could mistake for regular bums, and they *were* regular bums, and each one of them had a story, but the Evil One was in them, and maybe Jesus Christ could laser out the bad part and leave the rest alone, but not me.

Jack said, "Don't kill them. These ones are very stupid, but if we hurt them, someone smarter might get curious, and then we'd have our hands full, and it's not a good night for it . . . Are you okay, Lea?"

"Perfect." I was starting to wish my face was still dead. I was starting to wish the winter had never broken like it had for those couple days. It always snaps back, you know, and the cold is so vicious cold that you think the cold before was like a Jacuzzi. It clamps its teeth around you and shakes you and it doesn't let go till all your fingers and toes are numb, then your arms and legs and then your heart. When you don't move anymore or think anymore or feel anymore, it lets you go.

That's the way I saw it.

* * *

I snuck Jack into Bobson's place for the shower. We didn't see any of Sarge's hoods the whole way. We completely outfoxed them by traveling underground, and if Sarge ever looked at my papers to see where I lived, he would find out that I had put down the address of the goddam mayor's house on Prince Street on account of what business was it of Sarge's—I'd only wanted to wash dishes and empty the garbage.

We had underground all over us. We had to carry our shoes because they were stinking dirty and had gotten stinkier and dirtier from stepping through the mess of a dead dog that was lying on the sidewalk outside Bobson's, looking like its stomach had exploded.

Bobson was asleep in her room behind the glass door. She was snoring in her old lady rocker with the stretched fuzzy gold fabric and the rows and rows of upholstery tacks on it. Her lap was full of mementos. I saw a framed photograph of, must have been Lillian, and one of those World War II postcards with cartoons on them of guys peeling potatoes and bitching about the sergeant. There was other stuff. Her lap was full of them. There was a record going on the record player. The needle was riding up and down like a surfer and you could hear Bing Crosby hiccuping through the glass door. He said:

"My heart...
My heart...
My heart...
My heart..."

We tiptoed past. I gotta say, she looked sweet. She was wearing a strictly old lady black lace dress from some previous century and high-heeled shoes that laced up the back. Her hair was silvery in the lamplight. It was done up in a bun like she did sometimes, and it looked sweet in a prudish kind of a way, which almost changed my mind about her, but she was snoring like a goddam trucker. Also, her half glasses had slid down her nose practically to her lip, as if she were trying to see out her nostrils.

Me and Jack chugged some milk straight out of my gallon bottle from the fridge, then we went upstairs and I got to take a shower first, but I made Jack stay in the bathroom, where he sat on the toilet with the shag seat cover down because I was a little nervous about Mrs. Bobson finding him. The bathroom door had a lock on it; through a door, I could BS that cow any which way I felt like.

I was in the hot shower and I said, "Jack, where do you wash yourself? The utility sink in the spaceship isn't much good."

"I sleep different places. I eat and wash different places. I have a few disciples, like the *minyan*. They like to take care of me. It's a *mitzvah*, a meritorious act, to take care of the Thrice Chosen."

"Are any of your disciples girls?"

"We don't do anything funny together, Lea. Did Sylvia tell you something about me?"

"What the hell could that dyke tell me?"

"Don't call her that. God Tetragrammaton has a purpose for all kinds of people."

"If you're going to get moral on me, hand me in the soap. I forgot it on the sink. You can close your eyes or you can keep them open, I don't care."

He kept his closed but I kept mine open. I read about

a guy who turned into a stag because he peeped at Diana, the virgin goddess, in the woods somewhere in Greece. Jack would never do that. You could trust him, is what I was thinking. I made him stand there a minute with his arm in the spray while I looked at him, and he said, "Here…here…here, Lea…here…!" and I loved him.

I took the soap and he said, "So what did Sylvia tell you about me?"

I said, "Nothing, because she got sick to her stomach all of a sudden."

"I bet you wonder how I could deal hashish and be a *tsadik*."

"A what?"

"A holy person."

"Well, how could you?"

The hot water felt good. All the underground was washing off me and going back underground through the drain. I washed my hair, and there was really starting to be some to wash. I didn't really care how Jack could be anything and anything else. Whatever he was was okay in my book. I didn't have a problem with it, but he seemed to feel like talking. That's guys. I liked to hear him talk though.

The water on my head and down my back and in my face, and Jack's voice—it was all good. Every time I touched myself I pretended like it was Jack's hand touching me, which I liked it and there's nothing wrong with it. I was starting to see that I'd been dead all over, just like in my face, and I was coming back, because of Jack.

He said, "I don't know. I just know what I am. It's not a moral thing, what you are. You don't try to be it. I find myself in an alley handing someone a chunk of hashish with a Moroccan guild stamp on it, and some-body I never saw before is counting five hundred dollars into my palm. Then I'm talking to Reb Sabbatai, or God Tetragrammaton whispers in my ear, 'Use German gold leaf—the best kind. Don't scrimp, and here's where you can get it...' Or I'm eating *traif* at Burger King."

"*Traif?*"

"Unkosher food. No matter what I do, I'm still one of God Tetragrammaton's Thrice Chosen. Do you under-stand?"

"No."

"Me neither. It's just so."

I scrubbed and I scrubbed. Bobson kept a loofah in the soap dish. You'd think she'd be scared all her skin would come off and wash down the drain and she'd just be bones. I rinsed that loofah good before I touched my-self with it. I was completely clean except for two things, and the loofah couldn't reach them, because they were thoughts in my head.

I said, "Jack..."

"Yeah?"

"Tule's gone."

"If the *minyan* doesn't find her, you'll see her in the Promised Land."

I thought about that a minute. So I was definitely go-ing. I wasn't a *goyim*. Jack and me were as good as engaged to be married, is how I figured it. And so it gave me a little room in my mind to see what was obvious. And I knew that Tule had to be dead.

Tule, Tule, who's gonna tell me to be pretty and not to kill anymore, and who's gonna cold shoulder me when I go wrong?

And Tule said, *Yakov.*

But she wasn't there. But she said it. You know what I mean.

And then I said the second thing the loofah couldn't reach. I said through the curtain, "Jack, I killed my brother Julian."

And Jack said, "It was an accident. Lea, honey, you were just a kid! How could you have known what you were?

"In the mountains, if a bear touches a man—that's what it is for a bear: just a touch, like hello, shake hands—the man dies. A bear's touch is too much for him, claws and thunder.

"Maybe the bear is surprised. Do you think so? The bear watches the man fall down. He tilts his furry, ferocious bear's head. He makes a little confused sound. He kicks the man's body a little bit to wake him, maybe, and it breaks him and mangles him. Then the bear runs away into the caves and hollows.

"It was an accident."

And I said, "Okay."

I rubbed my face with my hands. I felt all kinds of muscles I'd forgotten about that Jack had told me the names of. I felt my *frontalis*, the muscle of attention, and my *zygomaticus major*, the muscle of joy, and other ones that used to do things before Julian fell out of the swing. And they were starting to do things again.

I turned off the water.

Jack said, "I'll go out for a minute and let you dry. I'll be okay. I can still hear your landlady snoring. I'll take my shower, then maybe we'll see about the spaceship, if they've staked it out or what."

"Jack, what if they got in and wrecked stuff?"

"We'll see."

I heard the door open and close. I pulled back the shower curtains and dried myself with Bobson's best white towels which she always said I could and it would make her happy but which I never did, if you want to know the truth, because I killed my brother Julian. But now I did. I wrapped one around my head, which was going to be full of beautiful hair pretty soon. I unfolded Mrs. Bobson's fresh pink bathrobe from a shelf in the bathroom closet, and I wrapped it all around me. When I pulled the knot tight on the terry-cloth sash, I practically squeaked.

I opened the bathroom door, but I didn't see Jack. He wasn't in the hallway. He wasn't in my room either. I stood still and listened hard. Mrs. Bobson wasn't snoring anymore. "Jack...?" I tiptoed downstairs, but I stopped cold before the last step. Jack was flat out on the kitchen floor, facedown, with his head in a pool of blood.

chapter nine

Mrs. Bobson's Hospitality

I ran into the kitchen and there was Mrs. Bobson standing in the corner by the refrigerator looking very confused. I just dropped to my knees beside Jack. "Jack! Jack! Are you okay? Please be okay."

Mrs. Bobson said, "Oh thank God you're here, dear. Your young man must have slipped and fallen in the dark. He hit his head, didn't he? I was just going for some ice— you look very nice in my bathrobe, by the way. I'm so glad you're using it."

Jack lifted his head and groaned. His forehead was bruised and bloody. He winced when I leaned over and kissed it. He said, "Why did you do that to me?"

I said, "Do what?"

And he said, "You know! I felt you do it. I felt you squeeze my mind, Lea ..." He saw me look up, and he looked where I was looking, and he saw Mrs. Bobson, and he shut up.

Mrs. Bobson turned her back to us. She opened the refrigerator and took an ice tray from the freezer compartment. She knocked out some ice cubes over the sink and wrapped them in a dish towel and handed them down to Jack.

Jack didn't even know to take them. He was staring at something else. He was staring at Bobson's eyes, and he said, "It was you."

"It's for the swelling, dear. Take it."

"You knocked me down."

"Land sakes, don't be silly. An old hag like me? Take this. You'll feel better. Go ahead."

"I can't believe it—you have a talent."

I saw Mrs. Bobson's face harden. She looked at me, and she was angry and embarrassed. "Well, what was I supposed to do?" She darted glances this way and that, at the lace curtains over the sink, at the marquetry "GOD BLESS OUR HOME" by the cup hooks, and at the open glass door by her memory room, as if they were accusing her of things that she had to answer them as much as me. "I thought he was using you, Lea dear. I didn't know you were here. I thought he had sneaked on back to steal things or to snoop."

I said, "Mrs. Bobson! You . . . you're like me."

And she said, "Does he know what you are, Lea?"

Jack pushed Mrs. Bobson's ice pack away. He grabbed a leg of the table, then the edge of the tabletop, and he pulled himself up and I helped him till he was standing pretty well. He said to Mrs. Bobson, "What is Lea, Mrs. Bobson? What are you?"

Mrs. Bobson's face tightened up some more, like the face of a scrub rag when you clutch it harder. Or you could say she was starting to look like one of the rats from under the city. Her eyes were slitted and her mouth squeezed tight, with wrinkles like rays coming off it in every direction, or like, say, the bottom of a rotting apple, when the meat is all shriveled inside and the skin bunches together. She shot a look at me. It felt like she read me in a second, and she knew that I didn't keep any secrets from Jack. Then she said, "We're Daughters of Satan."

I had to laugh.

"Why do you think I took you in? You looked like a hard little bitch who'd cut my old lady throat, and that's what Mrs. Cavanaugh said, and so did Mr. Hearst at Number 341. My dearest friend Amanda Ryan at 337, she said, 'Mrs. Bobson,' she said, 'Mrs. Bobson, land sakes, that new girl of yours will steal your money and kill you in your sleep. Give her notice tomorrow.' But I didn't. I kept you. And I'll keep on keeping you, too, because we are the Devil's daughters, both of us, you and I."

Jack told her, "No, what you do is not from the Devil…"

Mrs. Bobson flashed him a phony smile like he was a little kid that didn't know what he was talking about. I could tell by his face that Jack thought the exact same thing about *her.*

"My marquetry circle knew you were a catch, Lea. I know it, and now you know it, and he knows it, and all those others in the cellar know it too. Yes, they do! They know it now!"

And Jack said, "The cellar?"

Mrs. Bobson kept looking at me and talking to me—I

was the one who was her Devil's daughter sister. She said, "They came here wanting to hurt you, Lea honey. So I hurt them first. Three big, fat ugly men! I've never seen such rude men!"

I said, "Was one of them the nose ring guy?"

"No. That one hasn't been back. These were new ones. I thought they were a motorcycle gang, but I wasn't afraid. I'm never afraid. The Devil protects his daughters, and He gives them special powers.

"Those gentlemen said they were looking for you, Lea dear. I invited them in. I waited till they had all stepped across the threshold. Then I did it. The door was still open, but no one was around to see. Only a dog. I think that dog must have gotten hurt when I hurt them, because it made an awful noise. I'm not as accurate as I used to be.

"I think it might have been Mr. Loomis's dog from Radio Street. Roscoe runs off sometimes. Mr. Loomis will be upset, but Roscoe was an old dog. He didn't have much time left anyway. For that matter, neither does Mr. Loomis. Still, I'm glad Mr. Loomis wasn't out there with Roscoe. Mr. Loomis was a friend of my husband's."

Jack was standing like me, like an idiot, staring at her with his mouth open. A little blood dribbled down his face. "Are they dead, Mrs. Bobson?"

"No. They doubled over, the way they always do, and I closed the door and I made them go into the cellar just the way an elephant trainer makes elephants go where he wants them to go. I saw a special on it. If they don't do exactly what you want, you hurt them a little until they do. They always end up doing what you want, you know, because you're the elephant trainer, and they are just elephants.

"They were very noisy and self-pitying, I thought, for such big, tough men. But I opened the door to the cellar, and they went down the steps. They sat where I told them to sit—eventually. Then I tied them up. I stuffed some old nylons in their mouths and I tied an extra nylon around each of their faces so that the stuffing in their mouths wouldn't come out. I thought it would get on my nerves if they shouted. I was tired by then, and I just wanted to sit in my glass-door room and look at some of my old things and listen to my Bing Crosby. Land sakes, I get to do that, don't I, for all I've contributed to society in my time?"

I didn't feel like laughing anymore. Me and Jack looked at each other. I said, "Maybe Sylvia followed me one night, and she knew where I live, and she told Sarge, because I sure never told Sarge."

Jack nodded. I cleaned some of the blood off his face with the side of my hand. I was about to wipe my hand on the bathrobe, but I stopped myself.

Mrs. Bobson said, "Go ahead! Land sakes, I know how to soak blood out of things!"

Jack said, "Mrs. Bobson, can we see them?"

"Why?"

"Mrs. Bobson, there are some bad people who are angry at Lea and at me because we didn't do something exactly the way they wanted us to. I think those men are probably with them, and if they are, then we have to figure out what to do about it."

"Does this have to do with drugs, young man?"

"No. Not directly."

She raised her eyebrows. "Lea picked an honest one. You're an honest one, aren't you?"

"Yes, ma'am, I am."

"You know I am a daughter of the Dark One. You know what I could do to you if you tried to hurt me or Lea in any way."

"Yes, ma'am."

She softened up then. Her face unbunched and she breathed, which looked like she hadn't been for a while. "I'm sorry I hurt you, young man."

"Jack."

"I'm sorry I hurt you, Jack."

"I'm okay. Can we see them?"

"I suppose so . . . I would like you to call me Belle."

"Belle."

"You too, dear." She held out her hand for me to take. She did it so elegantly you would have thought you were at a Southern debutante ball, the way she held out that hand, and I took it, and she gave mine a little squeeze.

And I said, "Belle."

And she took us into the cellar. I have to tell you the truth: I was getting extremely tired of being underground. There is lots of radon down there that probably screws up your genes so that Jack and my kids might end up with two heads, for one thing.

Belle had a statue of the Devil down there next to the furnace, which you saw it when she pulled the string for the lightbulb. It was about four feet high. It looked like a lawn ornament, except that it was the Devil. You had your horns and your forked tail and your evil grin. You had your pitchfork and your fiery red eyes and your waxed mustaches. Probably the whole thing was out of an occult mail-order house like the ones in the ads in the back of some kinds of comic books. I bet it really threw a scare into those three elephants of hers.

Belle's old lady legs were doing pretty well tonight. She led us past the furnace to an old coal bin kind of room with a peeling whitewashed wooden door, and when she opened that door on its creaky hinges—there they were. I knew one of them right off: it was Benito, Mr. Toupee from the fights, only the toupee was lopsided and his mouth was full of Belle's stocking. The other two, one looked like a football player, young guy, with shoulders like the grille on a Mack truck, face the same, and the other guy, he had on an expensive overcoat with a black fur collar, but some of the buttons were busted and his belly poked out, big and round, through the slit in his stiff white dress shirt that was underneath. The three of them looked drugged. They barely looked at us.

Belle said, "These are the bentwood chairs I was talking about, dear. You can have one for your room when the gentlemen are done with them."

Jack stood very still, looking from one to the other. "That's Mr. Morano," he said, and he pointed to the guy in the fur collar.

Belle said, "From Morano's Restaurant?"

"That's the one."

"Wonderful seafood plate."

"He has a piece of every drug deal on the East Side— like a tax collector. I didn't know he was tied up with the scrappers as well." Then Jack nodded in the direction of Big Shoulders. "Here's his enforcement division. The other one is a concerned citizen, probably along for the ride . . . This is very bad, Lea. I've got the Powers and Principalities in my back pocket, but the downtown mob has got our number." He shook his head and laughed a sorry little laugh.

I said, "Maybe we could get the *minyan* to help us and we could knock through the wall and call together the thirteen and pull in the three and take off in the *Meschiach* tonight, before those hoods could say boo."

"Yeah, if they're not already there."

Jack thought a minute, then he said, "Of course, we've got some leverage now, and all we need is a little time." He turned to Belle. "Can you keep them here, Belle, just like this for, I don't know, maybe a few hours and maybe a few days? It depends. These men have friends who want to hurt Lea. If we have these men here, their friends won't be in such a hurry to hurt her. We can talk. We can make a deal."

Belle said, "You got her into this trouble, didn't you, Jack?"

"Yes, ma'am, I did."

She tightened her lips and cocked her head and looked cross for a second, but then she breathed out and dropped her shoulders and she said, "Go do what you have to do. These gentlemen will be safe and sound with me. And if any more of them come, why, I'm just a dotty old lady who doesn't know what they're talking about, and if they aren't satisfied with that, why, they will be safe and sound with me too. But I only have so many of these bentwood chairs, and the rest will have to sit down on the cold floor."

I hugged Belle. Yes, I did. I took her scrawny old lady body in my arms and I hugged her hard and I pressed my face against her shoulder and then I kissed her on the cheek. I couldn't believe it myself. It came right out of me just like that, as if it were something I did all the time. Maybe it was, once upon a time, before Julian fell out of the swing. But after I killed my brother, all that hugging stuff went the way of my *buccinator,* right up till now. I never even let James touch me after that.

Belle smiled so hard I thought her face would bust and the dimples and twinkles would go spinning off it like sparks off a match head. She said, "You are my Devil sister."

"Oh, Belle, it doesn't have anything to do with the Devil."

"It most certainly does, but never mind that now. Can you take care of yourself and Jack all right? I'm worried about you. Show me some of what you can do, Lea."

"Who to?"

"Why, me."

"You're kidding—I don't want to hurt you, Belle."

"You couldn't possibly hurt me, dear. Just go ahead and twist me around inside or whatever you do. Or try to kill me if you can't do anything subtle. I just need a taste of you, dear, and I'll know it all. I'm a very old hand."

I hunkered down inside my mind. It was a funny thing to do while Jack stood next to me with his hands in his pockets, and those three bozos sat lolling in their bentwood chairs, and me in Belle's bathrobe with Jack's bloodstain, and my wannabe hair all tied up in a towel. I concentrated and I did what I did at the Wee Spot the night of me and Jack's first date, when I kind of put everybody off their key lime pie.

Belle just smiled. "Go ahead, dear."

I squeezed again. It should have toppled a lumberjack.

Belle said, "Land sakes, I'm not made of isinglass. Go ahead, Lea."

Jack watched the air between us. Belle caught him at it, and she said, "That fellow knows what's going on!"

I said, "He's one of the sixteen, Belle," and I slammed her as hard as I could, and she blinked.

She said, "Hmm! Not much there, but I expect no regular mortals will get past a Devil's daughter without a good plan, and these men don't look smart enough. Are their friends any smarter?"

Jack said, "No."

"Go ahead, then. Go! When you come back, we can have some nice tea, and I'll teach you how to do some damage. May Satan annihilate your enemies! Be careful, dears...!" She stopped and covered her mouth with her hand. "Oh dear! Did I leave my phonograph on? Would you stop and see on your way out? It'll take me a while longer to get these old bones upstairs, you know, and I hate to think of Bing going on and on in my glass-door room with no one even listening."

It was only a few blocks to Sears Roebuck's. I threw something on, a faded blue jumpsuit that Lillian never should have bought, because it wasn't on her chart. I knew it wasn't, because it wasn't on *my* chart, and everything else of Lillian's was on my chart. Her chart was the same as my chart.

Maybe she had been having a bad day. Maybe it even had something to do with the accident that killed her, is what I was thinking. Maybe she was wearing this when she got hit and died. There weren't any bloodstains as far as I could see, but Belle had said she knew how to get rid of them.

I put a couple of sweaters over it, and I wore earmuffs under my beret. I stuck on some sneakers. I thought at first they were a little too big for me, but then I realized they were just the right size and that all Lillian's other stuff was too small on her and too small on me, and she must have worn these sneakers when she wanted to relax. They were relaxing. I relaxed in them, just like she must have relaxed, for all that it could be the last day of my goddam life on Earth, one way or another.

Jack didn't want to take the time to shower. He stayed inside his filthy threads with all the underground sticking to them. He just wanted to wash his face. I had to show him the posters on my wall, which he had thrown away because of the drips on them, and he smiled and I was happy. Then he looked at my bed where I slept and he looked at me and he kind of swallowed and he said, "Let's go."

We ran. It's warm that way, even in the cold. We only slowed down when we got near the parking lot. We walked in the shadows along the edge. We reconnoitered. We stopped by a tall hedge next to a chain-link fence at one end of the lot. We stood very still and watched.

You could see our fire escape from there. It looked deserted. It looked okay. Then somebody coughed, and this pile of dirty, rain-pocked snow turned into a kid smoking a cigarette, crouching beside the Dumpster near the fire escape. He was rubbing his hands together and cussing. Nobody had to tell anybody what this kid was doing there.

Jack sighed.

I said, "I could take care of him, Jack."

He said, "This whole business is just a distraction, you know that, Lea? This is of no importance whatsoever. I don't want to fight with them. I don't want to be involved with them. I want to be united with my brethren and do what God Tetragrammaton has given me to do."

He looked down at his shoes, and he half whispered, "I'm already a criminal to use you up on a dime store barnie. I thought it was the easiest way to satisfy Sarge's thugs, but I was all wrong. I'm so sorry!

"These people are not the Devil's any more than your landlady. If they were the Devil's, I would ask you to kill them right now. But they are big, stupid babies with their guns and their rolls of money. They have no idea of the real meaning of what they are doing or of what God Tetragrammaton's world is really about. If I asked you to kill them, it would be like Moses hitting the rock."

"The rock?"

"On the desert, my people were thirsty, and God said, touch the rock and water will spring forth. But Moses was frustrated, like I'm frustrated, Lea, that a little thing like thirst should threaten their making it to the Promised Land. So, instead of just touching it, he struck the rock. Because of this he was not permitted to enter the Promised Land himself. He only got to see it from the top of Mount Nebo, out near Jericho, the city of palm trees.

"Last night, Reb Sabbatai showed me everything in a dream, to warn me. I saw them bury Moses in Moab, among the palm trees. Palm trees are not the Promised Land. We have to touch, not strike."

Somebody was creeping toward us along the hedge. "Fine talk from a dope pusher." It was Sylvia.

I said, "Why aren't you holed up with Sarge, you bitch?"

She said, "I came here to save your ass, honey. Any girl who gets mixed up with Jack needs all the help she can

get." She must have caught the look I was giving her—
ever since I met that Yid, my poker game was shot to hell.
"Go ahead! Give me a stomachache, Lea! Knock my knees
out from under me, why don't·you? There are a dozen
guys up there in your savior's spaceship, just aching to
knock your teeth down your throat, and there are dozens
more where they came from, and, honey, they are profes-
sionals. That's what comes of being Jack's friend!"

Jack said, "As opposed to being Sarge's friend?"

I said, "What do you want, Sylvia?"

She said, "I want you to be alive, that's all. Get out of
here. You have any relatives in another state? Go visit for a
while. I'll lend you money, if you need it. I'll drive you
downstate where they won't be watching the bus stations.
We'll keep in touch. They won't stay this mad forever.
When things cool down, if you want to come back, I'll
fix it."

"What about Jack?"

"What about Jack? Jack is crazy. Jack is a dopehead.
Jack uses people. Can't you see that yet, for crissakes?"

I said, "Who loves me, Sylvia?"

Sylvia stood right in front of me. She was still fuming,
but her lip trembled, and her eyebrows twitched like she
was practically going to cry, and she said, "I do."

I said, "No, you don't. It's Jack."

Sylvia stepped backward, as if she'd just taken a right
to the jaw. Then she made all her soft weakness into a kind
of strength like desperate people do and she took hold of
my elbows with her hands. I held her elbows the same
way, only to keep her in control, and we pushed each
other back into the bushes away from Jack because of the
force of it, and she whispered hard, like steam hissing

from that underground pipe and she said, "He comes to the Spot and he *schmoozes* with his doper friends. He sells and he buys. I know dozens of guys like that. He makes himself up, Lea. He's like an actor. I know these guys. He even fools himself, like a kid with a clubhouse and a Superman cape. He thinks he's a space captain or a Messiah or God knows what.

"Then he runs into you. You're not like him. You're real. You've got something real. I don't understand it, you don't understand it, Sarge and his pals sure don't understand it, but you have a power. I saw some of the things he had you do in there, measuring you as if you were a freak. He's just like them, don't you see? Jack wants something out of you just the way Sarge does."

"Go to hell, Sylvia. You told them where I live."

"I wouldn't let them hurt you. I'd let them kill me first. Don't you see, it's better for them to get you than for him to have you? They're stupid. They only want you to make them some cash. The Yid wants . . . everything."

"What do you want, Sylvia?"

"I care for you, Lea."

"What do you want?"

Sylvia's hands loosened up on my elbows. She looked a little shy and she blinked and she whispered and she said, "You can kill little things as well as big things, can't you?"

"So?"

"Real little things, like an amoeba or a virus even."

"So?"

"I heard Jack tell you that he thought maybe you could cure a disease."

"The point, Sylvia?"

"Lea . . . I'm sick."

She let go of my arms completely, and her arms fell down at her sides like deadweights and she looked limp and sunken all over. I saw right through her makeup and her getup then, through all the getups, for the first time. She was tired. I felt bad that I ever knocked her down or gave her a stomachache.

She loved me, too.

All of a sudden I realized that Jack was gone. I nudged Sylvia out of my way and I saw him halfway across the parking lot, walking toward the spaceship, straight toward the kid with the cigarette. I started to run up to him.

Sylvia said, "Lea, stay here with me."

Jack heard her and he stopped and he turned around. He held up both his hands toward me, like a ref giving a fighter a standing count—"Ten!" I stopped in my tracks. He looked like Moses then, in the weird, mercury vapor parking lot lights, in his dry-cleaned trench coat which was all muddy now and hanging down like robes. He looked so strong and dignified and I loved him and Sylvia didn't know what she was talking about and if he said stay I would stay and if he said go I would go but please, God Tetragrammawho, don't let those bruisers hurt my Jack— I have enough of my family dead.

chapter ten

The <u>Minyan</u> Reconnoiters

I remembered the Noah's Ark guy—Arthur had bragged about the big tip he'd left him—and he was in the book, so I called him. Mrs. Solomon was a bitch—why shouldn't she be at one-thirty in the morning?—but she woke up her husband like I asked her to and she handed him the telephone, and I heard her saying, "Is she what you really do when you're going to goddam *minyan*, Noah? Because if she is, Noah, as God is my witness, I'll grind your *kishkes*! You'll have to make your own breakfast and do your *own* books, *und fartik!*"

I said, "They hit him, Mr. Solomon. They hit him and he wouldn't let me do anything about it. Even the kid hit him, the stupid lookout, and two big guys grabbed his arms and I started to do something but Jack, he shouted to me, no, don't do anything, I'll be all right. And they looked at me, out by the fence, which they couldn't see me, but they looked, and Sylvia said, go, and I knew Jack wanted me to go. All I wanted to do was stay and help, or die with Jack if he was going to, but they both said go. So I went."

"Whoa! Who is this?"

"I'm the girl from under the city with Jack."

"The *shiksie*."

"Yeah."

"They've got him where?"

"At the spaceship."

"Oy gevalt geshrigen gefilteh fish und lukshn!"

In the background I heard, "I'll grind your guts, Noah! You've got some girl in trouble, haven't you, you *chazir*, you *pig*?"

And Noah said, "Where are you? Give me a number I can call you back."

"I'm at the Wee Spot. It's just me and a waitress who let me in, who's helping me. We looked you up." I told him the number of the Wee Spot, and he hung up without saying good-bye.

I was standing in the phone booth, which was an old-fashioned one in the corner of the dining area for atmosphere. Sylvia was leaning in and when I hung up she said, "We can't stay here forever. They're going to come after you. If they find me helping you, they'll—" She cut off all of a sudden and she bit her lip and her chin trembled and then she said, "They won't like it."

I didn't say anything. I didn't do anything. I just gritted my teeth and waited for the phone to ring. A person can do that. A person can just wait, period, like a pillar under downtown: reinforced concrete. And Sylvia had to just stand still and watch me, period.

The phone rang, and I grabbed it off the cradle. "Yeah?"

"It's Abie, sweetheart, from underground. Tell me what's what."

I told him everything about Sarge and the fights and about Jack and me and about the three men under Belle Bobson's. And he said, stay where you are. He said, they probably have Sears Roebuck in their pocket or why wouldn't the Security come with all this *meshuga'as*. They could even have the police precinct in their pocket, this kind of guys. The *minyan* has in it a city guy who could even take care of this and that, but it's very delicate because we don't want to jeopardize the spaceship.

Which I said, if it comes to that, screw the goddam spaceship—I want to get Jack out of there.

And he said, don't go anywhere, don't do anything, we'll be there in half a minute. And he said, and we found your cat...

I breathed. I closed my eyes. I knew. I wanted to cry, but I didn't. It was almost a relief to hear it. I'd known my Tule was dead. I'd already made my peace with it in the shower. Maybe it comes with having a talent, is how I figured it—knowing what's dead. I always know.

And Abie said, "You want we should bring it to you, to the Wee Spot?"

It.

"No."

"Listen to me, honey—the *minyan* is coming. Call your landlady and tell her to expect a certain young gentleman who will want to take a look at her houseguests and who will stay with her and keep her company awhile. His name is Yakov."

"Jack? Yakov is what you call my Jack, right?"

"The other Yakov, our tenth man, the youngest, what we call Yakov the Bull. But just tell Mrs. Bobson 'Yakov'—you shouldn't give her a fright."

And he hung up.

I called Belle. She was awake. "Land sakes, what a night for visitors!" She didn't have a problem with anything.

And I waited.

I said, "Sylvia, I can cure you, no sweat, no question about it, but I'm pretty upset right this minute, so I can't focus up and I'd most probably kill you trying. Sylvia, I forgive you for everything, because you're sick, but you're two hundred percent wrong about Jack, and you gotta help me do whatever I say, and whatever the *minyan* says, you gotta do that too. Whether you believe in Jack or you don't believe in Jack, you gotta help us save him and call in the rest of the thirteen and the three and launch the spaceship up with the *Meschiach*. If you really love me, you'll do it—and otherwise you're dead meat."

Sylvia just nodded. She didn't know I was lying about being able to cure her. I felt like maybe I could, because of the Indian Summer and how my dead face had come to life and because Jack said so, but I'd never tried it before, and I wouldn't bet anybody's milk money on it.

We waited. I made a pot of coffee in the machine; the waiters always made me do that when it was busy, even though it wasn't supposed to be a part of my job. That night for the first time I figured out why I let them. In the middle of all my troubles, with my Tule dead, and with Sylvia slowly dying in front of me, thinking I was going to save her, which I couldn't, and with Jack maybe getting his ass busted in the hidden section of Sears and Roebuck, and with my landlady doing a Federal offense on three hoods in her basement, and with a bunch of Yids out of the hobo jungle bivouacking at the Wee Spot, and with some nose ring guy name of Shane or Shamus or Chad casing me and leaving notes at my goddam door—in the middle of all that, it finally came to me why I let those waiters tell me to put down my bus tray and make coffee: I liked it.

I liked helping them. That's why I even worked there. It was like making breakfast with the ones you love.

All kinds of things like that were lighting up in me, like nerves tingling back after your foot's been asleep. For example, while I was sliding the plastic coffee filter tray into the machine, I figured out that I liked Belle Bobson. I'd always liked her. I never would have even moved in there if I hadn't liked her. Only I'd been scared that if I melted up over Belle Bobson and over being chummy with the waiters and like that, then it would melt me up over some other things that I didn't want to melt up over—this is how I figured it—things like how Julian fell out of the swing and how I always loved that little jerk and how it drove my daddy crazy and wrecked our family and it was all because of me and I couldn't stand it.

Well, now the cat was out of the bag, see, which I had twisted it in so tight. I still could hardly stand it. But the numbness was starting to wear off.

Sylvia said, "Don't cry. Everything will be okay, you'll see." But she sounded like a ghost, and she didn't look at me when she said it. I just kept making coffee and sniveling.

Sylvia was too nervous to do anything but pull a chair down off one of the tables and sit in it and chain-smoke her Kools. It was like the chairs were growing there upside down on the tables, filling up with Sylvia's smoke in the dusty, empty light.

Eight of the *minyan* dribbled into the Wee Spot, and Sylvia let them in. Yakov the Bull was at Mrs. Bobson's, and Manny Baranes would be with us in a jiffy, Abie told me. Manny used to be an excellent thief as a juvenile. His police record was sealed when he turned eighteen, in prehistoric times, and now he was a manager at a Radio Shack. Manny was sneaking into Sears and Roebuck through the known section, in order to bug the unknown section from under the floor. That way we could actually hear what was going on.

We took the chairs down off three tables and pushed them together in back for the *minyan* to sit down. Each one of the *minyan* had a blue cloth bag the size of two fists, with funny writing embroidered on it and with fringe, some of them, and a zipper, which they were lined up around the edge of the table in front of the *minyan* like place mats. Mr. Solomon also had a crate full of ram's horns packed in old copies of a Yiddish newspaper from Canada called *Der Zun*, which means *The Sun*.

They were drinking coffee as fast as I could make it except for one guy who kept sipping from a flask he kept in the vest pocket of his corduroy sports jacket. He had this sports jacket all right, but no tie, and a *schmatte* for a shirt. Every time he took a slug he hiked up his shoulders and closed his eyes like that was supposed to make him invisible or something. For all that he was on the right team, I felt sorry for the guy. He was Manny's brother, and his name was Isaac Baranes or "Ishky."

I filled everybody in on what I knew about the fight deal. If any of them was surprised about my talent, they didn't show it. Abie said, "Surprised? We should be surprised? You want maybe a couple panels in *Believe It or Not?* Honey, all of this was prophesied in *Zohar Hagoyim.*"

And Ishky piped up, " 'And in those evil times there will be born, from out of the *goyim*, protectors of the Chosen who will protect them with many protections that they will be called witches and evildoers by those who have not the eye.' " Then he closed his eyes and hiked up his shoulders and took another swig.

"I got the eye," little Abie said. He twinkled. His pompon shook on top of his head.

"And I got the ear." Manny Baranes came in, skinny hunchback guy, all in black with a black watchcap—no pompon—straight out of James Bond, but a geek. Who knows how he ever made front office at a Radio Shack. He held one hand straight up over his hunchback head like he was asking to go to the bathroom, except there was a radio in it, a gray dingus with dials and grilles and an antenna from here to Wisconsin.

He had on his face the silliest grin I have ever seen on a human being, though once, before that breakfast I told you about, James took me to the zoo on our bicycles—James used to take me everywhere in those days because he was my protector and he was the one who loved me no matter what—and there was a snow monkey there who was poking his gums with a stick, and that monkey had a smile like Manny's.

I said, "Mr. Baranes, could you hear them? Is Jack okay?"

Manny said, "He's okay—so far. They're being polite and they're talking business—so far."

Then he said, "I loved it! It was a piece of cake! I haven't used my burglar tools since before the Flood, and the old fingers, I'm telling you, are as smart as ever! But you know what I can't figure from it? I was looking for the best place to put my machine, maybe by a high shelf, maybe over a lintel, and what do you know, the best place, it's a perch, a merchandise shelf, a cubby, up high. And I can see that I am not the first one to use it.

"In this perch, what do I find? Candy wrappers, would you believe? And an old peanut butter jar with piss in it. Piss."

One of the old guys said, "For a chamber pot, take it from me, Skippy is the best. It's hard plastic, so if you drop it, you shouldn't break it, what you spill peepee all over the place."

Abie said, "Probably some store clerk, his wife threw him out, and he had to spend the night!"

And Manny said, "No! No! It was like me, an eavesdropper. I also found an empty tumbler, and on the ceiling just above this perch, round marks precisely one hundred percent the fit of the mouth of this glass. Am I a Sherlock Holmes or what? This bird in his perch was listening."

Ishky said, "*Bubbe meisehs.*" The other guys shrugged and laughed, and they pretty much dropped it, figuring Manny was showing off. But I remembered what Sylvia told me at the Wee Spot when I showed her the quiver and arrows, and I thought, *Sylvia's mice.*

Some guys had comments to make about the fight while Manny set up his receiver on the table, for which he made Sylvia find him a long extension cord. There was this one curly white-haired guy in a silk shirt with the top two buttons open to show the hair on his chest. It was all gray but there was plenty of it and it looked like the guy pumped iron, from the size of those pectorals, which were a little gross on that old a guy, is how I feel about it. Everybody called him "Shlomo."

And Shlomo stood up and he said, "Y'know Jim Corbett come out of retirement on August the thirtieth, nineteen hundred, in Madison Square Garden. That fellow looked to be one washed-up pugilist, gentlemen, but he decked Kid McCoy in the fifth round, just like Denny Love got decked by that Ruiz fellow tonight, but Denny Love could have done it to Ruiz just like Corbett did it to McCoy. It could have happened that way. It was going to happen that way, it looked like to me, before the downtown mob had our *shiksie* friend intervene."

And Ishky took a swig and he said, "The mob wanted Denny to win, you blockhead. Weren't you listening? It was a mix-up."

"I'm saying if they wanted him to win, they should have let the whole thing alone, blockhead."

"Yeah, well I'm saying the whole Corbett-McCoy thing was a *farkakte* barnie, and McCoy took a dive, and anybody who knows anything about the fight game will tell you the same, Shlomo, you blockhead."

"Aw, have another drink, why don't you?"

Abie said, "*Liebe brider*, this is a matter from life

and death what we got here. I beg you, you should not forget that."

Shlomo snorted and sat down. Ishky slipped his flask away and buttoned up his corduroy jacket. He clapped his hands together with a little too much force, the way drunk guys do things, because the juice has worn down their brake pads, so to speak. Then he sat there like a schoolboy, with his fingers laced together. It reminded me of how Jack laced his fingers together one night to show me how it would be if he ever ran into another one of the thirteen.

"Almost done!" Manny said. His radio was spitting static. It looked like the hardest thing about it was how he had to reach across the table with his hunchback arms to fix the antenna and the dials. He was leaning in through two of the younger guys, CPA types, the both of them. One of them held his arm around Manny's back so brotherly it almost made me cry, melty like I was, and the other one kept craning his head in and screwing up his eyes behind these glass-brick glasses and saying, "Can I help? Can I help?" Manny kept saying, "No, I got it practically. No sweat."

Turned out that one of those young guys, the "Can I help?" one, was the city guy Abie had mentioned, Leonard Fine. Leonard Fine said it was an even bet that Sarge's crowd owned the Sears and Roebuck building one way or another. They owned several lots in the vicinity, like the building the Wee Spot was in, as a matter of fact, which could make a person nervous. Leonard Fine was familiar with Sarge's friends because they practically ran the Department of Public Works and handed out jobs and contracts to all the garbage trucks in town. Every now and again Leonard Fine would get a memo from his boss to speed something through for them. That's what he told us.

The other young guy was a guy they called Rabbi Metzger. He was a real rabbi, but he didn't have any congregation he belonged to. He had big soulful eyes, almost as big as Sylvia's, which made you love to look at him, and he was growing a beard.

"It's Israel versus Italy," one of the *minyan* said, guy name of Simon Black. He was a tall, very old guy with a chalk white face and jowls like dripstone hanging off the bottoms of his eyes. His bones looked too big, and he had trouble doing things with them, like a giant in a dwarf's room.

Abie said, "No, Simon, don't talk that way. For all we know, Romulus and Remus were two from the thirteen, Sicily could be lousy with Thrice Chosens, and the entire State of Israel, God forbid, from Haifa to Elat could be teeming with agents of the Evil One. Am I right, Rabbi?"

And Rabbi Metzger said, "Of course you're right, Abie. It has nothing to do with whose son or whose daughter."

And Mr. Black scowled at the rabbi and said, "That's why you haven't got a *shul*!"

That's when Waxy put his two cents in. He was a fat guy in a thick, black overcoat and a fedora that he kept on indoors. He had lips like salamis, and he never stopped sneering, like maybe he had a sinus condition. And Waxy said, "Yakov the Bull was not even a Jew when God Tetragrammaton sent him to us to be our tenth man after Menachem died. Does anyone have greater faith than our little Yakov? Mr. Black is a racist. I am not a racist. I am a businessman..."

And Black said, "We all know what kind of a business you do!"

Waxy gave Mr. Black a look like he could have shot

him dead but he wasn't worth the bullet, and Waxy said, "As I was saying, I am a businessman, not a racist. I work with many kinds of individuals from all walks of life in a variety of activities..."

And Black said, "Prostitution, gambling, pick-pocketing—a real variety!"

"...And I know lots of individuals who are ac-quainted with Serge and who have dealings with Serge and with Serge's associates in one manner or another, and I can tell you from personal experience..."

"Hah! Such an experience he's got, Mr. Bigshot! He's got a police record from here to Poughkeepsie, and all wool!"

Waxy turned to Black and pounded the table and shouted "Will you shut up?" so loud it hurt everybody's ears and made them wince. Black looked scared at first, but then he just huffed and got up to go downstairs to the bathroom like he had to anyway.

Abie patted Mr. Black on the elbow as he passed him, and I heard him whisper, "Simon, you don't always have to say everything you know. There is such a thing as too honest, old friend." But Black shook his hand off and walked away.

And Waxy said, "Gentlemen, I apologize for the out-burst. I'm sorry it was necessary. It's past Mr. Black's bed-time, and he is a little out of sorts.

"But as I was saying, I can tell you that Serge's people are all of them amenable to reason. This is what I want to emphasize. They are, it is true, nearly all of them, Italian individuals—except for Serge himself, of course, who is a nothing, frankly. Mr. Panaggio, who I believe is the CEO of the local organization—mob, if you will—I actually know to be a churchgoing man and a Rotarian of a fairly high order.

"These are businesspersons like myself. They do not act hastily against their own interests. If we refrain from going forward on some irrational basis, like racism for example, if we make it clear that we want Jack back safely, and that we want the continued use of the floor space Jack has been using in their building, and that we are willing to offer value for value, why, I'm sure we can come to a mutually satisfactory accommodation."

And Manny looked up from his wiring, and said, "Have you got a gun, Waxy?"

And Waxy said, "Do I look like a complete idiot?"

And Manny said, "I thought so. Me too."

And I said, "The whole reason Jack wouldn't let me help him is on account of Moses, how he hit a rock that he was supposed to just touch it, and then he couldn't get into the Promised Land. You think you can goddam shoot somebody for him, and God Tetrachloride'll just ignore the whole thing?"

The rabbi said, "The *shiksie* is right."

And Waxy said, "That's what I'm saying! We have to be reasonable!"

I kept pretty calm considering Jack was maybe getting his teeth smashed or his legs broken, and here's how I did it, in case you're ever in a fix like that: I counted and I felt. Feeling was my new talent anyway, which could make dead things come alive, like Jesus Christ, so I felt everything I could. I felt my heart beating all through me. I felt my blood swell out and suck back, like after you run around the block, but subtle, subtle, subtle! I counted my heartbeat until something made me forget my number, then I counted all over again. Does a person only get so many heartbeats and that's it? I never really knew I had a heartbeat before that, except that people said so, and people say all kinds of things.

I felt the people around the table too, and Sylvia, how they were feeling, from their faces and from their shoulders and their fingers and everything that you could see of them. Did you know that you can't look at any part of a person without getting a certain feeling from it? I didn't know that before. And all the time Jack was in deep shit in the unknown section of Sears and Roebuck, but I felt like: these are *Jack's* feelings, this is *Jack's* heartbeat, one, two, three...

Sylvia paced like a maniac sometimes and other times she would sit as still as a mummy. I told the *minyan* about our arrangement, how I was supposed to cure Sylvia, and Abie raised a brow, but he understood: We might need Sylvia to help save Jack. They asked her questions about Sarge and about Sarge's business associates—including herself—and they wanted to know what she thought of Jack, too, so they could figure out from her answer what to make of her and how far to trust her, is what I figured.

Sylvia was shaking, and she said, "I can't believe this. What do all of you think Jack is? Do you think he's some kind of angel, the way he says he is? He's just a dopehead, for crissakes. Lea's the one who's worth something, and to you she's just a *shiksie*. Like me, I suppose. I'm a *shiksie*. You, you're the Chosen People, and Jack is your angel. You all belong in a nuthouse. The only reason I'm sticking around and filling your coffee cups is that I told Lea I would."

"And because you need her," Abie said.

And Sylvia said, "And because I need her."

And Abie said, "So by you, we're all crazy. Jack is crazy. The *minyan* is crazy. Lea has a talent, all right; that you see and you believe. For the rest of it, *meshuga'as*, am I right?"

"You're right."

"But you still owe Lea for future goods receivable, so you'll go and do us crazy people one favor, and then you'll go someplace safe—you know someplace safe?"

"The Garden of Eden."

"Funny! So you'll go someplace safe and stay out of it altogether."

"What's the favor? What do you want me to do?"

Abie scratched his chest through his pajama top, and he thought a minute and he said, "I'm not sure yet. God Tetragrammaton will show us."

Manny kept saying that he was almost done, and he kept not being done. I know this kind of guy. The world could be about to end—which it was, by the way—and they just have to putter.

Sylvia, meanwhile, holed up in the phone booth, half-hysterical. She closed herself in with the folding glass door. "I'm sick! I can't take this! I'm sick! God, isn't it enough for me to be sick? Do I have to put up with packs of crazy people?"

The *minyan* shrugged. You could see centuries of practice in that little shrug. Yids got a tough row to hoe. And tonight they had the *Meschiach* to worry about.

Rabbi Metzger said, "Put on your *talleisim*! Pray! Pray! We don't know what we might be called on to do before the sun rises again." And the *minyan* zipped open their little blue sacks and pulled out the white-and-blue shawls I'd seen on them under the city and kissed the ends and put them on. But the rabbi kept glancing around from one to the other, and he looked more and more worried. "We only have nine! Where's Yakov the Bull?"

Leonard said, "We must have a tenth! A *minyan* is ten!"

Manny said, "I'm almost done!"

Abie said, "Rabbi, what can we do? Our tenth, Yakov the Bull is at Mrs. Bobson's house, where Lea lives!"

And the Rabbi yelled, "Is it far?"

And I said, "No, it's a few blocks!"

And the Rabbi said, "Call him!"

Which is about when the phone rang, honest to God, and if you don't think there is One after all this, you are reading with your eyes shut. You could hear the phone ring through the glass door. Of course, Sylvia was in there. She was sobbing hysterically with her face pressed against the glass, which looked deformed because of how the skin pulled down and you could see the pink under her eye and her mouth was open. Shlomo pulled up his *tallis* like a lady hiking up her skirts to cross a puddle, and he went over to the phone booth.

And Shlomo shouted, "Open!"

Sylvia just shook her head and blubbered.

It wasn't long before there were three *minyan* guys at the phone booth working on Sylvia—Shlomo and Waxy and Ishky. Shlomo and Waxy kept trying to elbow Ishky out of the way because he was drunk, but Ishky was full of *k'vanna*. Sylvia just wedged herself in there, and they couldn't open the door because they didn't want to hurt her.

But then Ishky said, "Honey, honey, I know what it is to be sick. Listen to me, honey. I know what it is to cry and cry and nothing changes and nobody listens, and you find yourself doing things you don't like because what's the difference, am I right? And it makes you hate yourself." Shlomo and Waxy backed off. They could see that Sylvia was listening to Ishky. They stared at him like they'd never seen this guy before. "Honey, open up. We aren't bad guys. We'll take care of you, honey. We don't care what you've done. I'll take care of you, personal. Come on out and let us use the phone."

It kind of moved me, and I couldn't help myself, and Abie had this Jiminy Cricket way of sitting near you, quiet and trusty, so I said, "My brother, he used to be nice to me like that, Abie."

Abie pricked up his ear. He said, "You have a brother, Lea?"

"Two. Julian died. He was little. He kicked me, Abie, and that's when I got my talent." I said it right out. I didn't gulp or anything. "James was the oldest, and he protected me, he was nice to me, like Ishky and Sylvia, I guess. Only nobody can protect you from everything, can they?"

Abie said, " 'James,' did you say? 'James' . . . ?"

But then Sylvia pulled the door open. She practically fell out on top of Ishky. He held her while he led her to another table, where he pulled down the chairs that were still on it. They huddled there, and Sylvia cried, and Ishky said, "There, there! There, there . . . !"

Waxy was on the phone. "It's the landlady. She saved us a call. She says Yakov the Bull never showed up, but she's got another one in the basement now."

Abie said, "Who's she got? Another one from Sarge?"

And Waxy said, "No, she says it's some guy who's been pestering the *shiksie*. She *klopped* him on sight!"

Abie said, "Lea, who is this person she's got?"

And I said, "I don't know! He left notes, is all, but I never even read them. All I know is that she said the guy's got a ring through his nose."

Waxy said, "Did you just say, 'a ring through his nose'?"

Suddenly it got very quiet.

Little Abie, he was tilting his head and staring at my face, and he said, "Bone structure."

And they were all staring at my face, and one of them said, and I don't know which one, because a lot of them said it then: "Yakov the Bull!"

I could hardly hear a thing for the thump of my blood. "Abie, tell me, does 'Yakov' mean 'Jack'?"

And it was like we were all in a trance, like the air turned to cotton. "It's Hebrew, sweetie. There isn't an exact translation. It could be Jack, or it could be Jacob or Giacomo or Sean or Jaime…"

"Or James?"

"Or James. And that's what it is—James. That was his English name, Lea—James. At the *mikvah*, under the bridge, we made Yakov the Bull a Jew, and we gave him his Hebrew name, 'Yakov,' which is to say, 'James,' 'James the Bull.' 'The Bull,' we called him because of this nose ring.

"Honey, I think your big brother, our Yakov, has been protecting you the whole time."

Then I fainted.

chapter eleven

Yakov the Bull Explains
Me Everything

When I came to, I thought I was Denny Love and my handlers were peeling me off the canvas after Ruiz's sockdolager. I heard somebody moan, and I figured at first that it was me, because my head hurt. Only it wasn't—it was old Simon Black. He had fallen on his way upstairs from the john; he had lots of scratches, which Ishky was swabbing with a hanky dampened from his flask.

I was lying on the floor near the waiters' station. I looked up then, and I thought it was me leaning over me, and I must be dead and out of my body, like I read about. Only it wasn't me up there. It was somebody with more hair than me. The eyes were root beer brown like mine, and there was my perfect, small turned-up nose, but there was a little ring through it.

I started crying, and James said, "Don't do that!" He

had on a *tallis* and a black *yarmulke*. I saw some other *minyan* guys standing behind him like surgeons when you're on an operating table. I didn't know what to do. He didn't know what to do. He kissed his two fingers and he touched my forehead with them. I closed my eyes, because I wanted to evaporate into the kiss on James's fingers.

You can't, you know. There are good things in this world, is the way I see it now, but that's not one of them.

I said, "James, what are you doing in the *minyan*? We aren't even Jews."

And James said, "I had a *mikvah*. I'm one now. At first I just fooled them, honey. A person can do that so easy when there's nothing inside; you know, like ever since Julian fell out of the swing. I was keeping an eye on you, Lea, and when you got involved with Jack, I kept an eye on him, and that led me to the *minyan*. I conned them so I could keep up on him, and when Menachem died, they made me one of them. But I didn't really con them…"

"He thought he was conning us," Noah Solomon said. "We were conning him. We didn't know he was anybody's brother, but we could see he had the *ruach*, the holy spirit." Noah shrugged. "It happens."

And my brother James said, "I was like cold, wet kindling, and the *minyan* warmed me and dried me and set me on fire. I saw the *Zohar Hagoyim*. Sabbatai Levi Hagodol appeared to me in a dream."

And I said, "Me too, James. At the fights."

"I heard." And he smiled at me so sweet, like your big brother who loves you and who's proud of you, that I could have died at that exact moment and everything would have been just perfect. "Why didn't you answer my notes?"

"I didn't read them. What do I care about notes? Why did you leave notes, James?"

"I wasn't sure you'd want to see me, honey."

"You're my goddam brother. Who loves me, James? You do. Why the goddam hell wouldn't I want to see you?"

"It's in the notes."

"I didn't read the notes!"

"I killed Julian."

I fainted again, but just for a couple seconds, not like before. I didn't hit my head this time—I was already on the floor. I opened my eyes and James's palm was stroking my cheek, which practically made everything worth it.

I said, "I thought you just said you killed Julian!"

And he said, "I did, honey." His eyes began to tear and his lower lip trembled and then his nostrils got wide the way they do when you force the tears back where they came from. "I killed Julian, not you."

"James, I'm the one who's got the talent."

"You're not the only one, baby. Oh, you were there all right, burning into him. You were mad as hell, but mad don't make dead. I did that. I sighted him down your sights and I pulled the trigger inside me. It was me, Lea.

"God Tetragrammaton knows I didn't mean to. Julian was the first person I ever did it to—my own brother! *Ne'bech!*" It must have been a Yid word that my James had learned from the *minyan*. He rolled his eyes up and it was like he was lifting off the lid of a cup full of tears, because they came gushing down, a sheet practically, and he had to wipe his nose with his sleeve. "My muscle inside me wasn't strong, wasn't sure then. I didn't mean to kill him, for Pete's sake."

I didn't want to look at him just then. It was too

much. I bear-hugged his arm, which was as strong and hard as an iron cable, and I buried my face in his side. "James, you said you sighted him down my sights. What did you mean, you sighted him down my sights?"

"I always could read you inside, honey. I read where you looked and I read what you felt. When you got horrible mad or scared or tight, I just did what you wanted to do. I protected you, honey. Who loves you, Lea?"

"You do, James!"

"I do. I do. But I let you take the rap, didn't I? You didn't have the power then, the day with the swing. You didn't get it till later. I knew you would. I felt it growing. Then I knew you'd think it was you who killed Julian. But I didn't have the guts to tell you the truth. Or, I did and I didn't: I decided, must be twenty, thirty times to find you and tell you.

"That's why I stole the car to begin with that landed me in Juvenile Hall. I'd decided to leave the foster home where I was at and come tell you everything. It was my foster folk's car.

"I was chugging my foster dad's Pabst Blue Ribbon and I was speeding and the cops chased me. I gave them a good chase, but then I landed upside down in a ditch with the car totaled. My foster dad, he decided he believed in 'tough love,' and I got a judge with a gavel up his ass, and that was that. But I don't blame anybody a thing, because it all brought me to the *Zohar Hagoyim*, and that is what my life is about.

"But I mean, I kept trying to see you and tell you, even after the crash. I kept running away from the Hall. I'd run, then I'd lose my nerve and let them catch me again. Same thing with the notes—I'd bring one, then I'd stay away,

then I'd come again. By the way, did you know your landlady can do that thing?"

"Yeah, I found out. She thinks she's a witch."

Manny shouted, "I'm almost done here!"

I said, "James, how did the *minyan* turn you around?"

Rabbi Metzger butted in then, and he said, "It's like a
riddle isn't it? How does a confidence man take a mark
who has ceased to place any confidence in worldly things?
Yakov the Bull was this confidence man, and we of the
minyan were the marks. Angels we are not; of sins we have
a million apiece—and then some. But: Each one in the
minyan has placed his faith in a thing which, by the lights
of this world, is utterly, completely, one hundred percent
crazy. *Zohar Hagoyim*. Sabbatai Levi Hagodol. The thirteen. The three. The *Meschiach*.

"So: Comes the confidence man, and he lies, you'll excuse the expression, like a husband with a social disease—
or such is his intention. He's a nice boy, already, a good
boy, a believe-in-Godnik, an Eagle Scout, an I-just-want-
to-hang-around-and-learn-from-your-great-wisdomnik,
a sweetie. Any ordinary person could look up his police
record or hook him up to a polygraph, or ask him a well-
chosen question of fact, and they would prove everything
he said to be a lie.

"Not us. This was not our way. I'm telling you, to lie to
us, it's like trying to punch a lake. We didn't care what the
man said. We were looking at his heart.

"And in this heart, what did we see? I'll tell you." Rabbi
Metzger's face sweetened. He stopped looking like a priest
on a pulpit and started looking like your mom. He even
tousled James's hair. "We saw a nice boy, a good boy, a
believe-in-Godnik, an Eagle Scout, an I-just-want-to-

hang-around-and-learn-from-your-great-wisdomnik, a sweetie. Yakov the Bull thought he was lying, but in his heart—which is the only thing that these marks can see in a man, when it matters—we saw that he was telling the truth."

Behind Rabbi Metzger the *minyan* was collecting things, putting some chairs up on the tables again and even washing our coffee cups. You could see five thousand years of splitting hairs in every sponge stroke.

Rabbi Metzger went on: "When a person is believed, he begins to believe himself, and this is an old law. Yakov the Bull saw us how we saw him. He saw his reflection in our eyes, and lo, a sweetie! Tears flowed. Of embraces, a bushel and a peck. Soon Reb Sabbatai came to him for a confirmation. Yakov the Bull joined the *minyan*. And then it was now, *und fartik*." The rabbi laughed, and he went to help Ishky dress Simon Black's wounds.

Simon pointed at James and he called out, "He's still a bad boy. He's on the path—okay. He can make a *minyan*—fine and good. But you got to watch him."

And James said, "Simon, I have to watch myself."

Manny piped up from his wire-twisting and screw-driving and fiddling about, "Watch, listen . . . I just put two and two together, and you know what? It's four. It was you, Yakov, with the cup to the floor, you, Yakov, bird in a perch, your piss in the peanut butter jar. You were watching over the little sister, weren't you?"

"Yeah, it was me. I was underneath the spaceship, on the next floor down. I was protecting you, Lea, like I told you, like I always did. I listened up through the floor with a glass, which worked like crap, but I could hear when one was talking and when the other was talking and enough words to get the gist. I could feel you inside clear as a bell. A few of those cockroaches and mice—and some of the microbes—I killed them, sighting down your sights, honey. That was interesting. I know why you wanted to do it, too. It wasn't because you were afraid or angry, like usual. It was for love. You're in love with him, aren't you?"

"Yes."

"Maybe you'll go to the Garden of Eden with him and the sixteen."

"That's what I figure. That's what Reb Sabbatai told me."

And James said, "Good. Good," but he looked miserable—until he caught me looking at him, seeing how miserable, and he forced a kind of smile.

He smiled like that for a minute, then his eyes seemed to go someplace else. For some dumb reason he started to laugh, but it turned into a kind of snarl instead. He wiped his face as if it was just that his nose felt funny—though I could see that it wasn't. Then he got a dark look, like he was ashamed and he didn't want me to see him. He shrank inside his collar. It was like somewhere in his mind he'd hit black ice, and he was skidding off the road.

He said, "When you were with Jack at the Wee Spot that night, why did you kill the cat?"

"You were watching me, huh?"

"Yeah, from across the street in the liquor store behind the car where that cat was."

"It was because Jack said to. He saw the Devil in it, and nobody knows how to kill the Devil without killing who it's in."

"He was sure it was in the cat, huh?" That dark look again.

"Yeah—who else was over there, for crissakes? Say, you tailed me everywhere, huh? Did you, like, do it to any others, sighting down my sights?"

His face tightened. "Some." That's all he would say just then. He was like a door that slams open and the cold blows through and makes you shudder. Then he was my James again, just like that. Maybe it was the fainting. Maybe it screwed up the way I saw things, like how a concussion can make you funny for a while.

The point is, my big brother James was kneeling over me. See, that's what I mean. That's how it is. The world is turning to liquid shit, and there's something so sweet and lovely that none of the bad stuff even matters.

After a while he said, "Julian was an accident. I came to see that. I didn't know if you would see it that way, though. I didn't know if you would blame me. That's why I wrote those notes instead of just coming to you as soon as I got out of Juvenile Hall."

I swallowed hard, and I sort of took care of my face a little. I wiped the tears off, and I sniffed my nose clear, and so on. I didn't want to cry at that particular moment. I wanted to know something. "James, where's our mom?"

James looked away. "She didn't make it."

"What do you mean, she didn't make it?"

James didn't answer. He kept looking over at the table where the guys were huddled over the radio, which Manny was still working on, and which there was nothing particular for James to see there. I was sitting up by then. Guys were passing out ram's horns. Leonard was asking Sylvia questions and she was answering them and he was writing things down and drawing things on a piece of paper, and he had his thick glasses on.

And I said, "Leonard works for the city, huh?"

And James still didn't look at me, but he nodded. "That's what he does, all right."

And I said, "That's what I heard."

And I said, "I bet that's a good job."

And I shouted, "Look at me, James! What the hell do you mean, she didn't make it, James?"

And James said, "Mom killed herself about a year ago. They found her hanging from a beam in a housing development across from where she was living. She did it on a Saturday. It was a three-day weekend, so nobody found her until Tuesday when the carpenters went back to work. It must have been an awful sight. They told me at Juvie. Not the whole thing. I found out the ugly parts later, when I ran. Then, when they came to take me back, I let them."

I said, "Three days, huh? She might not have been rotted so bad. It would have been cold, if it was a year ago. What was it, Presidents' Day? It would have been like a refrigerator. Like me. I'm a refrigerator. Look how I'm preserved."

And James hugged me tight. I kind of fell apart then—again. It's like, ice melts—okay!—but what you don't know until it happens to you, is that water melts and steam melts, and whatever steam melts to, that melts. Everything melts.

James said, "You're no refrigerator, Lea."

And I was crying again, but I said, "Oh James," I said, "yes, I am. Yes, I am." I said, "Only I'm on defrost." And the way it sounded to me coming out of my own mouth that way, I had to laugh.

And James laughed. And Abie, who was looking on, he started to laugh. Then they all of them laughed, the whole *minyan*, which half of them didn't know why; but they were tapping one another's shoulders and cocking their heads and saying "*vooz-vooz*," which is Yid talk for "*What?*" It was a regular yuck fest. Even Sylvia was laughing.

When I get to the Garden of Eden I want somebody to tell me why you don't get any straight flavors in this stupid life. Everything is bittersweet. Everything is: dancing the hokey-pokey on somebody's grave or crying in the middle of a clown show. Sometimes, don't you want to just clap yourself into a phone booth like goddam Sylvia—but then the phone rings. Bittersweet.

All the *minyan* had on their *talleisim*, and all the *minyan* had ram's horns tucked under their arms which they called *shofars*. Noah Solomon went from one to another wagging his finger that they shouldn't mark up the *shofars*, because they were only rentals which had to be returned for the High Holidays.

Ishky said, "You bourgeois *schmuck*, what is it worth in the Promised Land?"

And Noah said, "Who's a bourgeois? And who's going to the Promised Land today? Not us. Not the *minyan*. Only the sixteen. For us, the whole world is the same, and payment is due on every rental, jot and tittle, with interest—you hear me?—and with postage and handling thrown in. So you'll watch the merchandise, thank you very much."

Then Manny yelled, "Am I a genius or what?" and we all heard Jack's voice.

chapter twelve

Rats

"Denny, you were fabulous, you were a house on fire, and everybody knows you would have kayoed Ruiz if it had been on the up and up. You had every round. He didn't know where you'd be coming from next. It was the most scientific fighting anybody's ever seen," is what Jack was saying.

And Shlomo said, "Is that what I was just saying, or what?"

And Ishky said, "Is that what he was just saying or what. Shut up, *maven*: They got Denny Love up in the spaceship."

And Denny Love said on the radio, "Can I slug this Yid, Mr. Panaggio? Can I give him just a little one to re-member me by?"

And somebody we all figured to be this Panaggio guy,

he said, "What did you say you call this thing here—the 'Fleshpot'? Jeez, this is a fucking perversion. I mean, you got gams here with boobs in-between. And what's this—half a rear end?"

"Yes, Mr. Panaggio."

"Shut up, Yid. When I want you to talk, I'll ask you, see? The kind of dough you lost me in that arena, you'll never see in all your Yid life, and I ain't reconciled to it, see...? What's this, somebody's nipple?"

"That's it, Mr. Panaggio."

"Shut up. It's sick."

And Denny Love said, "What about hitting him a little? Can I slap him?"

Rabbi Metzger started praying in Hebrew, leaning back and forth and mumbling with his eyes shut. Some other *minyan* guys were saying "Amen, amen, amen."

But Abie was pacing his itsy-bitsy midget paces and shaking his head and clucking his tongue. "This is not good. I'm not talking a racism, but to have in the spaceship *goyim* that don't believe in the Thrice Chosen, this is a danger to the whole coming of the *Meschiach*."

And Rabbi Metzger said, "Our Abie is right. Isn't it written in *Zohar Hagoyim*, 'The spaceship is built of *k'vanna*,' which means, *a believing and enthusiastic spirit*? If this disbelief, and a scorn and a spitting, are allowed in the heart of the craft of the Thrice Chosens of the earthly realm—catastrophe."

I felt everything and I counted my heartbeats, but I was still scared for Jack up in Sears and Roebuck's. He was laying it on thick, but nobody was buying it. I felt sick and weak all over. I decided, if this keeps up, I'm gonna run over to the Sears and Roebuck and I'm gonna climb up and I'm gonna jump down and bust in and do some damage, Moses or no Moses.

Then some guys in the background of the radio, it sounded like they were jumping and yelling. One of them said, "There are rats in this place! Look at the size of them!"

And I said, "There can't be rats, because there are mice, and mice always keep the rats away."

And Abie said, "The Evil One knows that something is cooking."

And Jack was saying, "Please leave the fabric alone. That is the Holy of Holies over there ... Oww!" It could have been a slap. All around the three tables the *minyan* shuddered. It could have been a stick like Moses's on the rock. It could have been the famous around-the-house right that Denny Love had been saving for the Detroit Pile Driver and had felt cheated out of at the arena. I hated that sound, and I wasn't going to stand still for another one.

I could hardly see straight. There were tears brimming in my eyes, and my blood was pounding inside me, and I lost count, and I charged through the kitchen for the alley door. I knocked past the steam table and clanged all the hanging pots, but Abie came after me. He could really make tracks for such a little guy.

And he said, "Lea, Lea, wait."

What was it about that guy? I waited.

He came up to me. He was all out of breath and he said, "You know Jack's heart, honey, but his life you don't know. He's one smart, tough cookie, our Jack. Nobody's going to hurt him. He couldn't speak English until he was six, he had a Yiddish accent till he was twelve, and where

Jack grew up, he spent the whole time defending himself against people who wanted to throw him in front of a truck. And he lived."

I said, "You're wrong. He'd be dead meat right now if I hadn't saved his butt when some guys wanted to beat up on him right outside this door."

Abie said, "It's as God Tetragrammaton wills. The *minyan* is here to protect him if it's necessary. We have no other goal in life but this, Lea. I know what I'm talking about. If it were necessary, Waxy and Manny could be there in one minute, and everyone but Yakov would be a corpse, *und fartik*."

"It's necessary now."

"It isn't. Not yet."

From Manny's radio there was another one of those sickening sounds. Then we heard a bunch of confused voices and static, and someone was saying, "How the hell did that happen?"

"How the hell did that happen?"
"The Yid did it."
"He didn't. He couldn't."
"There's blood coming out of its fucking mouth."

Abie and I looked at each other, and we ran back to the *minyan*. They were all looking at one another and at the radio: what were those hoods talking about over in the spaceship?

And Shlomo said, "Shut up and listen."

And Ishky said, "Was somebody talking besides you?"

And Waxy said, "Shut up, the both of you."

And the rabbi hit the table and said, "Shh."

* * *

"The other one's dead too, and one in the corner is lying on its side and shaking."

"I tell you, it was the Yid."

"I thought you said the girl was the one."

"The girl is *the one."*

Sylvia said, "That's Sarge." She had to be right, but his voice sounded a little funny to me, not just on account of the radio, but on account of he sounded scared. I'd never heard him like that before. He was always the guy on top.

And Mr. Panaggio said, "Yeah, well I hope rodents is the limit that this Yid can kill because otherwise, boys, we may be in deep shit here."

And Sarge said, "How the hell did the Yid get a goddam talent?"

And I said, "Julian kicked him."

"Praise God Tetragrammaton," is what Rabbi Metzger said. "The Thrice Chosen One, having come into the fullness of his powers, has directed his talent not at the human enemy, who is but a wayward sheep in the pastures of our God, but at the agents of the Evil One, who burrow and gnaw and who wrap themselves in filth to delay the coming of the *Meschiach*."

We were all crowding in around the radio, cheek to cheek practically, and Noah Solomon, the dry goodser, said, "Rabbi, you mean rats?"

But everybody else said, "Amen."

Abie asked me, "What did you mean, 'Julian kicked him'?"

And James said, "I know what she means, Abie. It's how the talent came to us. Our little brother Julian kicked

Lea and she got mad and something awful happened. It was an accident, but our talent did it, me and her being so young. It was because Julian kicked her. That started it."

And I said, "Jack, he made meters and a biofeedback dingus, and he's been studying me and measuring me..."

Noah said, "So that's what it was for, the electronic stuff he made me get."

"He's been practicing to do what I do—and what James does. He never could, but now Denny Love punched him, sounds like, and it flipped a switch, like Julian's kick, and he's got it."

Just then there was a staticky rumble. Those rats must have been stampeding right over Manny's Radio Shack receiver. It was like the walls were full of rats and they were all emptying out onto the floor. I could practically see all those pink tails like baby boy dicks and their dirty gray sausage backs and their idiots' heads with the fangs sticking out. They made squeaks that spoke straight to the place you shiver from.

Over the din of the rats' feet, I heard Jack say, "*Do you believe in the Devil, Mr. Panaggio?*"

And Mr. Panaggio said, "*Where did all these fucking rats come from?*"

And Jack said, "*The Devil.*"

"*Serge, you fucking asshole, you didn't tell me anything about any fucking Devil. You said he was a psychic.*"

And Sarge said, "*I said the girl. The girl's a psychic, not him. He's a dopehead. He's a Yid.*"

"*Yeah, well he's a fucking rat-killing Yid, isn't he? Look at those little fuckers keel over. You're doing that, aren't you, Yid?*"

And Jack said, "*I could do it to you, Mr. Panaggio, but I*

don't want to hurt you. I don't even want to hurt the rats, but it's the only way I know how to get at the Devil in them. I'm new at this."

And Panaggio said, *"Sock him, Denny."*

And Jack said, *"Please, Mr. Love—I'll bet you're a Christian, aren't you?"*

Then I heard Denny Love say, *"Yes, I am a Christian. That's how come I win fights. Jesus gave me my whole comeback, Jesus and Lou Panaggio, my whole comeback that I'm having after I slowed down and lost those decisions to butt-faced Johnny Hacker and the new kid out of Texas, Ben Wylie, who your mother could beat on a bad day. God was punishing me, and then I was born again. I went down in the name of the Lord and I come up a winner—except for tonight."*

And Panaggio said, *"Jesus Christ!"*

And Denny Love said, *"I am a Christian, Mr. Panaggio. Ain't you a Christian?"*

"I am not a goddam Christian. I'm a Roman Catholic. Punch him."

"I don't know, Mr. Panaggio. Look, he's fighting the Devil here, Mr. Panaggio. Look at them rats hit the canvas."

Manny Baranes pasted his ear to the radio. "Maybe Jack is making a progress. Maybe the Panaggio *goyim* would come to believe, and they would keep the *k'vanna* of the spaceship, it should have a liftoff okay."

On the radio, Jack was saying, *"Mr. Panaggio, honestly, what harm has been done? The referee called off all bets. Everybody's going to get their investment back. If you want to hold me responsible for lost interest, I'm sure I can manage that..."*

"Yowch!" That was Panaggio yelping. *"You sonuva-*

bitch, you missed one. If I get bubonic fucking plague, Yid, we'll guild stamp you and smoke you in your own fucking hash pipe. And don't talk to me about interest. You Yids got some nerve, you know that? I got a Boxing Commission to deal with now. They'll be thinking I'm a crook, for crissakes. Me, Louis Panaggio, for crissakes. And what about my word, my honor, my reputation? I've been insulted here. How are you going to make up for that, Yid?"

Somebody yelled, *"Kill him, boss."*

And another guy said, *"Yeah, kill the little fucker, but let's get the hell away from these rats first."*

And another guy said, *"Yeah, otherwise, when the Yid buys it, they'll swarm all over us."*

Then I heard Denny Love say, *"He's got a point about the Christian thing, Mr. Panaggio. I mean, you know I'm grateful to you, Mr. Panaggio, for all your assistance that you've been giving me, but without Jesus Christ, our Lord and Savior, a person can't even win a fixed fight. I mean, that's what all this proves, don't it?*

"I don't think I should hit the Yid. And besides, he's casting out demons here, which is a Christian thing in my book."

And Mr. Panaggio said, *"Nobody's reading your fucking book, you stupid has-been."*

And Jack said, *"Mr. Panaggio, I know you believe in the Devil."*

"What if I do? Yowch! Will you keep them off me, dammit?"

"We have the same enemy, you and I, Mr. Panaggio."

"You little shit, suppose I grab your girlfriend and aim her at you like a big goddam bazooka and blast your ass to hell? I don't need you. I could get her to come and kill these rats and you along with them. Am I right, Serge?"

And Sarge said, "*You're right, Mr. Panaggio.*"

Mr. Panaggio said, "*Don't think I couldn't get her to do it, either, Mr. Yid. I got my charm, don't I, boys?*"

And they said, "*Right, boss. You got lots of charms. Kalashnikovs and stilettos and piano wire—all kinds of fucking charms.*"

"*And dough. Lots of dough. We bought you. We can buy her. Right now as we speak, Mr. Yid, three of my associates are accompanying Miss Tillim the psychic, the other psychic, to our present venue from her little domicile which we know her to be sharing with a sweet little lady name of Belle Bobson.*

"*Harry, go down and tell them to come up from the lot and bring the girl.*"

And some kid said, "*They ain't come back yet, Mr. Panaggio.*"

And he said, "*What?*" You could hear a smack then, and the kid yelped.

The rats were squeaking and stampeding; thousands of little feet scratched and tapped like dry rice on a drumhead. The kid on the radio was crying. "*I don't know why I didn't tell you before, Mr. Panaggio. Please don't hit me again. I figured they was just detained. I didn't know they was expected at a certain time—owww!*"

And Jack said, "*That's the other thing, Mr. Panaggio. That's the other negotiating point. We have three of your people.*"

"*You sonuvabitch...Yowch!*"

"*I'm sorry. I missed that one. Honestly, I'm trying to control them. You could help me, Mr. Panaggio. I know you believe in the Evil One. I know you don't like the Devil any more than I do.*"

And Denny Love said, "*Help him, Mr. Panaggio. Christ ain't coming back until all the Yids are in their Promised Land, you know. Everybody's got to help.*"

And Mr. Panaggio said, "*Shut up. Shut up. Is everybody going crazy?*"

And somebody said, "*Boss, I bet Waxy the Grifter is behind this. I bet his boys is got Mr. Morano and Aces and Benito in one of them Yid hideouts underground. Damn! I can't take these rats, boss. Please let me go outside. Or help him, help the goddam Yid, like Denny says. Nobody wants the fucking Devil to win, am I right?*"

And the radio said, "*I'll kill him. I'll kill him, do you hear me? Morano and Aces and Benito can all go to hell. If anybody says one more word about the Devil or the fucking Promised Land, goddammit, I'll break this Yid's neck with my own two hands.*"

Waxy started pacing and making funny sounds in his throat. "Gentlemen, I don't like this. Louis Panaggio's up a tree. He's got a mutiny there. There's no telling what he's going to do anymore. Tempers may flare. Injuries may be sustained. I do not like our Yakov's odds so much anymore."

Simon Black had been bent over, worrying all the little bruises on his leg, but when he heard Waxy, he unrolled himself like a potato bug, and he said, "What have I been saying all along? Watch, he'll kill him. We sit here listening to our gangster maven, and the Thrice Chosen One is going down like a chicken in a sack."

Then Waxy looked like he was going to get physical with Simon, but Abie placed himself between them. "There's no need to *putshky* around. It seems to me that we are all in agreement here: It's time the *minyan* went up."

"It's time," is what Rabbi Metzger said. "As the psalm says, 'Thou layest affliction on our loins, and thou dost let men ride over our heads, as a goad, that we should go for Thy sake through water and through fire.' Brothers and sisters, it's time."

Abie sidled up to me and gave me a little poke, and when I looked, he motioned me closer and whispered, "Don't let Simon Black upset you. Jack will be all right. Mr. Black expresses himself poorly, that's all."

"You mean, he sees everything upside down and backward and paints it dark."

"No, no, he sees things more clearly than anybody. Simon can't be fooled. But you have to take him with a grain of salt. He overstates."

"I sure hope so, Abie."

We herded ourselves through the Wee Spot. We massed through the kitchen, to the alley door. James kept his arm around me, which wasn't like Jack's arm, but I felt at home there, in James's hug, like I was back in the house I grew up in, before the world got shot to hell. Sometimes I grabbed James's hand, the way a little girl would to pull his arm a notch tighter.

I said, "James, are the Chosen Ones gonna leave today?"

James said, "Who knows? Maybe."

"Tule'll be there, won't she, James? Tule'll be in the Garden of Eden."

And James said, "Huh?"

"Don't dead people go there, I mean, if they're good? I mean, and dead cats. Tule was good."

And James said, "Tule's not dead. She's at Mrs. Bobson's. Who told you Tule was dead?"

"Abie told me on the telephone."

We pushed out into the alley. Me and James were in the middle of everybody and it was warm there and we were walking in a cloud of all our breath: *ruach. Spirit.* And James said, "You must have misunderstood. We found her underground. Some mongrel had her up a ledge where she couldn't get out or he'd eat her. We got her down though. Abie told me he'd asked you and you said you didn't want us to bring her to you at the Wee Spot."

"I thought he meant her dead body."

And James said, "Nope. Tule's alive, all right, though she's missing a bit of fur. She even had a message for you, honey."

"A message? What did she say?"

"*Meow.*"

The jerk laughed, and I punched him. He punched me back. It was practically like breakfast with the ones you love.

Abie heard us talking, and he made his way over to us, and Abie said, "You thought Tule was going to be in the Garden? Hah! Not unless she's one of the thirteen. Or unless she's the *shiksie* Reb Sabbatai was talking about, the protector and the interpreter—*Tule* and not you." And he laughed.

Why not? We didn't know if maybe we were going to get our blocks knocked off by Panaggio's thugs. Waxy looked grim. Manny kept checking his pocket, where everybody knew he was packing heat.

The point is, Tule was alive.

Abie was like a little jester, like he didn't want us to get scared and shit in our pants when we got close to the parking lot, or maybe he was just joking around because he was nervous. "Who can tell who's Reb Sabbatai's *shiksie*? Maybe it's Tule. Does she know languages?"

And Sylvia, who just caught the tail end of that, said, "I know languages. I majored in linguistics at NYU uptown."

chapter thirteen

The Minyan Sings Ghi Diddy Di on Top of Mount Nebo

Here is the part of my story where extremely weird shit starts to go down, so you can stop here if you want to. I mean, for everything up to now, it's just life. My little brother dead, my father dead, my mother hung herself, and the CPS guy and the city councilman and the frat jock who died in the alley, and the others, it's all just life; if you don't believe it, read the goddam newspapers.

You can chalk up Jack and the *minyan* for a bunch of kooks if you want. I don't know what you want to make of all those rats, but I'm sure you could think of something. As far as me and my brother James's talent and Jack's and Belle Bobson's, hell, half the people in the state of California believe weirder shit than that, but if you don't happen to go for that stuff, you can mark all those deaths and stomachaches down to coincidence.

Nobody's going to tell you not to, and it's no skin off my teeth.

But when the *minyan,* that my brother James was one of, went into that Sears and Roebuck parking lot, there were flames of glory licking the awning of the Garden Shoppe. I looked up into the little window that Jack never let me clean, and there was flickering firelight and explosions of color coming out of it like what you see if you press your eyeball with your thumb.

Sylvia looked really sick. She'd cried off her makeup. Her clothes were mud and shadows. Her skin actually looked gray, and it made you realize how much a good presentation can compensate for what nature didn't give you, or in Sylvia's case, for what it took away. Ishky had his arm around her. Time was I would have thought the guy was coming on to her, but that wasn't it. He was doing Sylvia like James was doing me: brotherly.

It exists.

We were halfway across the lot when two barking dogs ran in front of us, scruffy mongrels the both of them, and one stopped near me and started to sniff at me and wag its tail. The other one stayed away and barked for the friendly one to come join it, but the friendly one kept sniffing at me and wagging so hard and squatting down its hindquarters so low I thought it was going to pee. I was so melted by that time I figured even dogs liked me.

I was leaning down to pet it, when James stepped in my way and he cocked his leg and he gave that puppy a kick in the gut just like it was a goddam football. It yelped and scrambled away about ten yards, then it stopped and licked itself a little, then it limped away into the shadows as fast as it could. The other dog was already gone.

And I said, "James, what are you doing?" and he got that sheepish dark look again. He didn't say a word.

Simon said, "Pay attention, Yakov."

Rabbi Metzger clucked his tongue. "Good and bad. Bad and good."

It was a lousy night for dogs.

The moon rose right over Sears tower. The moon was skinny, pale yellow, and its horns pointed to the right, which means that it was getting smaller: not good. There was a gigantic aura around the moon, as if it was a hole in the sky, as if the sky were the flesh of the Earth and somebody had gouged out a chunk. The *minyan* shuddered, and Rabbi Metzger said, "Blessed art thou, oh God Tetragrammaton, who created the Lesser Light to rule over the night!"

And the *minyan* said, "Amen."

And the *minyan* kept on walking toward Sears and Roebuck, toward the fire escape. In the sickly light from the hole in the sky, the rust looked like blood. When we got to the bottom of it and looked up, we couldn't see the top, because awful, fiery tongues glowed in the upper stories. Those tongues were like swords with two edges and they were like spikes on a dog's collar and they were like a sunburst and they were like when they open the door of a smeltery and it shines as bright as the inside of the sun—that's how bright and awful it was. It was as if that fire escape went all the way up into heaven, where God is supposed to live, which I used to doubt, but I don't anymore.

Sylvia said, "You don't mean to say we're going up there?"

And Ishky said, "Poopsie, it's nothing. Don't worry

from it," but it took him four tries to get all the words out, because he was shaking and stuttering like all the rest of us.

Me, I was clutching my James so tight I think he would have yelped but he was too scared of the burning bloody sky to even notice the pressure. And James kept saying, "It's okay. It's okay," the hysterical way that guys do when things are completely out of control.

The Earth moved. You wanted to duck and cover, but it was the Earth, the sky, everything: Anyplace you could think of to hide in was a place you had to get away from.

And Rabbi Metzger bellowed: "It is a portent of the coming of the supernal *Ish-ra-el*, the true Promised Land, and this fire escape is the ladder of Jacob, of *Yakov*, upon which the angels of God Tetragrammaton ascended and descended in the dream he dreamed at *Luz*, which Jacob named *Beth-el, The Lord's House.* And it was this same Jacob, *Yakov*, who was called *Ish-ra-el*, which means, *the man who wrestles with God.*"

And I said, "That's Jack all over. That's what my Jack does. He wrestles with God. Just like me, goddammit." The words just ripped out of me before I knew I was saying them; otherwise, I couldn't have peeped.

And everyone shouted, "Amen."

And Abie leapt up like a circus acrobat onto the lowest landing of the fire escape, and he tucked his *shofar* into his belt and he pulled his *tallis* over his head so that the fringe covered his face like a shawl. He thrust out his arms and made the sign of the priests, and his hands were like the lattice that the gazelle peeks through. He sang:

"Kohani-im!"

The rusted bars of the fire escape were burning red hot. Clumps of ice were raining down, red with rust, if it wasn't God's blood dripping off the moon. Mr. Black yowled from under his elbows that he had up over his head like a boxer getting lambasted in the corner, "You *shi'ker*, you *drunk*, are you a *Kohayn*? Only a *Kohayn* could make this sign. And are we *Kohayns* what you want us to make a *Kohayn broche*?" But everybody else draped their *talleisim* over their heads the same as Abie, so Mr. Black grumbled and did the same, and they all bowed from the waist, back and forth, back and forth, like Mongoloids, and they howled, and they sang:

"Ghi di di di! Ghi di di diddy di di!"

I saw smoke curling up from Abie's shoes and I smelled the burning shoe leather. The sky was burning open around the moon, and fire was pouring out along the edges of the hole. When they all, the whole *minyan*, raised their arms, I thought I saw the *Zohar Hagoyim* appear in their hands with the pages fanning and burning like Moses's burning bush, which wasn't consumed. Then I remembered what Jack told me about how you could go blind from looking, that's how holy the *Kohayns* got when they did their *duchening*, is what he called it, so I shut my eyes tight and I shouted, and I said, "Sylvia, close your eyes." But she only said, "What? What? What?" which is how loud they were *duchening* right then.

I shut my eyes and let the crowd move me along. I felt shoulders and bellies and backs push me and lift me and rub me. I was scared of the red-hot iron of the fire escape, but if Abie could manage, I guessed I could too. *Ghi di di,* we clanked up the stairs. I smelled the rubber soles of Lillian's tennis shoes burning, and I felt them sizzle under my feet. Maybe it was because my eyes were closed: It seemed like we climbed up more flights than we should have to reach the roof. *Di di diddy di*, and I was starting to wonder how thick those rubber soles were, because the smell of the sulfur was choking me. We went up about thirty or forty stories, felt like, and we were still climbing, and everybody was still *duchening* like a house afire, when Sylvia screamed, "I can't see! Help me! Everything's black!"

And Ishky, he stopped *ghi di di-ing* a minute to say, "There, there! There, there!" but it didn't help, and she screamed and she screamed, and Ishky went back to his *duchening*. We carried her along. I felt her flailing and dragging through all the bodies in between, which pushed against me when she pushed, because we were all so close.

I saw a litter of puppies once, before Julian fell out of the swing, with their eyes still closed. They squeaked and yawned and pushed—Roll over! Roll over!—like one big gut, and if those puppies had been on fire at the time, it would have been exactly like us.

Then I could feel with my feet and my knees that we were on the roof at last, on the gravel-and-tar-paper roof, and the *duchening* stopped. I opened my eyes. The bottoms of Lillian's sneakers were completely burned through, and I could feel the tar paper under my feet, and my feet were blistered and they hurt like hell, but I still had feet, is how I figured it, and thank God Tetragramophone for that. I saw Sylvia's head peekabooing through *talleisim* and *yarmulkes*, and her eye sockets looked like the hole in the sky. Only, there were no moons in them.

I said, "Let me show you the rest of the way in!" but as soon as I said it, I felt extremely stupid, because nothing was the same. We were standing in the clouds, in moon steam, which felt like dead souls spidering and curlicuing and sticking to our clothes. I thought maybe it was Mount Nebo, where Moses saw the Promised Land but couldn't enter it, like Jack had told me, because he'd hit the stone. Maybe down below was Jericho, the city of palm trees, where I'd been living my whole life and didn't even know it.

You think you know everything, who you are, where you are, who other people are, then one little thing changes, and suddenly it's Mount Nebo, and you've been in Jericho the whole time and didn't even know it, is my general principle now.

Oh, the wind! That precious wind on the roof of Sears and Roebuck! Down in the plains of Moab, and in Gilead and Dan, in all Naphtali and Ephraim and Manasseh and all the land of Judah unto the utmost sea, no one knows how to breathe. But up there, swimming in moon steam, you know what it is to fill your lungs. Everything that goes in is alive, and everything that comes out is alive, and the air is made of diamonds.

Then the spirits of the wild animals came. They stampeded out of the hole in the sky, lions and wolves and rhinoceroses and wild boars, roaring and trumpeting, and something that looked like a pterodactyl, along with swarms of wasps and locusts, in a storm of bloody hail. They were the *spirits* of them, which didn't have any bodies.

They charged at me from the sky, but when they reached me they didn't trample me or eat me or push me aside; they ran right through me like a wave through water. I felt the hamstrings of the wolves stretching in my knees and I felt their wet snouts move through my face and my head, front to back. Even their pizzles were made of my groin flesh when they passed through me. And their dark red animal thoughts filled my head, their beastly bile filled my guts, and inside my fingers I felt claws and wing feathers and talons and insect electricity.

And between yelps and cries Mr. Black shouted to Waxy, "*Nu*, Waxy, maven, businessman—you call this 'Mr. Panaggio being amenable to reason'?"

And Abie said, "Hush, Simon, because these creatures are not from Panaggio. They are from the Devil, it's no mistake."

There was nothing you could do when the Evil One was streaming through your own body, because you would kill yourself trying to kill him. But while the Legions of Hell were coming at us from the sky, before they had reached us all the way, James and I made a stand.

James said, "Hold on tight. You aim and I fire." There were Apocalypses sweeping through my brains, and my heart pumped the blood of dragons, which used my veins while they flew through me, but I swiveled my head like a gun turret and wherever I looked the air crackled and nightmares exploded in flame. When one creature exploded, all the ones nearby were horrified. You wouldn't think those horrors could be horrified, but it's so.

They cringed and slowed and it made it easy to pick them off. James got better and faster at reading me inside. We got so I could sweep my head left and right like a machine gun or a water cannon, and whole bunches of beasts would just turn to butter or dust or sparkling mist. Pretty soon, we were ahead of the game, so that not a one of them reached us. Our bodies belonged to us again. James and me were picking them off as soon as they spilled, rode, flew, galloped, or slimed over the lip of the sky hole.

And James said. "What a team!" and my *buccinator* was pumping iron.

If you're thinking, this is *bubbe meisehs*, you can take your pansy ass the hell out of my book, because the way I'm telling you is exactly how it happened, and I warned you, and you're still here, so take a little responsibility. That's the point. I hope you don't imagine it was like the goddam hokey-pokey for me either.

The rush of terrors dwindled like a rainstorm petering out. But then the bad wind came. *Talleisim* flagged and whipped. We were thrown around and tangled up, and we finally had to grab on to one another and hunch down against that poison wind. It stank like sulfur and shit and rotting meat and blood—and worse.

Some smells make you remember things and some smells make you feel things that you don't know the name of. There are smells that you've spent your whole life staying far away from, like how mosquitoes shepherd people around a field and put them where they want them to be, and people think it's just some stupid annoyance, but the mosquitoes are up to something, is the way I see it. And that's what smells do. Some smells, you just get the tiniest whiff—you don't even know you've smelled it—and you feel so depressed you could jump in the river and drown; I've had some nosefuls of that smell myself. The Devil leads you by the nose, is the truth of it.

And there we were on the bare roof, in the thick of it, and killer depression was puffing up our coats and gusts of sheer nastiness were pasting back our cheeks like a god-dam face-lift. You had to burrow down deep to see who you were under that garbage or you would get fooled into thinking that all that wind was yourself, and you'd give up; you'd become an agent of the Devil, or you'd get blown down into the plains of Moab.

Rabbi Metzger got danced backward to the gutter along the west edge of the rooftop. He was spinning and flailing, which his *tallis* got twisted over his eyes, and for a minute it looked like he was going to fall off. Abie was holding on to him by the arm, then by the hand, and finally by the fringe of his *tallis*, when the rabbi started to spin out of it like a top. Then his eyes were uncovered, and he could see he was about to fall down a kajillion stories into broken and scattered stones of the wall of Jericho, and he said what anybody would say at a moment like that, he said, "*Fuck!*" And Ishky hurtled across the tar paper and tackled the rabbi, and they fell onto the rooftop together. He saved his life.

That night Ishky the Shi'ker scored big in the Book of Life that God Tetracycline keeps in his right hip pocket, and if you judge people too quick, you'll never get to read it.

I have to say, if Julian had never fallen out of the swing, if I'd gone on just having pancakes and maple syrup and biking to the zoo with James, and if my life hadn't turned to liquid shit, while I ranted and cried in every black hole in my heart, so I knew all my shadows inside and out—if not for all that, I'd have been blown away, no mistake.

Ishky pulled Rabbi Metzger back to the clump of us, the way a lifeguard drags a bloated swimmer under the arm and by the chin. We all hugged together, and the bad wind was whistling and shrieking past us and through us.

Abie said, "So *nu*, Lea, you're going to show us in?"

I peeked up through one clenched eye. The sky was practically all hole now. The moon had turned blood red. The moon's horns were dripping as if it had been storming around heaven trampling and goring every soul worth a nickel, and we were next. I looked at where the elevator shaft should be, is the way I thought about it, where it *should* be, because I wasn't taking anything for granted now that the Sears and Roebuck was as good as turned to Mount Nebo. Lucky thing the shaft was still right there where it had always been, and the plywood board was clattering and flapping on top of it.

We crawled to the shaft. None of the others had ever been inside the spaceship. They didn't know about the decompression chamber. They didn't know about the jump. They only knew that it was in the hidden section of Sears and Roebuck and that you got in by way of the roof. I led them like a slug's feelers, and they were the slug squirming behind.

I mean, me, Lea Tillim, I led them! I led the Jews across goddam Mount Nebo, is how far I'd come from Julian's swing and dirty, killing looks and my dead face workout video. I led them and they followed me, and my own brother James, he was holding me and inching along behind me. You can give me the fish eye from now till Kingdom Come—which is just around the corner, don't forget—and it's all still gospel true.

The black wind pinned us down. The tar paper buckled and waved underneath us. It slapped our faces.

Roofing nails shot out like bullets—with the business end down, thank God Tetragrammy, or we would have been perforated. Black feelings thundered through us too, and the ones that you weren't wise to stuck.

Noah whimpered and he said, "I love my wife. She treats me like hell, and I love her. I can't help it."

And Leonard Fine said, "I love all women. But they don't love me, Noah. None of them can keep her eyes on me for half of a minute, I'm so ugly to them, and I lack manhood."

We were grappling inch by inch, tearing up tar paper to pull ourselves along, and bits of it flew across our backs like gnats, like shrapnel, like black flies, and like bats, but we were almost there.

Waxy said, "I've had all the women I want, and what good has it done me? Simon's right: Mr. Bigshot is a nothing. In a couple years it'll all be history. I'm slowing down, Leonard, and a new pair of balls or a bucket of Vitamin E won't change things. It isn't manhood that counts, Leonard. You're a saint and a wise man, Leonard. Crawl for Reb Sabbatai and the sixteen. Crawl."

Simon howled, "You want to talk women? A life like mine, nobody's suffered. I had it a body like Adonis— such a face, it would make you fall over dead to look at it. And brains? Nothing missing. And natures? I could satisfy a complete House of the Rising Sun from Rosh Hashanah to Yom Kippur, what they would insist to pay *me*. And still, three wives left me. Go figure. Oy, what I've suffered at the hands of the daughters of Eve!"

Even James said, "When you *tsadikim*, you Righteous Ones, have to live at a placement where the boys and the girls have to go to school in separate buildings on the same grounds and you have to not look at them out the window during their gym class and not say hello to them when they pass by, tits first, giggling like they do, and you've got a boner the size of an Olympic springboard and you can't do a thing about it—then you can talk."

And Shlomo said, "*Ne'bech!* Pity! Pity! Is life even worth living? You can't help but wonder."

My head felt like it was going to explode if I didn't put my two cents in. The Devil's breath curdled the air all around us. The Sears Roebuck was shaking, and the sky was dissolving on top of us. Nobody knew if my Jack was dead or alive. But I said, "You pricks, you don't know what it's like to be a female and to have you guys sniffing at your butt and treating you like crap if you don't roll over and die every time they try to lick your face. You make me sick."

And Abie said, "It's just the wind, the *farkakte* wind. *Liebe brider—und shvester*—don't listen to your heads." That shut us up. Then he said, "And if I wanted to, I could tell you things that would make the bunch of you feel ashamed that you would even claim to have from the other sex a suffering next to what I have a suffering. You should all be midgets like me."

But we reached the shaft. I careful sneaked my fingers under the cover board at a spot where it was warped, because otherwise, the way the wind was flapping it, it would have crushed my fingers. I couldn't budge the thing. I torched every muscle in my body, from my scalp all the way down to my toes, which they got charley horses tractioning against the roof. Big Shlomo pitched in, and the wind beat him down too. So the whole *minyan* leaned into it, and Sylvia put in a hand, and we did an Iwo Jima, Devil be damned, and we levered the front edge up about a yard and we balanced against it, weight for weight, and we crept along both sides of the shaft and we walked it up to vertical—and then the wind took it.

If you ever saw anything like it, God bless you, God Tetragram, Who is the A and the Z, Who was, Who is, and Who's going to be, the whole entire time up to the end, which is pretty soon now, and *yud, hay, vov, hay*, is how to spell Him, *YHVH* in English, if you don't know the holy language, which I'm definitely going to learn pretty soon. God Tetragram bless you, if you ever saw anything like that tar-papered plywood twisting and dancing on top of the roof and launching up into the black sky.

I watched its tar paper shred and shed like clothes off a stripper. The thing leapt all over the roof and every time it touched down, it splintered and it sent shattered wood flying like daggers and arrows. That board was alive. That board had the Devil in it, because I gave it a look and I squeezed James's hand, which he was pressed flat to the rooftop next to me, and James understood and he did his part, and that plywood board exploded into wood pulp and blew away like snow.

And the wind stopped. And the sky opened up like a peeled stomach that they pin back for an autopsy. Everything was as still as the grave. The Devil was eye-balling us, that's what. The Devil was done batting us from one paw to another to watch us scramble, is how I felt, and now he was about to bite and swallow. The *minyan* was scared to death. We were shivering at the edge of the shaft, and Abie started to sing again:

"Ghi di di di! Ghi di di diddy di di!"

And all the *minyan* sang:

"Ghi di di di! Ghi di di diddy di di!"

And I said, "Do like this."

And I swung my legs over into the shaft and I jumped...

It was like when something's on your mind and you think you've come to the last stair, but there's one more step down that you never figured on, and your hip goes out of whack, and your knees buckle, and your arms fly up.

It was all dark. Then it was all light. I could see the pain flash around me like the hull of a falling satellite burning white hot. I counted the order of the parts of me that hit: foot, other foot, knee, thigh, hip, ribs, shoulder, head, head, head, head...

Then it was all dark again.

chapter fourteen

Israel and Italy

This is the unknown part of my story, like the unknown section of Sears and Roebuck. I'm busting through the wall of my story—*vohu*—and me and you readers out there, we're coming together like the thirteen and the three, the way Jack laced his fingers, which is how the Thrice Chosens melt together when they meet. We're coming together like a deck of cards when you shuffle them and bridge them and knock the edges flush.

Most people have everything they want in the known section of Sears and Roebuck; it's full of merchandise of every variety, and different prices if you want a regular or a deluxe or practically anything you could think of. You don't have to go anyplace else. You don't have to go pounding on the walls to see if they are hollow and maybe there's a hidden section with other stuff, if you can get everything you want right there where everybody gets it. What's the point, am I right?

So this is what I am saying here: I'm giving you another chance to get out with your regular world in one piece. Maybe you don't want to get knocked flush with a person like me. Nobody's going to call you a name. I'll even tell you how things come out, so you won't worry about stuff.

First of all, I was okay. I wasn't hurt bad in the fall, and nobody got killed that night. You can take all the *meshuga'as* on the rooftop for what they call an "atmospheric anomaly," or for an aftereffect of Jack's hashish, which I had smoked in the taxi. (Later on, when I asked a guy who lives in one of the welfare apartments over the liquor store across Monroe Avenue from the Wee Spot, how about that weather the other night, he said, what weather? Also Simon Black insisted that he never said any of the things I heard him say up there, and that everybody was crazy.)

Mrs. Solomon didn't divorce Noah Solomon or grind his *kishkes*, whatever those are supposed to be; she just cold-shouldered him for a week or two, which he was used to. Ishky, he didn't get on the wagon and he didn't get any worse either; he was the same *shi'ker* as always. The *minyan* kept on meeting, but they mostly played contract bridge and gin rummy after that, which they argued and *schmoozed* and ate pickled herring and other Yid food items, instead of *ghi diddy di* and all that. Rabbi Metzger got a job with a congregation in Cleveland.

There were a few things different, but you could live without knowing about them. It's like Jack said to me once: "All the *goyim* will stay below. You don't have to worry. For the *goyim*, everything will stay the same. You have your reward."

So you think about it and do what you have to do.

When I woke up, everything hurt, and I felt my arm dangling under me like a sausage on a string. I figured out that I was looking up and that the gargoyles lining the hole I was looking up through were the heads and shoulders of the *minyan* looking down at me. I was sprawled out on the roof of the elevator car. Somebody had slid the cover plate out from under me and was shining a flashlight up into the shaft. Lit from below, the *minyan* looked like goblins with faces made of shadows.

Then I heard Sarge down in the decompression chamber. He said, "I'm a sonuvabitch, it's Lea Tillim. Shit! If she's dead, Panaggio gonna eighty-six us for sure."

And I said, "I'll eighty-six you, you Uky asshole," which I shouldn't have, because it made my chest hurt and my head ache just to talk. But I gave him a little punctuation at the end with my middle finger of my goddam pendulum arm which I hoped was sticking right in his twisted sausage face. And it was like I found my bones and my muscles one at a time and I collected them and nothing was broken. But if I wasn't black-and-blue in three-quarters of a kajillion places, rain falls up, which it doesn't—even still.

From above: "Lea, you okay?"

I said, "Somebody moved the goddam service elevator! It's a floor too low!" On my aching back, I wiggled and slid away from the hatch. Right away, Waxy and Manny pulled out their guns and aimed them down at full arm's length at the hoods in the decompression chamber. I peeked in, and what I saw made my blood run cold, even after the shit storm up on the roof.

There were three guys in there—Sarge, a punk in a black motorcycle jacket with chains and studs and with Vaseline in his hair, and a guy who looked like a prize porker, practically round, but with a puss like a steam shovel, grit and steel. Each of them was holding a chain saw, and the elevator car was loaded with red gallon cans of gasoline.

I looked up, and I caught James's eye. Nobody had to tell me which one it was; it was my brother's eye. And I looked down at Sarge with a look that could kill, and I felt James get behind it, and Sarge winced, and he said, "No! Stop it! Please don't hurt me! You don't understand!"

The Vaseline kid hit the elevator control stick, which I never even knew worked, and the car shook and started to move up. Manny squeezed one off, and the report nearly busted my eardrums, and the bullet ricocheted off the floor of the elevator and pinged and the car stopped with a jerk so sudden and strong that I flew up a whole foot and crashed back down like a pancake being flipped.

Sarge said, "Jesus God damn me! We're all on the same side together here for crissakes. Get your psychic goddam claw off my gut and stop shooting a man."

Abie shouted, "Talk." James and me let up.

Sarge said, "What do you think, we got a Texas chain antimacassar? We don't want to hurt the Yid. You think we want to hurt the Yid? Mr. Panaggio and the Yid, they're big friends now. Mr. Panaggio, he say, go down to Hardware Department and bring us up some merchandise, that's all. Sonuvabitch, we gonna help make *vohu* out

of the goddam Light Sponge. That's all we're doing here.
Everybody family here. Israel, Italy—and goddam
Ukraine. All family. All bust through the sonuvabitch
wall. Goddam Messiah don't come back till the Yids are
back in the Promised Land, I'm gonna say. All big pals,
huh?"

Abie said, "What do you think, Waxy?"

And Waxy said, "I think we should blow their fucking
heads off while we got a clear shot."

And Manny said, "Sounds like a plan."

And Rabbi Metzger got down into his lower octave
and he did a Humphrey Bogart that I know they didn't
teach him in rabbi school, and he said, "Kill the fuckers.
I'll say the prayer for the dead over them," and he started
to chant:

"*Yisgadal v'yiskadash sh'may rahbaw...*"

Sarge and Porky and Vaseline all dropped their chain
saws, and they got down on their knees and they raised up
their hands, and it was one of the tastiest little bird's-
eye views I ever had. They said, "Please, please, don't hurt
us. We're on your side. It's all of us against the Devil," and
like that.

And Abie, he said, "You know what Lea can do to you,
without even a gun?"

Sarge said, "Yes. Yes."

And Abie said, "Lea, can you make it down into the
elevator?"

And I said, "Sure thing, Abie. I'm okay." Which was a
lie, but I'd been in plenty of pain before, and I knew I
could manage.

And Abie said, "Go in. If anybody bothers you . . ."

The three guys in the elevator said, "We won't. We won't."

". . . Kill them all, *und fartik*."

And I said, "Sure thing, Abie. No sweat. *Fartik*." I careful eased my legs through the hatch, which hurt in my joints and on my skin, but I lowered myself in. I used all the arm muscle I could, so I didn't have to jump more than a few inches. I knocked aside a few gasoline cans coming down, and I was in the middle of the bruisers. I looked bloody murder at Sarge, and I swear he flinched, and I enjoyed it, but it was a lucky thing James didn't take me serious and kill him on the spot.

Then Abie said, "Bring the elevator up a floor to the spaceship."

The Vaseline kid worked the lever again, and we moved up to the spaceship floor. Panaggio's thugs, including my boss Sarge, were regular lambikins. I looked at my face in the polished metal cover of the old emergency phone box, and I could hardly recognize who I saw there. Never mind the purple swelling on my fine goddam cheekbone and the black smears of tar paper—I had *hair*.

Can hair grow that much in a night? You tell me. From a crew cut, which is what it had been the last I remembered, when I was Estée Laundering and Maybellining and L'Oréal Colorviving and Cover Girl Long 'n Lushing for the fights, in Bobson's bathroom mirror, it was up to a pageboy practically. I could tell that when I washed my face and when my swelling went down and my internal bleeding healed up, I was going to be a world-class looker and no mistake.

That's what life is, believe me. That's how the Big Tet

has it all laid out: shit in a cone, but with jimmies. It keeps you going.

Once the elevator was up to the right place, the *minyan* jumped down one by one. Waxy and Shlomo and hunchback Manny climbed in first to make sure Sarge and his two pals kept acting peaceable. Ishky helped Sylvia inside last of all, right after old Simon Black, who creaked and moaned like a loose plank. Sylvia hung on to Ishky. She didn't say a word. She kept shifting her head and looking around as if her eyes still worked, except that the eyes were out of synch with how the head moved, and you could tell.

We all of us just fit in the decompression chamber, with maybe enough spare room to hiccup and maybe not. The *minyan* straightened out their *talleisim*, which there were elbows in people's faces and shoulders in your neck and a butt against your stomach. Then they stood very tall and solemn in their blue-and-white striped shawls with the fringe, which said on them in Hebrew, "Blessed art thou, oh Lord our God, King of the Universe, Who commanded us concerning the wearing of *talleisim*!" They were facing the door to the spaceship, and they were ready to rumba, never mind that they were every mother's son of them so scared to death that the elevator trembled from their shakes.

James leaned over and whispered in my ear, "Lea, there's something I have to tell you. Sometimes I do bad things and I don't know why. It scares me." James looked around to see if anybody was listening, and, yeah, a couple guys were craning their stupid necks, but when James looked, they looked away and tucked in the fringes of their *talleisim* or whatever.

So James went on. "I mean, I'm okay, I can take care of you like always, but I'm scared of doing bad things, is all. If I do anything bad, please, I gotta know you'll forgive me."

Guys. I gave his arm a special squeeze, and I whispered back, and I said, "James, you're a goddam angel. Now that you and me are back together, everything is gonna be aces. Don't worry about a thing, you lummox."

I pulled the metal gate open, me, Lea Tillim. Shlomo reached past Porker to the big, steel-braced wooden doors, which they were always half out of their tracks. He was going to pull them open, when this noise came from inside the spaceship: slamming, cracking, and crumbling. The elevator doors shook. We heard yelling inside, too. The shaft rumbled all around us, and Simon said, "*Der Teivel klopt zich.*"

I said, "What?"

And Sylvia said, "The Devil. It's medieval High German. He's saying that the Devil is knocking about." Sylvia herself, she sounded like the Devil knocking about. That girl had stripped a couple of gears on the way up Mount Nebo.

Sarge started to talk, but Waxy smartened him up with a tug at the collar. James snaked his hand through two or three bodies to find my hand, and we held hands, and I was ready. The pounding kept up, rhythmic and hard. I knew that Waxy and Manny had a hand on their guns, but everybody was looking to Abie, and Abie gave a nod, and Shlomo pulled the wooden doors. The doors screeched and groaned and jumped into their tracks— and they slid open.

The spaceship was thick with plaster dust and sawdust,

which wrinkled my nose the minute the doors opened. Bright light poured out. Our eyes were squinty from the dark of the decompression chamber, so it was a minute before we could tell what was going on. They had run extension cords through a hole in the west wall and clipped up floodlights in aluminum shells all along the Gold Sky. Light bounced up from the Gymseal on the Mirror Below and it twinkled through the dust like swamp goblins.

The Fleshpot was on my left, which a couple guys were sitting on the floor mopping their foreheads with *schmattes* and staring at it. The Holy of Holies was on my right; it was still covered with the purple velour, only there was a transparent plastic drop cloth over it. Some kid was poking under the drop cloth, whisking off the cope and feathering it with a lint brush. It was the same kid who had stiff-armed Jack in the parking lot, is what I was thinking, but now Jack was telling the kid what to do, and the kid was doing it. Matter of fact, Jack was telling everybody what to do, which I'll come to in a second.

I told you about the Gold Sky and I told you about the Mirror Below. I couldn't see the Pyramid Wall, because my head was in the middle of El Gizah, where I was peeking out of the decompression chamber at the time, but the point is: They were busting through the west wall. It was all fractured drywall, two layers of it, a sheet on either side of the upright two-by-fours. Pieces of busted drywall hung by their flat black latexed skin. As the dust settled, you could see through big holes into the known section of Sears and Roebuck.

A security guard on the other side was even helping break off the loose chunks. He shuffled and yes-manned

Mr. Panaggio, which proves who runs that particular Sears and Roebuck.

Everybody had a hand in. Guys had peeled down to their T-shirts, even Panaggio, the big man himself. You could tell who he was by the elevation of his chin and because he kept his John B. Stetson on. They were swinging sledgehammers, busting through the wallboard, and knocking the studs right off their toenailed spikes or shattering them outright. Plaster showered from the ceiling where the studs pulled out.

That's what the racket was. It wasn't the *Teivel klopping*—it was Jack and the hoods making *vohu*.

"Rabbi," I said, "I figured something out." I caught an edge of his *tallis* and tugged. "The sky and the Light Sponge are opening up together. The bad guys pour through the sky hole, just like the *Meschiach* hitches up at the *vohu*. Equal and opposite, like Newton in second period General Science, just before I stopped going. Every *klop* against the drywall *klops* through a piece of sky at the same exact time."

I said so, and Rabbi Metzger tousled my brand-new hair and he said, "A *chachem*!"

And I said, "*Chachem*?"

And Sylvia heard me, and she said in her shell-shocked voice, "Hebrew: *wise person*. Or else, *stupid person*—according to usage." And I looked at her, which she had this empty grin on her face.

But the point is, I was a *chachem*.

Sarge said, "I told you we were all on the same team, yeah? We brought up the sledges—twenty pounds, forty pounds—and lightbulbs and wire. That's what we was doing moving the freight elevator. Then we get the chain saws, just like the Yid tells us. Louie Panaggio, he says do what the Yid tells you, just like the US of A Army working for a goddam UN general—in Gaza or what. We're all fighting the Devil here, and even the Pope hates the goddam Devil's guts, don't he? Sonuvabitch, you gonna believe a guy, or what?"

And Rabbi Metzger said, "*K'vanna*. The *goyim* have realized *k'vanna*, praise God Tetragrammaton, and the spaceship will be preserved."

I squeezed out of the decompression chamber and I ran to Jack, and I didn't feel my sprains and bruises one iota, and I threw my arms around him and I kissed him with my whole face practically. He was bare-chested; he was wearing long underwear, but he had peeled out of the top and it hung out the back of his pants, with the sleeves trailing down like tux tails. And he was sweaty and gritty, which I felt with my hands all over his back and his shoulders. He was trying to talk, but I swallowed him up, and he started laughing.

Denny Love was nearby. He was swinging his sledge, and on every swing he sang a line of a song. He sang:

"Were you there when they crucified my Lord?"
BAM!
"Were you there when they nailed Him to the
    cross?"
BAM!
"Oh, sometimes I just can't cease from trembling!"
BAM!
"Were you there when they crucified my Lord?"
BAM!

* * *

Finally, I let Jack get a word in, while I just laid my cheek in the hollow of his shoulder, and he said, "Are they here yet? Are they coming in?"

James came out of the decompression chamber, and he said, "We're all here, Yakov. All ten."

Jack wiped the sweat out of his eyes, and he said, "Ten? Who are you? Ten? Not thirteen?"

And James said, "I'm the other Yakov, Yakov the Bull, the guy who replaced Menachem. The whole ten of us are here, Yakov, the whole *minyan*."

And Jack said, "*Minyan*. Ah. Good. Good. But haven't the thirteen started to arrive? The Evil One is reaching the height of his power. Didn't the sky open up? Have you had the bloody moon and the tongues of fire and the beasts and the wind?"

Abie made his way out of the decompression chamber between everybody's legs and he came up to us, his *tallis* dragging behind him. While the others shoved and slipped out through the elevator doors, Abie said, "Yes, yes, Yakov, the sky opened and we had everything. But we haven't seen the other Thrice Chosens yet."

Panaggio threw down his sledgehammer and barked at Jack, "I don't know why the fuck I should bust my ass if you're going to stand there jawboning."

Jack didn't seem to hear the guy. "It's got to be soon. They must be on their way." Then he did a double take at James. "The nose ring—are you Lea's nose ring guy?"

I said, "Jack, this is my brother James."

And Jack screwed up his eyes at James, and he said, "You've got a talent."

I said, "He's like me." And I explained to Jack how it

worked and how we all knew that he, Jack, had got the talent too.

And he said, "It's because the time is upon us. All the Thrice Chosen are realizing powers and circumstances that will enable them to come here faster than thought, once *vohu* is established in the Light Sponge. This is the word of Reb Sabbatai."

And the *minyan* said, "Amen."

Panaggio's boys were fueling up the chain saws now, and it stank gas stink. From the looks of them, they might set the whole place on fire or saw off everybody's arms and legs by accident before they came in range of the Light Sponge.

Waxy introduced himself to Panaggio, who doffed his Stetson to him. Then Waxy took a chain saw and started cutting down studs, and Panaggio helped Shlomo *shlep* the fallen wood the hell out of the Light Sponge. The lookout kid was running around spilling buckets of water on everything to wet down all the dust, which somebody was afraid would ruin the albedo. Guys in the *minyan* were starting to pitch in, sledging and sweeping, and mainly arguing about the best way to bust out the rest of the west wall.

But all this time Jack and James, they were standing eyeball-to-eyeball in the middle of the spaceship. Jack still had an arm around me, but I could feel it going kind of itchy and cold. I said, "Jack?" but he didn't seem to hear me.

And Jack said to my brother: "It's you, isn't it?"

Panaggio heard him, and he came over and he said, "Is this one of them? Is this one of your fucking thirteen? Then how come you ain't going like this?" And Panaggio laced his fingers together like Jack must have shown him.

James didn't say anything. He had that dark look again. Then he kind of smiled in a way that made me nervous. I said, "James?"

And Jack said, "Isn't it?"

And James said, "The game is over, Jew boy."

chapter fifteen

Mrs. Bobson's
Marquetry Ladies

You figure the worst is over. You've bottomed out. Things are still plenty bleak, but there's a patch of blue. Maybe the world is falling apart, but, hell, inside your heart, you figure, you've been to hell and back; so whatever comes, you can take it.

It's like, you're back in the kitchen now, having breakfast with the ones you love. There's a splash of sunlight on your plate, your belly is full of pancakes, and the taste of maple syrup is on your tongue. Maybe you open up the papers, and you read where those killer bees that wiped out all the cattle in Texas are headed north. In five years or so those bees will be buzzing up your nose and licking the maple syrup off your tongue after they've stung you to death along with everybody else.

And you figure, okay. Because, actually, that's not the

big deal. Bees are not the big deal. The big deal is inside your kitchen, where the ones you love are. Inside your heart, there is peace.

Then the light shifts. The sun goes behind a cloud. You look around and you notice how stiff and phony everybody is smiling. That song Mom likes to sing, actually, the words are pretty stupid. And in your heart, all the warm and lovely items turn out to be lies. You think about bees.

All at once I wondered why it hadn't registered how much James's eyes had become like sky holes. They made you cringe to look into them with their jaundiced little moons. Eyes like that don't see you. Eyes like that just want to do something to you. Eyes like that don't see anything. They twist the whole universe into whatever pleases them.

Those eyes bored into me, and I felt the names of everything I loved change, so I could never call them or find them. The nearest things became so far away, it would take years even to begin to think about them. I was all alone—except for those eyes. I couldn't find Jack's arm. I couldn't find my body.

Sledgehammers dropped. Chain saws went dead and clickety-clicked until they stopped. Denny Love started to say the Lord's Prayer. And the rabbi, dumb with fear, elbowed little hunchbacked Abie, and Abie sang:

"*Kohani-im!*"

And James said, "You've only got nine."

Abie stopped. Everybody stopped. James reached over and eased Jack's granny glasses right off his nose. Jack looked so weak without his glasses! And James held the granny glasses up with two fingers right between his eyes and Jack's eyes. Then James opened his fingers and let the glasses fall. He twisted his foot and he crushed them and ground them into the Mirror Below.

Mr. Panaggio said, "You..."

And James turned to look at him. "What?"

"You...you...you..." Panaggio fell to his knees choking.

And James's voice was as smooth as Slivovitz and he said, "You're not quite through the west wall, are you? Don't you realize that every mote of dust and every bit of plaster and wood must be entirely cleared away before the other twelve Thrice Chosen Ones of the earthly sphere respond? Did not the great *Talmud chochem* Sabbatai Levi Hagodol tell you that?"

I wanted to say, What have you done with my brother? I wanted to say, Wake me up, someone, please, because I'm having a nightmare. But I couldn't. I was lost in a vast strange city where people took me for a dustball or a vapor or a wrinkle in someone's brow. I cried and I cried— Here I am! Here I am!—but no sound came out, and no tear fell. I felt like a TV ghost, half an inch out of my skin and on a funny channel.

We were like department store mannequins, all of Panaggio's guys and all of Jack's guys, and James was strolling through us. He cocked his head at one, raised his brow at another, twisted one's nose, and pushed another one to the floor by his hand on the guy's face. He spat in Manny's face, then he pulled out Manny's handkerchief from his hip pocket. Manny's pistol was caught in the hanky and it fell to the floor, bang! Then James wiped his spit off of Manny's face for a joke, with Manny's own hanky.

James laughed. "The congregation of the thirteen has been delayed. But my congregation has not been delayed. My congregation will be arriving momentarily."

He strode to the west wall, to the couple of remaining studs and broken soda crackers of drywall. The uniformed security guard on the other side was drooling like an idiot and staring at the sign that said *Returns and Repairs*. James said, "Go down to the main floor. Go to the front entrance and let in the people whom you will find there."

The guard crossed the known section of Sears and Roebuck, which was all carpeted and lit with neon lights and air-conditioned and full of items and with stanchions that had signs on them that told you where to go for bedding and for appliances and for cutlery and for men's casual ware and for the restrooms, and he turned a corner and went out of sight.

Time passed, but there was nothing in it. It was just cold and empty like a dead child's room.

James strolled. He stopped in front of the Fleshpot, and he touched himself like he was going to jerk off right there in front of us all, but then he turned and winked and made a joke of it. He checked out the pyramids. He said, "I had you then. I held you faster than you know. Moses was mine. I gave you manna on the desert. I led you in a pillar of cloud by day and by night in a pillar of flame. And how did you repay me, faithless ones? You betrayed me utterly and prostituted yourselves unto him whose name is four letters, cursed be he." He stormed over to Jack. "You want to kill me, don't you?"

Jack didn't say a word. He stared straight in the Devil's eye.

And James said, "You have the talent. Go ahead. Kill me." And James laughed. "You can't kill me without killing the *shiksie's* brother."

Rabbi Metzger inched forward like a locust cracking out of its old, dead skin. Through his locked-shut teeth, he managed to say, "Prince of Lies! It was Lord God Tetragrammaton Who led us through the desert! Moses was His servant!"

"No, Moses was mine. My hand was mighty. My arm was outstretched."

Jack croaked, "What do you want?"

And James said, "I want you to face reality, Jack. There is no supernal *Ish-ra-el*. Look around, Jack. This is the world. If you want it, take it. Lay up your treasure here."

Then, in a voice like a steam leak from a radiator, Noah Solomon said, "He's got a point."

Laughter tinkled from far away, through corridors and stairwells in the known section of Sears and Roebuck. It came closer. Heels clacked and slippers shuffled. I thought I heard panting and scratching too.

Then, from across the crumbled partition: "Land sakes, girls, wouldn't that coverlet be just perfect with the light greens in my upstairs room?" And then Belle Bobson sashayed around the corner with the security guard at her arm. She was with four other old ladies in slips and night-ies, and one of them had on a nightcap, which looked like a doily bonnet. Belle was the only one wearing normal clothes, because of how she'd been up entertaining guests in the cellar.

The last one rounded the corner, walking backward and tugging at three leather straps. "Come on. Come on. Be good boys." There was some wheezing and growling and huffing, and then three creatures at the other end of those leashes scrambled into sight: human beings. They had choke collars around their necks, and they were down on their hands and knees. Their clothes were so ripped and ragged that it hung off them like peeled sunburns, which they looked practically nude, and it was Morano and Benito and Aces, slobbering like dogs. Mr. Morano's civvies were shredded so that every time he stretched a certain way, his penis would poke out through the cloth.

Mr. Morano shook himself all over, and slush flew off his skin, first from his head, his jowls flapping like a boxer dog's, then from his shoulders and his gut. He even shook his hairy ass and his legs, one at a time. Benito and Aces shied away from Morano like fine ladies on a rainy day when a car splashes.

The dogs' mistress said, "Heel. Heel." And they heeled. And then they jumped in front of her. Aces, the big-shouldered one, was frothing and straining at the choker. His hind legs were on the floor but his arms were up in the air, pawing. He just stayed so, like a kite on a string, turning red in the face, until his mistress gave him a yank and he settled down. She led the dog-men to where Belle was drifting around through Returns and Repairs.

Those ladies were Belle Bobson's marquetry ladies. I had seen one or two of them coming out of her house after I closed the Wee Spot, and I'd wondered why they would be there so late. I figured I knew now: They'd been worshipping their King of Hell. All they'd ever seen of him was maybe a fork-tailed red guy on a bottle of hot sauce. This was going to be their first run-in with the genuine article.

The leash lady said, "Belle, these dog-people are a handful. These are the most spirited ones ever. Do you think we should sacrifice them, or what?"

But it looked like Belle didn't hear her, because she had wandered right up to the known side of our west wall, and she was shading her eyes from the glare of the floodlights and staring in. And Belle said, "Dixie, Mabel, Sisi, Jonette, come and look at this."

James smiled at her and waved.

We were mummified from the spell that the Evil One in James had cast on us. Panaggio was still on his knees, head bowed, breathing through his mouth. His wall-buster guys were planted like statues, staring into space. The *minyan* was scattered around the spaceship, every one of them looking like they had quite a bit to say, but not one syllable came out.

James fixed those moon-hole eyes of his on the marquetry ladies. "It is I, Satan, your sworn master. I spoke unto Belle, and I bade her summon you to me."

The four of them huddled behind Belle broke out in a terrible fit of screaming and shrieking and carrying on all over Returns and Repairs and on into Catalog Orders. The three dog-people howled and ran wild until Belle made them all shut up and calm down. She made the leash lady rein in Mr. Morano and Benito and Aces again, but they kept whimpering.

And James said, "Come nigh unto me that I may tell thee my pleasure, dark sisters."

One of them shook her head full of different-colored

plastic curlers and she elbowed the others and she said, "Oh my God, this is it. All the stuff Belle ever told us and showed us was gospel true, and, ladies, if I ever disbelieved one word of it, I'm deadly awful sorry." She gawked at the Fleshpot and when she saw the Pyramid Wall, her mouth dropped open. "This is the Devil's Temple, and it's right here on Monroe Avenue!"

And the oldest one of them, who looked like a boiled prawn in a pink nightie, said through the side of her mouth, "Sisi, shut up." And Sisi shut up.

Jack was like a guy trying to wake himself out of a dream, trembling and fidgeting. "I won't let you do this!"

And James smiled. "So kill me, Yakov."

Belle's marquetry ladies tramped after her right through the shattered studs. They came into the unknown section of Sears and Roebuck, is what I'm saying, right through the *vohu* and smack into the spaceship, them and their dog-people, who were sniffing and sneezing and raising their legs to piss. There wasn't a goddam one of them, ladies or dogs, that had a pisspot's worth of *k'vanna*. It was going to totally disable the spaceship.

And Jack couldn't stop them.

Belle Bobson stood square in front of James, but her eyes moved around the room, taking everything in. I saw them go wide when she spied me in Jack's arm; then her lips did a tightening, old lady thing. She didn't even say hello.

Then she said to James, "Land sakes, you don't look like the Devil."

"You want me to have horns and a forked tail?"

Sisi quickly said, "That's all right." After a minute, though, she got up her courage and she said, "Could you?"

And the old prawn lady said, "Shut up, Sisi."

Belle said, "You're using the body of the young man with the nose ring, aren't you? Oh, but that's not who you really are, is it? I mean, you've entered him. He didn't have you in him when he visited me before."

James said, "I've been in and out of this person since he became interested in Jack, because I am also interested in Jack, and I found it convenient to reside in someone who was getting close to him. The girl loves him too much, and the *minyan* is too feeble."

Belle Bobson bowed her head low and she said, "Oh Evil One, what will it please you to have us do?"

Then the other marquetry ladies bowed their heads low. They kind of curtsied and said, "Oh Evil One, what will it please you to have us do?"

James walked around from one guy to another, all still dopey and paralyzed. He dusted Shlomo's shoulders. He cleaned the side of his shoe on Panaggio's pant leg. He slapped Abie's cheek like it was a lump of clay. Nobody moved, but their eyes did. Their eyes followed James around the room, and so did mine. The Evil One played us like a pipe organ, now *you* can talk, and now *you*, and now *you* can drool, and now *you* can sigh.

And then he said, "The real world belongs to the Devil. Because you know this, you worship me."

The marquetry ladies, all except for Belle, they said, "Because we know this, we worship you." Belle was giving him the fish eye, watching him real smart and careful, is what I thought.

James said, "The real world is flesh and blood and sticks and mud and sea and air and fire. All this is mine."

"All this is yours."

"But these people want to subvert all that. These people want to milk and bleed the real world in order to puff up their *Ish-ra-el*." He said that word with a sneer that made you feel ashamed that you ever took it serious. Tears dripped down Rabbi Metzger's cheeks like splash dripping down a rock when the wind whips the waves up. Waxy got so red, I thought he was going to bust an artery. Simon Black's skin looked like a rubber dental dam, and I figured it was fifty-fifty he was already dead. James gave Manny Baranes a push, and he fell over, rigid, and rocked on his hump like an upside-down turtle.

James said, "I am the Great Physician. I am he who heals the minds of deranged and misguided beings. I have summoned you, my disciples, to cure their madness, to restore them to harmony with the material world, the Mother of all beings."

Sisi was so excited she was tugging at her curlers. She moved her head all around like a camera, like she was watching a Stephen King movie and loving every dreadful minute. "What do you want us to do?"

And the old prawn lady, who had skin like week-old filo dough, said, "Shut up, Sisi. He'll tell us when he's ready."

And Sisi said, "I won't. Because I love him. I love you, Satan, and I want to kiss you." And she charged him. The prawn lady grabbed her arm, but Sisi was stronger, and she dragged the prawn lady along, and the others shrieked like band freaks and charged James. The three dog-people on the leash plowed ahead of the four of them, and before you knew it, James was flat on his back. I thought, well, maybe the Devil isn't all he's cracked up to be. But then he stood up, flat as a plank, like a drawbridge rising. The four marquetry ladies and the dog-men, Morano and Benito and Aces, fell back.

"I am hellfire and damnation to those who obey not my will!"

"We obey!"

"Remove your clothes and defecate on the floor."

Sisi said, "What's 'defecate?'"

And the prawn lady said, "Shit! Shit!"

James said, "Do it there, by the pyramids. Do it there, under the pictures of women. Do it there, beside the Holy of Holies. And there, along the west wall. Defecate everywhere." He reached in under a flap of his coat that he was wearing and he pulled out a bottle of castor oil that I recognized from Belle Bobson's medicine chest—a blue bottle with a curly-edged label.

I was like a brain in a jar. I thought and thought: James in Belle's bathroom pocketing the castor oil, James in the alley kicking the dog. Good and bad. Bad and good. My James.

He said, "First, drink. Drink sisterhood in the Devil. This draught will fuel your ardor." They grabbed the bottle, and they passed it around and sucked most of it up in no time.

And James said, "Belle, you aren't drinking. Come, my prize, my beauty, my powerful one. I love you better than any of the others. I gave you your talent..."

"You didn't give me my talent," Belle said. The other four ladies swung round and stared at her like she was crazy. Even the dog-men stopped barking. "Land sakes, I always had my talent. You came after." Seemed like even the Devil was at a loss. "I spoke your name, I called on you and prayed to you and bent my knee to you after Lillian died, because the other one wouldn't help me. Now I see you right in front of me, right in the Monroe Avenue Sears and Roebuck's—and I want my *quid pro quo*."

"*Quid pro quo?*"

Belle Bobson looked the Devil in the eye, and she said, "I want my Lillian back. I'll shit, all right. I'll strip and I'll shit. I'll do whatever you want—but give me my Lillian."

"Done." The Devil walked to the Holy of Holies, smooth as a gurney, unnatural smooth. He threaded through the statue garden of me and Jack and Rabbi Metzger and Ishky, next to Sylvia, and Manny, still slightly rocking, and the others, which all of us were in the hell of wanting to stop him, and we couldn't. He took off the plastic drop cloth and he took off the purple cope between the bookcases, and there were like doors to a wardrobe, two narrow doors of old, dark, stained, and coffered wood. Each one of them had the sign of the *Kohayns* burned into it, the fingers spread like the latticework that a gazelle peers in through it. James the Devil opened them, and a dank smell and a chill wind came out of there—and Lillian was inside.

She was wearing a yellowy cream-colored shroud. You could see her bare feet underneath it, which they looked white and crumbly as feta cheese. Her pale little hands were folded together over her chest like two Thrice Chosens meeting. She was petite, just like her clothes, some of which I was wearing that exact moment. She had a pageboy haircut like the one I was working on. She was wearing so much makeup, I don't think she could even smile if she wanted to, but under all that foundation, I could tell, even though she was older and paler and had a happy childhood, it could have been me.

"Mother." Her voice was like dry rock cracking, and when her mouth moved her face split into little lines like a spiderweb.

"No." Jack's voice boomed out of him, but his lips barely moved. "This is a defilement and an illusion. No such abomination can come from the Holy of Holies. She is a mirage, Belle. A mirage."

"Lillian, dear?" Belle turned to James and she said, "I want her alive. I want her like she was before. I don't want the dead and stinking corpse of her."

And James said, "The earth is mine and everything on it and everything above it and everything under it, just as it is—no *Ish-ra-el*. I have given you your daughter, just as she is. Undress, Belle. All the coven, undress."

Jack shook a little bit out of the spell that James had put on us; he sweated and huffed like a carny busting the chain around his chest. He faced Belle and he said, "Belle, is that what you want?"

And I heard myself say, "Belle! Belle! Belle!" like my voice was a heartbeat. She looked at me and she looked at Lillian, and she looked at James, who was smiling. The coven was taking their clothes off, and the dog-men were yipping and howling.

And Belle screamed, "No!"

Belle's feelings flooded past me in waves like heat from a heat lamp. I could feel all the colors of them. It was like when I would see someone inside, the squiggly glow of them, before they died. I could feel her like I felt the cat on the car top on Monroe Avenue the night Jack had said, "Kill for me. Kill for me now."

James's eyes and mouth shot open so wide that I thought his face might rip apart. His arms and legs jerked out; counting his head, which his hair was all on end, he was practically a perfect pentacle. He had to squeeze and grunt his face and his body back together as if he were peeling them off a crucifix where Belle had nailed them. "Hag!" His voice was a landslide now; it hurt my ears. "You think you can harm me, decrepit mortal?"

Belle fell back onto her butt as if she'd been punched in the gut. She took a few deep breaths and lifted her head. Her eyes were as fiery as his! "For her I can." I couldn't tell if she meant Lillian or me.

She nodded slightly—that's all I saw Belle do, but James gasped and stumbled backward until he hit the wall. Then he staggered forward a few steps, he tried to say something—all that came out was "Ak...ak...ak...!"— and then he fell flat on his face, like a sheet of plywood tipping and slamming to the floor.

Belle stretched out one trembly hand in front of her, like when you go to take a rat out of a trap which you're not completely sure is dead. She crept toward him real slow. She touched his hair—and it was my James's hair, and she tousled it and began to get weepy. And she touched his forehead, and it was my James's forehead, and she started to fall down onto her knees to cry, but then she touched James's cheek, and his body jumped like a live power line. Sparks shot out of his skin, and he did his drawbridge trick again, and it was the Devil.

He shot up so fast, as if his toes were hinged to the floor, that his head knocked Belle under the chin, and she lurched back practically to the *vohu*. One more dead, is what I thought. I lost Julian, and I lost my dad, and my mom didn't make it, and my James he came back but then he was the Devil, and now I was going to lose Mrs.

Bobson, the old bag who loved me, and I realized: I loved her too.

From where I stood frozen, I could see Belle clutching her heart and panting. The Devil, who I saw from behind, rushed toward her. He could have been lava flowing down from a volcano, from which you can run but it's going to get you. He could have been gas from the showers at Auschwitz. He could have been water rising and the ship is sinking and everybody's life is history.

Then Belle did something funny. Her head kind of angled and she squinted and said, "James, honey?" And he slumped forward into her arms, that she had to bend her knees to keep from getting knocked over, but she caught him and she held him up, and it was James, and the doors of the Holy of Holies crashed shut.

I shouted, "James!" and I ran to him, and I laid my cheek on his head.

And he turned his head, and he looked at me, and it was my brother, and I kissed him, and he said, "What happened?"

I only just began to tell him, when he started to cry, and he shook his head and said, "I'm sorry. I'm so sorry. The Evil One badgered me and burgled my mind and defiled me and used me, and I should have told everyone, but I thought I was strong enough to control it. Lea, I nearly killed you once, at the Wee Spot. Oh, all I've done! All I've done!"

chapter sixteen

We Establish <u>Vohu</u>

The marquetry ladies whooped and pulled up their drawers. They galloped out of the unknown section of Sears and Roebuck and scattered down the hallways looking for the little room. Panaggio came to himself and barked at the three dog-men, and he said, "Jesus fucking Christ, look at yourselves! Get your asses over to Men's Casuals and dress yourselves decent, you crackpots!" They didn't know what was going on or how they had gotten to be that way, but they did what Panaggio said. Practically before he was done saying it, they were hopping and sprinting out of there with their arms crossed to hide their butts and their balls.

Then Panaggio looked at Waxy and said, "You okay, my friend?"

Waxy looked shell-shocked. He glanced around here

and there like a chicken pecking, like his mind had to take in a little bit at a time because, brother, the main gates were shut. But he got over it quick, and he said, "Yeah, sure. Sure I'm okay. So, are we clearing out the goddam *vohu* or what? Manny, pick up your weapon, for heaven's sake. Shlomo, what about that chain saw?"

The *minyan* came to life. Mr. Black was still breathing and even bitching—didn't anybody care that his scratches were bleeding through the dressings? Ishky had Sylvia in tow.

Jack joined me over my brother James, then I heard Belle shuffle near, and she was all over me. She was kneeling beside me, which I knew was hellfire on her joints, and she was kissing me on my head—I had practically a pageboy, remember—and she was saying, "It's you, Lea. You're my Lillian, honey. You're alive and she's dead. You can stay with me always."

And I said, "No, Belle, I'm going with the Chosens. I have to go along to the Promised Land to interpret the *goyim*. Reb Sabbatai told me in a vision at the Memorial Arena."

"Oh, Lea, dear!" She was about to fall apart if she didn't have a quick dose of Bing, is what I was thinking.

But then Jack said, "Belle, you saved us all. How? How? I thought you couldn't kill the worm without killing the host."

Belle covered her mouth with her hand. She held herself and trembled and cried petite, civilized little old lady tears. She didn't look up, but she said, "Land sakes, I've had my talent forever. You're just a chick, is what you are. I know how to do more than that. I know how to do things that would make your hair stand on end, even after all you've seen—but I am a discreet person. I just want my little family, goddammit to hell. Why can't I have that anymore? It's not like I'm headed for *Ish-ra-el* like you boys. I just want my little nook."

And Rabbi Metzger said, "The Devil is no match for a woman who knows her own heart."

Simon Black said, "Nobody saved anybody. This is a mass hysteria. Nothing happened here, *und fartik*."

"Help me." That's what Sylvia said in a strangled mouse voice. "Can you help me, Mrs. Bobson?" She was still snug to Ishky like a spoon on a spoon. "Can you kill the things inside me that are killing me, and make me live?"

And Mrs. Bobson said, "No, honey, I'm afraid I can't. If I could, don't you know, I would have saved my husband Al. His lungs were full of cancer, and I could see every cell of them like you're seeing me now, but they were too many for me to pick them out from the good ones. I'm so sorry. I don't know how to do that."

"Like amoebas and vorticellas," I said, but nobody understood except Jack and James.

Sylvia's head fell like a puppet head with a chopped string. I felt pretty awful about things. I'd promised Sylvia I'd help her, but it had been a dodge, a rotten dodge, even if it was for Jack.

Abie came then, and he helped Belle up. Panaggio called over the guard who had let the marquetry ladies in and said, "Take her home. Do you think you can manage that?" And the guard came and took her under her shoulders and led her away into the known section of Sears and Roebuck.

Before they were out of sight, I shouted after her, and

I said, "Belle!" She turned her head. She was tired. She was old. She wasn't going to live much longer. I said, "Take care of Tule for me." And she smiled.

Abie said, "Yakov, won't he come back, the Devil? What will we do then?"

Jack said, "We've got to finish opening the west wall. The thirteen have to gather. Things have gone too far to stop."

Shlomo started up one of the chain saws, but Rabbi Metzger yelled, "Stop. Wait." And Shlomo turned it off. It whined and clicked and went dead. "On the High Holidays, we blow *shofar* to fool the Devil into thinking that the Messiah has already come. What do you say? Maybe it would buy us a minute."

Abie looked at Jack. "We remembered Jericho, and we brought the *shofars*—for the liftoff, Yakov."

Jack nodded.

Rabbi Metzger shouted, "*Tekia!*"

All the *minyan* guys scrambled for their *shofars*. They pulled them out of pockets and pouches and belts, five rams' worth of them, and they blew. They came in at all different moments. They sputtered and slid up and down the scale, and flapped their lips like a Bronx cheer, some of them, trying to make the long blast of the *tekia*, which is a Yid musical note. They were not the Boston Philharmonic. They weren't even a mariachi band. But they definitely had *k'vanna*.

And Rabbi Metzger said, "*Shevarim-terua!*" And they blasted and blasted and the whole Sears and Roebuck shook, both the known and the unknown, and Panaggio and his guys all squinted and plugged their ears with their fingers, which so did me and Sylvia. They must have blown fifty *tekias* and twenty or thirty *shevarims* and I don't know how many *teruas*, and everybody was mostly deaf, and Rabbi Metzger said, as near as I could make it out, "Now the west wall!" and guys started in with the chain saws again.

Dawn comes so late in the goddam winter. Up where we lived, up in the snowbelt, what with the lake effect and the sky which is so overcast all the time there are kids who wouldn't know about the sun except they've seen pictures of it in storybooks, and there's practically the equivalent sunshine of maybe a square inch on the ocean bottom, and under a rock down there—a rock that's buried in the sand—it's not unusual for dawn to come sometime in the middle of the afternoon. But you could feel it beginning to insinuate daytime. You could feel the smudged window of the south wall start to brighten.

The whole spaceship was scrubbed immaculate. The ex-dog-men were giving the Mirror Below a spit and polish. Panaggio's guys *shlepped* the busted wall right out through Returns and Repairs in wheelbarrows they got down below in Hardware. Guys were starting to clean up. They were washing their hands. They were straightening their clothes or they were getting replacement items from Men's Casual. *Minyan* guys and Panaggio guys were waxing intimate. Shlomo had learned how to say "*Mingya!*" properly, and he was working on "*Bafungu!*" Old Simon taught Panaggio himself the difference between *shlimazel* and *shlemiel* and why it wasn't so good to call a person a *schmuck*, but Sarge said *shmegegge* actually was a Uky word, but the Yids could have it if they wanted, and it was okay by him. Sylvia said Sarge was right, by the way. She was sitting by the sink, humming and rocking.

The point is, everybody was very friendly, though they had hated each other's *kishkes* a few hours before. I was starting to think maybe, yes, the *Meschiach* is on its way.

We sanded all along the scar in the walls and ceiling and floor where the west wall used to fit in. We filled and smoothed and feathered. There was hardly a grain of dust to show that there had ever been a partition there, but Leonard Fine found one. He licked the tip of his ring finger of his right hand and he touched it, and it stuck to his finger, and he removed it—and suddenly the Gold Sky turned jet-black. The Mirror below emptied of light, and it felt like you were walking on the stars and space that were the sky for all the people on the other side of the world. The Light Sponge glowed with supernatural light.

I don't know how we saw it. You would think that if you could see it, if the glow could touch your eyeball, then it would touch other stuff too, and guys' faces and stuff lying around would have some of that glow reflecting off of it, but no! We just saw it, but it wasn't pumping out any light, not even like moonlight. We just saw it. It was a bubbleskin of something like light.

Mr. Morano, who was now wearing a blue blazer with a fleur-de-lis on the pocket from Men's Casual, was on the other side of the Light Sponge when it lit up. He seemed like he was a kajillion miles away, like on television via satellite, but he could stick his arm through or his whole body and walk through, and back and forth, and other guys back-and-forthed and nothing bad happened to them, and they didn't feel like they had gone a kajillion miles. Only, there, you felt like you were walking on the floor of Sears Roebuck, Monroe Avenue, and here, you were walking on the sky over China.

And Jack said, "We have *vohu*."

Everybody cheered. Panaggio got down on his knees and started saying Hail Marys. I was so excited I could have jumped through the Gold Sky, which was pitch-dark now. I threw my arms around Jack, and I kissed him, but he wasn't paying much attention to me. He was smiling and looking around the spaceship, at the *vohu*, at the service elevator door, and at the window in the Fleshpot. I kissed him harder and I hugged him harder, and he didn't respond and he didn't respond, and so I let my arms go limp and I pulled my face off him and I took a step back—and he still didn't respond.

James hugged me then, and he said, "Isn't it wonderful?"

And I said, "Yeah."

And then James hugged somebody else and said, "Isn't it wonderful?"

And suddenly Sylvia was all over the place. Sylvia. She was going from *minyan* guy to *minyan* guy and from Panaggio guy to Panaggio guy. She was hugging them and laughing and crying and she didn't need a seeing-eye dog either, because the minute she set her eyes on the *vohu* it restored her sight, *und fartik*. She blabbed in Italian and Aramaic and Hebrew and Yiddish and Ukrainian and Moon, for all I know. And then she was in Jack's arms. In Jack's.

The point is, I wasn't.

Which is when the regional sales rep from the textiles supplier in Indiana comes drifting into Returns and Repairs, calling, "Hello? Hello?" We see her through the *vohu* as if it were on TV. And she sees Jack. I see her seeing him. I see him seeing her. She is wearing a dress suit with a snazzy red silk foulard, if you can believe it, and stockings and heels, and a sensible do, the whole deck, forty pips, twelve picture cards, and two jokers.

And the Yid lets go of Sylvia and he heads for the Light Sponge. Miss Dressed for Success drops her attaché and heads for him. Their arms penetrate the *vohu* like soaped fingers through a bubble, and it's just like what the Yid said it would be like when two of the earthly thirteen met, which they inter-goddam-lace. The rat bastard, what about me?

Tule said: *Oh, take it easy, Lea.* I heard her all the way from Belle Bobson's. I heard her in my mind. *You let yourself get pretty, didn't you, just like I told you, and it grew you up, honey baby. Your heart opened up, and you made a friend, and you got your brother back. Now you have to let Jack be Jack. It's not that he doesn't love you. He's got God Tetragrammaton's work to do, is all.*

And then I turned around, because someone was touching my shoulder, and it was James, and James said, "You understand, don't you, honey?"

I was angry. "You mean, I have my reward?"

The new woman was astonished. Jack waltzed her into the spaceship, and I watched her face. She was very mixed up, but it was the kind of mixed up where it's not because you don't know something, but because you do know something and you can't figure how you could possibly know it.

She said, "That's the Fleshpot. That's the Pyramid Wall. That's the Holy of Holies. I dreamed all this—over and over. Are you...Yakov?"

And the Yid said, "Yes," and he kissed her on the mouth.

At that particular juncture I had a regular civil war in my brains, and my talent was nowhere in sight. So I whispered to James, "Are you still my protector? Would you still kill anybody I wanted you to, no questions asked? Would you still follow my feelings down to who I want to kill, and kill them for me? Would you, James? Would you?"

James didn't answer right away.

Everybody started to circle around Jack and the saleslady, like it was a ceremony. But then we heard more voices coming from the other side of the *vohu*. A giant in baggy saffron pants and a dirty white linen shirt with a yoke collar wandered in from the far hallway. He must have been seven feet tall, including the turban, but he was skinny as a ladder. There were two other guys with him; one was a fat, shaved-headed black man in a natty suit and tie, and the other a coffee-colored little boy, maybe eight or nine years old, wearing a skullcap and a robe with flowers embroidered all over it in thick cords of colored thread. The black man was holding a street map, all unfolded and dragging along on the floor, and the guy kept turning it and turning it like trying to find a dry spot on a hanky when you've got a cold—and you can't quite. "Where's Court Street Bridge?" is what he kept saying, but there were snakes' tongues in all the r's and flapping doors in the t's.

When they saw the *vohu*, these three guys first off looked at one another, then they charged across it and glommed on to Jack and his new girl. The *vohu* clung to them like a bubble to a wand that a kid waves, before it snapped back.

There were five of them now—interlaced.

All at once, there was a ruckus in the elevator shaft. Our circle opened up, and we non-goddam-Chosens looked to see what was going on there. And in through the decompression chamber hatch came this babe. I saw her gams first. They were sculpted prime beef in fishnet stockings, practically with a price tag, and she wiggled down through the hatch. Her water balloon tits jiggled in the halter, and she hardly had a stitch on under her fake fur boa. Her blond wig, which looked like a carpet sample, caught on an edge of the hatch and pulled off partway, so you could see her real hair bunned up underneath. I would have liked her face if I hadn't hated her guts. It was an Arab face, dark and small and perfect, with big dark eyes. She looked up through the hatch and yelled, "Ma! Ma!"

And from above her, this crackly geriatric voice yelled, "Fatima! Run, girl! Run!"

But then Fatima saw the Thrice Chosens in their huddle, with Jack and his saleslady in the middle, and she was hypnotized just like the others. She left her throw rug hair in the hatch. She shed the boa like a used-up bath towel. She opened her mouth and gave a whoop. Some of her big, perfect teeth had lipstick on them. Ma, who I thought wasn't Fatima's ma, really, but her pimp, was climbing down the hairpiece. She was a real fossil, only in black velour pants and a velvet vest. She was two or three facelifts to the left of "natural aging." The old one, she said, "Fatima? Fatima? He's still coming after me, Fatima."

But Fatima didn't care. Fatima broke both heels running to join the orgy. She cut right into the middle with Jack, a hot knife in butter. Then they closed up, and what was going on in there, I couldn't see, but I wasn't that much of a dope, is what I was thinking, not to have some idea.

And I said, "James? Well, James? What about it?" My throat was so tight and my heart and breath so wild, I felt about to explode. I was going to do a Frankie and Johnny on that Yid.

The fossil lady lifted both arms up toward the Gold Sky, which was almost as black as my heart felt, and she geysered tears. She looked up, and she said, "Oh Fatima, oh my daughter, our suffering is over, the Angel Gabriel has opened the well of Zamzam, and the People is saved!" I wouldn't have known that that's what she said, because it was all throat-clearing and gum cracking to me, but Sylvia told us. Then the fossil lady, she galloped into the knot of the Thrice Chosens, which made seven of them.

That's when the window in the Fleshpot busted and we heard the helicopter outside. Panaggio and Waxy and Manny and Morano conferenced. Numerous individuals were clutching hardware in their vests or in their hip pockets. Some of Panaggio's people, including Sarge, were inching back toward the known section of Sears and Roebuck to hedge their bets.

Guy swings in through the busted window on the end of a rope ladder. He's all in black, like Manny, and he has fingerless black leather gloves and linebacker smears under his eyes. He's got some kind of high-tech machine gun slung over his shoulder. He's as lean as a wasp. "Police. Nobody move. Fatima, Layla, come on out. Give yourselves up..."

Ishky straightened his *tallis* and stepped forward. "Please, there must be some mistake. It was only a couple of *kurvehs*—you know, *streetwalkers*—come in out of the cold..."

"You, step back and keep your mouth shut..." Then the SWAT guy saw the meltdown of the Thrice Chosens, and immediately you could tell that his confidence was flagging. Then he looked at the *vohu* and at the other walls and at the floor and the ceiling. His *frontalis* and his *orbicularis oculi* started to *déjà vu* just like the saleslady's had done. He gulped and he quick reached out the window and made a sign for the chopper to lift away. Then he glommed.

The eight of them were talking a language that even Sylvia didn't understand, never mind me. I was so completely on the outside of everything I had thought I was in the middle of—namely, Jack—that I practically wished I had my dead face back, with my cadaver dimples and my heart of stone. "Well, James, would you do it for me?"

Is enough enough? A guy came in through Repairs and Returns wearing a hospital gown split down the back, and he still had the needle from a drip tube stuck in his arm. He was one. A high school kid, an exchange student from South Africa, came and glommed. He was one. A movie star was one—you would probably recognize his name, and then you would know why all the rumors about how he ran off with somebody or got assassinated by the Mafia are a lot of baloney. He didn't look all that great up close—I figure lights and makeup do a lot for those celebrity types that you would never suspect.

And the two last ones arrived, up through Sears and Roebuck, the known way. One of them was an international airline hostess. Her plane was iced over and she thought she had come into this place to buy souvenirs for her nieces in Cologne. The other one was some kind of a junkie. He hardly even looked like a human being. He was definitely out of some very foreign gene pool. His face was almost a perfect triangle, if it was his face, which I wasn't sure, because he was so stooped over and dirty and miserable-looking. He said his "voices" told him to follow the airline hostess up to this floor, but he glommed before her.

The airline hostess was, strictly speaking, to my way of thinking, a dish. And when she glommed, putting yet another layer between me and Jack, I said to James, "Dammit, I'm talking to you. Answer me, James. Will you do it for me?"

"Kill for you? Who? Jack? The female Chosens? I didn't think you were serious, honey."

"I'm serious. I'd do it my goddam self, but I'm feeling a little distracted."

"Lea, you can't expect to own Jack. He belongs to God Tetragrammaton. But Reb Sabbatai said that you would go with the Thrice Chosens aboard the *Meschiach*, didn't he? You'll be with your Jack, honey. More than any of us."

I felt so stupid. I felt ashamed and mean-hearted. Of course, James was right. My whole life had been leading up to this moment, and here I was making something bad out of something good. I was going along to the Promised Land as the interpreter of the *goyim* for the Chosen of the Chosen of the Chosen.

Then the Thrice Chosens spread apart a little bit, and Jack looked out, and he said what I bet you knew he was going to say, but the jerk I am, I still didn't get it for two or three minutes after he'd said it, even though it made so much goddam sense. A person's mind is made up fifty percent of wishful thinking, is the point of it all, and that's just how it is, and you never know which half.

Jack said, "The *Meschiach* will be here any minute now. Sylvia, are you ready to go?"

chapter seventeen

The Coming of the Meschiach

You could say the place was crowded. At last, the whole thirteen Thrice Chosens of the earthly realm were in the spaceship, which I helped gold leaf for crissakes and now they were going to leave me behind with the *goyim* to have my reward, thank you very much. There were thirty-seven human beings in the unknown section of Sears and Roebuck's, so I don't think you could even call it "unknown" anymore. We had:

MINYAN GUYS = 10 of them

Abie
Rabbi Metzger
Manny Baranes
Ishky Baranes (out of booze now, and he looked it)

Waxy

Simon Black

Noah Solomon (who kept looking at his watch
because he was afraid his wife might beat up
on him for being out so late in spite of how he
was redeeming the goddam world, supposedly)

Leonard Fine

Shlomo

Yakov the Bull (my brother James)

THRICE CHOSEN GUYS OF THE EARTHLY REALM = 13 of them

Jack

The saleslady from Indiana

Layla, the fossil lady

Fatima, the *kurveh*

The SWAT cop

The small round bald black guy in the suit

The tall skinny sadhu guy

The coffee-colored boy in the embroidered cape

The airline hostess dish

The movie star (which I won't say his name)

The hospital patient (which you could see his butt)

The South African exchange student

The beggar with the triangular puss

PANAGGIO'S BUNCH = 12 of them

Louis Panaggio himself

Sarge

Mr. Morano (who had the seafood plate Belle
   liked)
Benito (who had lost his toupee while he was a
   dog)
Aces
Porker
Vaseline
Denny Love
The security guard
The lookout kid
Nondescript Number One (packing heat)
Nondescript Number Two (likewise)

MARQUETRY LADIES
NOT PRESENT = 4 of them, which don't count
them, though

Mabel
Dixie
Jonette
Sisi

(All of them were picked up, white as sheets, on
Monroe Avenue by police after the helicopter guys fin-
gered them with infrared binoculars leaving Sears and
Roebuck, and our SWAT guy got a walkie-talkie call saying, is that them, and he unglommed for a minute and he
said, yes, and they have disguises and two accomplices, ar-
rest them, and I have some cleaning up to do, he said, I'll
report in later, I guess that does it, case closed, and see you
in the funny papers. And what those marquetry ladies
told the cops, and what the cops made of it, that's some

kind of laff riot I wasn't privy to, but I found out later from Belle that Mabel boosted some pillowcases from Bedding, and a police lady found them tucked in her girdle during the strip search.)

OFFICIAL INTERPRETER FOR THE THRICE CHOSENS = 1 of them

Sylvia

MISCELLANEOUS INDIVIDUAL = 1 of them

Me

TOTAL = 37 of them

See what I was, is the point: miscellaneous.

A rumbling began, and Jack addressed everybody from where he stood, at the center of a half circle of Thrice Chosens, and he said, "*Liebe brider*, beloved brothers—and sisters—the end of time is coming fast. We thirteen have assembled, the holy congregation of the earth, thanks be to God Tetragrammaton."

And the *minyan* said, "Amen."

"You helped us, all of you, and we'll see you in the Promised Land on the appointed day, after the Thrice Chosen have prepared the way, according to the plan of God Tetragrammaton, Who is, Who was, and Who will be forever and ever, hallelujah."

Denny Love yelled, "Hallelujah."

And the *minyan* said, "Amen."

And Louis Panaggio said, "Are we done here? Can we go home to our wives and our gambling debts?"

Rabbi Metzger said, "According to *Zohar Hagoyim*, now that the thirteen have gathered, the *Meschiach* will be docking at the Light Sponge momentarily. I think all of us who are not going along should be at least as far away as the public side of the front desk at Returns and Repairs, so the *Meschiach* would have some maneuvering space and we shouldn't be crushed and popped like zits in a pinch. Abie, is this advice worth a penny?"

And Abie said, "It's worth a penny."

And Jack said, "That's the word of Sabbatai Levi Hagodol." And he hugged Abie. And he hugged all the *minyan* guys one by one, and they filed across the *vohu* one by one into the known section.

And Panaggio said, "I guess I should stick around and see this. God knows the fights weren't all that great." And he shot Denny a black look, then he shook Jack's hand and he went through the *vohu*, and everybody went through the *vohu*.

Only I didn't. I just stood where I was while everybody got subtracted away from me, and Jack was going to get subtracted away from me, and I couldn't believe it, and I felt my *buccinator* start to reatrophy. Sylvia and the thirteen were glomming and *kvelling*, which is a kind of beaming, and nobody even noticed me for a while. On the other side, the *minyan* were straightening their *talleisim* and standing all together like the Vienna Boys Choir, and the Panaggio guys stood behind them, craning their necks as if it were a car accident.

Jack was filling Sylvia in on something, and he happened to turn his head in the middle of a sentence and catch sight of me and did a little double take. He finished his sentence and came up to me and said, "*Nu?*"

And I said, "*Nu?*"

And Sylvia called over, "*Well?*"

And I said, "Goddam you, Sylvia, I know what that one means," and she shut up and turned away.

And I said, "She thinks she knows everything."

And Jack said, "Sylvia was going to die here, Lea. It wouldn't be long. In the Promised Land, she'll be whole again."

"I'm going to die here, Jack."

From the known side, Abie was shouting, "Lea! Lea!"

Jack said, "No, you're not." He took my hand. I looked away. He kissed me—on the goddam top of my head. I whipped my face back toward him and I laid my palms on his cheeks and I held his head and I kissed him on the lips—hard.

But he wasn't kissing me back. So I stopped. I looked at him, which he wasn't looking at me the same way, but he was already a kajillion miles away in the Garden of goddam Eden, and I pulled my hands off him, and I said, "Fine." I did a dress right dress and marched for the *vohu*, till I felt his hand on my shoulder. I felt so soft and so melted, don't you see, I had to make myself hard as a turnstile, and he turned me and he kissed me on the lips and he held me and I held him and we were wrapping around each other like ribbons on a maypole.

Abie was calling, "Lea, Lea, quick—it's coming."

And Jack said, "I love you. I never kissed a girl before."

I said, "No!"

And he said, "It's true. But you'll kiss lots of boys, Lea, before God Tetragrammaton calls you to join us."

"Oh Jack, I want to go."

"You can't. Not now." The floor started to shake. The *vohu* flashed and rippled. The purple cope exploded off the Holy of Holies, its doors flew open, and inside you could see an endless sky full of cherubim singing.

Abie said, "Lea, Lea, run."

Jack said, "Run, Lea. I love you."

I ran through the *vohu* into the known. It was streaked with rainbows. I was streaked with rainbows. James reached out for me, and he took me under his *tallis* as if it was a wing and he was a mother bird. He guided me back to the mass of *minyan* guys and Panaggio guys, where *talleisim* were starting to flap and flutter—a wind was picking up. Some of Panaggio's guys ducked and covered.

The *vohu* glowed so bright, you couldn't look at it but it made your eyes tear, like looking at the sun. And it was even brighter than the sun, which was so bright, it went over the top of brightness, which you weren't looking at it anymore, but it was looking at you, and the *vohu* was like a great eye in the middle of Sears and Roebuck. Then it was two eyes, then the two were four, and finally the four were six, and the *Meschiach* had arrived.

We were forty of us in the known and in the unknown. The three supernal ones, the Chosen of the Chosen of the Chosen, were standing just inside the Light Sponge. You couldn't see any *Meschiach*. Manny, who knew ohms and volts and impedance and Michaelson and Morley from Radio Shack, he said, "It's docked in another dimension," and even old Mr. Black nodded.

The three supernal ones had eyes like a flame and feet like burnished bronze, and one of them had the morning star in the middle of his breast, and another one, it looked like he had all his ancestors walking in his skin, which you could see them like pips showing on the corners of a fanned-out poker hand. The other one, flowers and tiny glittering birds steamed out of his pores every time he moved. Aside from that, they were ordinary people.

You couldn't tell if any of them was a male or a female though, and as for wardrobe, you couldn't focus on it, but when you tried you might catch the glint of an accessory. Mostly, though, you couldn't focus. It was like trying to make one of those floating paisleys you see in the sky stand still, which you can't. Clothes was not one of their priorities up in the supernal realm, is how I figured it.

And the morning star one said, "Lo, in heaven, an open door!"

And Mr. Pips said, "The *Meschiach* has docked, and she stands at the ready. Is the fuel at hand which will propel us to *Ish-ra-el*? Is it ready?"

Rabbi Metzger shouted, "Is it ready? *Oy*, is it ready!"

Then Birds and Flowers said to the thirteen, "Who is worthy to open the cockpit and press the seven panel controls?"

Jack said, "I am."

And Morning Star said, "You? A dope dealer? A masturbist? A gambler? A thief?"

And Jack said, "Yes."

And the three supernal ones sang out:

"Holy! Holy! Holy!
God Tetragrammaton!
Lord God of Hosts!
The world brims with His glory!

Behold *zohar hagoyim*,
The perfection of the imperfect ones!"

Noah Solomon was standing near me. I could feel him tremble. Hell, we were all trembling, weren't we? But Noah was mumbling to himself, and he said, "She can wait! She can wait! This is the end of time. Everything after is the reading of a book that it's already written and the counting of a number that it's already piled up. Everything after is no more sweating and climbing and worrying, but it's jumping and falling and coming to rest, and who shall die and who shall live has been sealed and it is a thing past and done. My wife can wait!"

Denny Love, he gave Noah a *potchkee* on the shoulder—a little slap—and he said, "I understand everything! You Yids are finally catching up, God bless you! The whole world is all saved in our savior Jesus Christ, the Messiah, and now you're getting a playback to get you up to speed. All's I can say is I'm grateful to God Almighty to be here to see it, and it's even worth losing in five to a dumb side of beef like Orlando Ruiz."

I don't remember hearing the ten, nine, eight, and I don't remember hearing anybody shout, "*Kohani-im!*" the way they do, but the *Meschiach* lifted off while the *minyan* sang "Ghi di di di!" over and over with so much *k'vanna* it would blind God Tetrazzini if He forgot Himself and looked. Me, I clenched my eyes like little fists, but the tears busted through, the way grass busts through concrete. Damn Indian Summer! There was a time I could have diked that juice up—not anymore.

The *minyan* provided the fuel. They sang their hearts

out. They sang themselves hoarse. They sang themselves inside out with both joy and terror. The *Meschiach* was one with our spaceship now: It was so bright, I could see it through my eyelids, and it shot into the supernal realm in a lightning bolt of quicken-and-killing passion.

I think I was still saying, "Jack . . . Jack . . . Jack . . . !" when the *Meschiach* roared and vanished into the sky and into our hearts, is what it felt like, deep and high at once.

I opened my eyes. Salt foam blew across the Gymsealed floor, which was only a floor now, and the Gymseal was bubbled up and crackled and peeling like a sunburn. The Holy of Holies was charred, and it stank of smoldering wood and melted synthetic fabrics. The Gold Sky, you could see tin panels of it bent and twisted and hanging down by a corner. The gold leaf was just a glint here and there out of the blackened metal, and if you blinked, it would be gone. Every few minutes, another panel would clatter down.

Waxy said, "Well—it's gone."

And Simon Black said, "*Shmendrick*, it's not gone. It's still here yet."

And Leonard Fine said, "Simon, it's gone."

And Simon said, "It isn't. You're *meshugeh*."

And Leonard said, "Look who's calling who *meshugeh*! Abie, is it gone?"

And Simon said, "So now Abie is the *maven*?"

Abie shrugged. He was watching me, and who needs it, because I'm perfectly one hundred percent fine, why can't they leave me alone for once, was what I was thinking at that moment. I walked away and started to leaf through a catalog, the summer one I think, but my eyes were a little blurry.

Shlomo stomped across the gone *vohu* into the charred and stinking remains of the hidden section of Sears and Roebuck, over crumbling boards whose edges still glowed when a breeze hit them, and he said, "What, am I crazy? Is this mess the *Meschiach*? Can I believe my ears? Can Simon be saying that the *Meschiach* has not yet left, and can somebody be taking him seriously?"

And Simon laughed and he said, "What a *naar*! The *Meschiach* is still here, and he thinks it's gone already!"

"It is!"

"It isn't!"

And Shlomo said, "Rabbi Metzger, you tell us, has the *Meschiach* come and gone or not?"

And Rabbi Metzger said, "Could be yes, could be no."

And Simon stuck out his tongue at us all, and he said, "You see? Could be yes, could be no. I'm telling you, nothing happened."

But for me it was settled. Jack was gone. I felt like a river made of melted snow from the top of a high mountain, which the sun finally warmed up, and it trickled and it streamed and it rushed and it flowed, and it wore away rock and it carved out basins and when it reached the ocean, the ocean wasn't there. I didn't know where to go.

There is nothing that can drive a heart deeper into the muck than a little jollity at a time when your *buccinator* is disinclined. About twenty minutes after liftoff, the Devil came in off the street, which by that time everybody was wise to him, and he looked like a chauffeur of a limo in a white tux with lots of buttons, and he said, "It just left. Holy Toledo, it just left, didn't it, you sons of bitches, not half an hour ago? I thought it left before that. I heard the *shofars*, for crissakes. You mean to say that fucking *shofar* trick got me again? I could have been back in time to stop the motherfucker." The poor guy was going one to another, and we were having a yuck fest over it.

Simon said, "What, 'left?' It's still here." And Simon laughed till he nearly had a stroke. The Devil left, humiliated, with both of his hands in his pockets, and we saw him roaming up and down Monroe Avenue for a long time till he just gave up and went back to Hell.

I'm sitting in Office Supplies in the known section of Sears Roebuck with a word processor that can't be beat. It's been weeks and weeks since the *Meschiach* took off, but I've got lots of time, because, let's face it, nobody is about to scoop me. Mr. Panaggio's friends have closed down the Monroe Avenue Sears and Roebuck for repairs after the fire, is the official story. Panaggio's got it worked out to make a pretty good return off the fire insurance, and I think Waxy has some of that action.

I could take the word processor home, but I like this arrangement. I like being close to everything. I like being able to stroll over and see the scarred walls where the *vohu* was, which the *Meschiach* docked there, just like Sabbatai Levi Hagodol always said.

I'm not in with Belle Bobson, by the way. I don't live there. I live with my brother James now, in his apartment that he rents. It's temporary while I figure out what's next for me. Maybe I'll have a *mikvah* and turn into a Jew like he did—but mainly for the company. I see a lot of the *minyan*, and they want to give me jobs and, like, college money, and cheesecakes in white cardboard boxes which have flaps with rounded edges and string on them. The way those flaps fit so perfect in between the outside of the box and the inside, where the waxed tissue paper and the goodies are, I never saw anything so beautiful, and for a while it made me think I might try to go into packaging and design eventually. Something like that.

I'm taking good care of my James. Maybe you think that when Belle knocked the devil out of his bones, James's dog-kicking days were over, but that's a lot of *chazerei*, which means pig fodder. Fact is, a person gets used to certain ways, like when Charlie Chaplin was getting married in one of those movies, and he put his foot up like he expected a rail at the altar, as if he was at a bar. It takes you a long time to stop putting your foot up, is the way I see it.

James watched over me practically forever; now I watch over my James. I help him catch the mean words that seep out of him; he might be bitching or dog-kicking or looking for that rail with his foot, and at times like that, I kiss him and coddle him and generally mommy him. Because, like I said, you have to reward people after they do bad; otherwise they just keep on doing bad, because they stay unhappy.

And it works, too. A lot of people don't believe it, but it's definitely true. You should see my brother James, how nice he is to small animals nowadays, and how alive his facial muscles are. He's hardly ever mean. I'm the one who taught him, and I'm proud of it. Now he's practically better at it than I am. I think I might even like to be a teacher instead of making packaging products. I forgot to tell you that I'm going for my high school equivalency diploma now, and it's a piece of cake, frankly, except for some things along the lines of relative goddam pronouns.

If you think about it, I bet you won't be surprised when I tell you that I could help James another way too, because James has completely the same color chart as me. I took him shopping for a wardrobe at Noah's Ark, where Mr. Solomon got us a real generous discount. James squawked and fidgeted like a nine-year-old, but I kept rewarding him, like I said, and he made it through our shopping spree, and he looks like a million bucks. He's got my features for crissakes. I think he's gonna land mega-girlfriends, which is a good thing, too, because then he won't be so jealous of Anthony.

Never mind who Anthony is, it's not really any of your business, and I wasn't going to mention him, but he's Mr. Panaggio's nephew, a couple of times removed, and he's a freshman in college at Brockport, New York, where they've got a teachers' college. I like the idea of that line of work, is my main thought here, so I am kind of profiting by our relationship, and he tells me stuff about how you teach kids' eyes to go from left to right for reading, for example. Who would have even thought about a thing like that, but it makes so goddam much sense when you do. That's the kind of thing Anthony tells me about, you know.

Yeah, okay, we kiss sometimes too, and I'll admit to one hickey, the one on the side of my neck; but the other one, which it's none of your business where that one is, it's not a hickey at all, no matter what anybody in goddam Brockport says, where I visit my Anthony sometimes but never overnight—it's abrasions from when I hit the top of the decompression chamber, remember?

Of course, I still have a bunch of Lillian's nice clothes, and Anthony is positively crippled by the sight of me. I have to admit, I don't mind that one bit. You should see my hair, too. I have lots of it, and it's pretty gorgeous, I gotta say.

My *buccinator*, listen, I practically forgot about it, it's so natural now. Abie says I have a beautiful smile, and he's not the only one, I guarantee. I'm getting into it, and I don't feel the least little bit like a sap when I do it, either.

I still see Belle once in a while, and we sit and listen to Bing in her glassed-in room, and I eat whatever she makes me. Tule rubs me and sits in my lap if she wants to, but she never talks to me anymore; she saves herself up for Belle, is how I see it. That's okay by me. Sometimes Belle, she gets to talking about our talents, but I don't encourage it. Me and James, we're kind of letting that muscle atrophy. We figure we've seen more important things. That talent, when it comes right down to it, now that the *Meschiach* has come and gone, it's just a distraction.

Sometimes Belle starts to go on about how we are Dark Sisters and the Devil is our master, and then she remembers herself, that it was never really like that, and she kind of trails off and plays with her napkin or what have you. If you want to know the truth, the Devil isn't much interested in this world anymore, because he has pretty much lost the ball game. I don't think he even had that good a lineup to begin with, do you? All the things that happen now to keep people's souls out of the Promised Land, they are up to them—to us, is what I mean. The Devil is out of the picture. Maybe he's got other worlds he's working on. I wouldn't be surprised. But he's basically a wimp, is my take on it, and he'll probably screw up in all of them.

I guess you could say things are really great all around. Really wonderful, you know? Very happy time for me.

That about says it. I'm doing great. The *Meschiach* has been and gone. I've been up on Mount Nebo and I've been down under the Memorial Arena. I've seen live people die and I've seen dead people come to life, namely me, that you wouldn't have thought had a chance in goddam hell. But here I am buccinating and learning tenth grade geometry and sparking with Anthony in Brockport, and I'm very happy, extremely, no kidding...

And if Anthony were Jack, and if Monroe Avenue were the Garden of Eden, and if it was me there instead of goddam Sylvia, hell, everything would be aces, wouldn't it? Just aces.

I don't think about it.

Listen, here's how great things are, actually. I didn't even tell you yet about the great time that everybody had at the Sears and Roebuck.

I got this phone call, see—I was staying at James's then, and I was supposed to get a double-time pay temp job in Catalog Orders starting early next morning, at dawn practically, because Mr. Panaggio had arranged it for me. So I went and I was sitting on a bench waiting with my carmine red handbag and my dress suit—and whaddaya know!—suddenly Panaggio peeked in from the hallway and he was wearing a white chef's hat, if you can believe it, and he had on one of those HOT STUFF! aprons, and he yelled, "Well, are you coming?"

And there was Abie next to Panaggio, holding up a spatula like it was the key to the Kingdom, and he said, "We're down on the second floor in Major Appliances—but somebody bring down a few card tables from Furnishings, would you? We don't have enough places."

And out from behind these white partitions—it was

the whole gosh darn Panaggio's gang and Denny Love
and the *minyan*. Even Rabbi Metzger from Cleveland was
there. And every *meshugeh* one of them was smiling like
their heads would bust from the pressure on those facial
muscles.

It was breakfast!

We moved out into the hallway and tramped down
the stairs, the whole crazy, hungry lot of us. We were
laughing and backslapping and making jokes in poor
taste. We followed the smell of pancakes all the way down
to Major Appliances, and we plunked ourselves down at
the card tables in stackable plastic chairs, and James and
Abie piled up the pancakes on everybody's plates, which
were fine china from Syracuse, New York. There were
lakes of Vermont Maid and oceans of melted butter.

Mr. Black reached in front of me for the syrup once,
and, through a mouthful of mashed pancake, he said, "It
never happened, Lea. It's a mass hysteria. Panaggio made
a fortune here. Did you know, he and his friends own the
building, and his brother-in-law was the insurance un-
derwriter? Somebody put something in somebody's
Manischewitz, that's what. Ach, but who can argue with
pancakes, am I right?"

I said, "You're right, Mr. Black," and he winked at me
and smiled, and he filled his plate with syrup.

Denny Love sulked a little because nobody would let
him say grace, but the point is, a person can take only so
much holiness. The way I see it, that's the hidden meaning
of *Zohar Hagoyim*, which is the brilliance of the *non*-
Chosens.

Right in the middle of everything, Sarge sang his Uky
song to me, which I blushed:

"You are my spring.
Your family gives me goats and chickens..."

...and the rest of it. Everybody made a big fuss over me. Abie and James must have put them up to it, and I bet Waxy coaxed Panaggio to come on board. Everybody loved each other so much after that incredible night with the *Meschiach*, you could have gotten them to do just about anything together, just for the pleasure of each other's company.

Me, I ate so many pancakes—it must have been practically noon before we called it quits—that I could hardly get up for the warm weight of them inside me and for all the laughing I'd been doing. James and Abie had to take me home, one on each side of me helping me walk. We laughed and laughed.

Well, okay—so Jack is gone. Jack was my first love, is how I see it. You could say he left a hole in me the size of the La Brea Tar Pits, and there's never gonna be an end to picking bones out of there. You could say that, all right! But I know that what he told me is true: I'm going to have lovers up the wazoo and lined up down the street, and Anthony is only the goddam beginning, see? I mean, hell, I'm only sixteen. I'm nowhere near done thawing, you know, and I already have looks that could kill.

You got to keep a stiff upper lip—there's a muscle for that too.

I mean, the fact is, I'm never going to see Jack goddam Konar again until *Olam Habaw*, the Kingdom Come. It kills me that Sylvia's going to be the one up there translating me to all the Thrice Chosens, like some UN guy with earphones in a booth over the General Assembly. I'll get in, though. Nobody's going to not stamp my goddam passport after all the shit I've been through, and I didn't even get to go along. The way I figure it, God Tetragram owes me.

So I don't care that much. I'll probably wind up getting married to some *zhlub* and having half a dozen kids and getting *zaftig*, which is *fat*, and *naarishe*, which is *stupid*. I'll "have my reward."

That's all.

I'm glad you decided to keep reading into the unknown section of my story. It's been helping me a lot to write everything down. Abie and Rabbi Metzger said it would, and they were right, and Mr. Black was wrong: it's the farthest thing from *meshuga'as,* from *monkeyshines,* that anybody could think of.

Now I'm going to stop this blathering before I short-circuit the goddam word processor with my salt tears, which Manny, the Radio Shack *maven*, tells me conduct electricity. They conduct electricity, and they even turn to gas, when the electricity goes through those tears, and you get hydrogen at one pole and oxygen at the other pole, and those are what water comes from, hydrogen and oxygen, and I bet they go straight back up into the sky—like moon steam—which is where water came from, and we came from water, so we came from the sky too, and that's what we're going back to, is how I figure it, *the end*.

ABOUT THE AUTHOR

ELIOT FINTUSHEL has published short stories in *Asimov's, Analog, Strange Horizons, Amazing Stories, Lady Churchill's Rosebud Wristlet, Crank!,* and in the anthologies *Jewish Sci-Fi Stories for Kids, Jewish Detective Stories for Kids, Nalo Hopkinson's Mojo: Conjure Stories,* and *Polyphony 4.* His fiction has appeared in the annual anthology *The Year's Best Science Fiction* several times. He has been nominated for the Theodore Sturgeon Award and the Nebula Award, and has twice won the National Endowment for the Arts Solo Performer Award.